D0810302

The Hallelujah Revolution

The Hallelujah Revolution

The Rise of the New Christians

IAN COTTON

 **Prometheus Books**

59 John Glenn Drive
Amherst, NewYork 14228-2197

Published 1996 by Prometheus Books

00 99 98 97 96   5 4 3 2 1

Library of Congress Cataloging-in-Publication Data

Cotton, Ian.
    The hallelujah revolution : the rise of the new Christians / Ian
Cotton.
        p.   cm.
    Includes index.
    ISBN 1–57392–055–X (cloth : alk. paper)
    1. Pentecostalism—Great Britain. 2. Evangelicalism—Great Britain.
3. Great Britain—Church history—20th century. 4. Christianity—Fore-
casting. 5. Psychology, Religious. I. Title.
BR1644.5.G7C67   1996   96–2658
                                                                    CIP

Printed in the United States of America on acid-free paper

Contents

Acknowledgments

There is a long and a short version of an acknowledgments list: this one will stay reasonably short. I am of course indebted to innumerable Christians, historians, scientists, psychiatrists and librarians who have, one way and another, helped this project to its end. There are certain individuals who have been especially helpful. First of all, my wife: suffice to say that everything they say about living with an author is true, except that the reality is far, far worse. Secondly, my editor at Little, Brown, Alan Samson: Alan displayed conspicuous energy and patience throughout this long gestation. Thirdly, my agent, Sara Menguc of Murray Pollinger, who fought unfailingly for this idea from the start. Also, several good friends, old and new, all of whom have helped unstintingly, each according to their expertise. Peter Martin and Dennis Hackett read my drafts and gave invaluable advice. Jean Liedloff, Paula Binns, Belinda Beeftink and Chris Trengove all made critical contributions. Michael Persinger of Laurentian University, Canada, and his excellent staff, gave their time and ideas. Maggie Fielden of the Evangelical Alliance and Michelle Webb of the British Library helped above and beyond duty. And academics like Peter Fenwick, David Bebbington and Abe Rotstein were an inspiration. Finally, The Institute For the Study of American Evangelicals helped, at a crucial stage, with a grant. My thanks, again, to all.

Preface to the American Edition

The United States has lived with "right wing fundamentalism" for years: noisy, conservative, tear-jerkingly emotional. As American, in its way, as apple pie.

So Americans may be surprised to find that the British have long been into something very similar—a version, if anything, even *more* impassioned than that in the U.S.A. But surely this is utterly un-British! The Brits of all people, the ineffably formal Brits, getting into such capers as charismatic arm-waving, the roaring and floor-rolling of the so-called Toronto Blessing, even such *capo di capo* faith healing excesses as the (putative) raising of the dead.

Yet this is what is happening, and this book—largely centered in the United Kingdom—shows how and why.

Some Americans read the overseas Evangelical/Charismatic movement as U.S. cultural imperialism: I disagree. U.S. influences are, undoubtedly, very great, and to an ingenuous Brit our charismatic services do indeed look distinctively, even alarmingly, American. (Less so to Americans, I should add.) But this is just a part of it. As the following pages show, the eruption of the supernaturalist "new" or "house" churches in the U.K.—as around the world—was largely a local, self-generating process, and has more to do with the postindustrial, postspecialist instincts of the world "do-it-yourself" movement—"do-it-yourself" religion, in this case—than with any U.S. role-modeling. And, significantly, a large part of this book de-

scribes the ways the U.K. movement (largely through its burgeoning global creation, the "March For Jesus" network) now influences the United States: in the States alone, this British-dominated
movement has gone from 1,200 marchers in 1990 to 1.5 million in
1994, the year in which, incidentally, MFJ's world figures leapt sixfold to over 10 million. And for those who find British "tolerance"
a further reason why British evangelicalism comes as a surprise, it's
worth noting that the quality U.S. evangelicals value, above all, in
the British movement is its instinct for cross-denominational "reconciliation." So different from the feuds and schisms of the traditional U.S. denominations, say the Americans, especially in the cities.

But if this book in any way undermines the myth of an Evangelical Pax Americana, I hope it shatters other, related preconceptions
too. It underscores, for instance, that—far from being exclusively, or
even especially, a U.S.–U.K. Anglo-Saxon phenomenon—the current
Evangelical/Charismatic revival is now a gargantuan, *global* reality:
conservatively there are now 400 million Christian "charismatics"
worldwide. And where in 1906 less than 1 percent of the world
Christian communion was "charismatic," today at least 25 percent is.
By the year 2000 this figure will climb to an estimated 30 percent, a
staggering one "new" Christian in three. It demonstrates that this
movement stretches from South America to Europe, from Canada to
mainland China, and that it is above all characterized by growth. In
the Henan province of mainland China, for instance, a million converts were reported in 1994, while in ex-Soviet Russia, at least 30 percent of the population now consists of believers; while in Korea,
where at the end of the Second World War Christians represented a
mere 8 percent of the population, by 1994 Christian churches comprised over 50 percent of South Korean religious denominations.

But in a highly charged subject there are other myths too. There
is, for instance, that most supercharged matter of politics. So dominant (and high-profile) has the right been in U.S. religious circles
lately—above all, now, with the Christian Coalition—that it often
comes as a surprise to realize that there are any other Christian pol-

itics at all; that one in three white U.S. Evangelicals, for instance, votes Democrat; or that the proportion of white Evangelicals voting Republican actually dropped between the 1988 and 1992 elections. For while Bush landed 83 percent of the white Evangelical vote in 1988, in 1992 he managed only 55 percent. Tom Pelton, American coordinator of the U.S. March For Jesus, is typical of this posteighties, post-Reaganite strand. For not only is he anything but "right-wing," he actually proclaims himself a "Clinton fan." A Clinton *fan?* A leading U.S. Evangelical? Now this is news.

So here, too, the British movement comes in, because it is precisely the continuing high profile of right-wing conservatives like the Christian Coalition that is leading "liberal" U.S. Christians like Pelton to look toward Europe. Hence the great U.S. interest I found, during my American research, in the neosocialist communitarian work of U.K. inner-city churches like London's Ichthus, interest underscored by the fact that the Ichthus leadership is in turn at the forefront of that same, reconciling, international March For Jesus. Their different roles and gears overlap in a way typical of the fluid, amoebalike new church global culture (just one of many "Aquarian" qualities they share, incidentally, with the ad hoc, postspecialist traditions of modern business, not to mention postindustrial culture generally).

Nevertheless, as my American friends also say, "American fundamentalism remains basically a right-wing phenomenon." Undeniably so. But, it is fair to ask, which way will the pendulum be swinging, longer term? Will the Christian Coalition or Tom Pelton's "Countercultural" Christians, as I have called them, be the dominant mode in 2020? Which is most in tune with the information age, as it ever-more-swiftly unfolds? To some the answer is obvious: the Christians are headed ever further to the right. And yet, as Peter Drucker has so well observed, each historical development of the last one hundred years has been utterly unpredictable at the time, and the one thing that *has* been demonstrated is that societies develop discontinuously, by opposites and paradox. This is inevitable, perhaps, since the underpinning of virtually any societal state of mind is the screening out from consciousness of whatever forces spoil the pattern. My own bet is that while right-wing Evangelism will indeed gain ground, perhaps spectacular ground in the immediate future— for very good information-society reasons, not least the coming, desperate insecurities of unemployment—the liberal version will turn out to be the one with the legs over the longer haul.

Why? This too I explore hereafter, but suffice it to say here that I believe this for another very good information-society reason— namely, that the "Counterculturals" are so instinctively in tune with our evolving postindustrial modes of thought: their feel, for instance, for holism; for configuration; for what I have called "paradoxicality"; for gentle, feminine Jesus over macho, stern Jehovah. Meanwhile, as with the postindustrial counterculture and the neoclassical reaction against it throughout society at large, the two forces will unquestionably continue to bounce off each other for decades: the more counterculture, the more reaction, locked in an intense, escalating union-of-opposites embrace. (Not for nothing is the word "counterculture" so rarely off Newt Gingrich's lips.)

There is another important point, not always recognized. It is this: within both the right and left of the Evangelical movement there is a comparable generation gap, and the organizational instincts, let alone any others, of the coming generation in both right and left Christianity have more in common than either might readily admit. For whereas old-style religious conservatism like the Mormons' is, in business terms, strictly fifties-corporate ("top-down," as the sociologists would have it), both Christian Coalition and March For Jesus are effectively Nineties-style franchises (decentralized, citizen-led, "bottom-up"). Indeed, Ralph Reed, Christian Coalition's executive director, has described the coalition as nothing less than a "McDonald's"—which is exactly how I, for one, would characterize (organizationally) March For Jesus. This much is sure: as with parallel developments in business, education, even policing, it is these postspecialist, "do-it-yourself" organizational forms that have the future, whatever their political complexion. No doubt, in fact, there will be a left and right in postindustrial Christianity, just as there has been a left and right in "Fordist" Christianity.

So it is a mistake, in my view, to swallow too readily the notion of the Evangelical movement as mere cartoon conservatism, not least because it can distract attention from what is genuinely new about the "new" churches, and thus lead to underestimating the movement's long-term potential. But overemphasizing the politics can be a mistake for other reasons, too. Not only is there the notorious fluidity of political labels—both Mussolini and Jim Jones started their careers as "socialists"—but, more fundamentally, it is limiting because it focuses attention exclusively on the *results* of conversion processes at the expense of what I believe is the deeper truth, the processes themselves. For these are common to entering, or leaving, virtually any belief system, religious or lay.

For just as left and right in the new postindustrial Christianity share postmodern organizational instincts, so their converts share a common process of coming-to-belief: a process described fairly rigorously in the following pages, analogous in many ways to seemingly nonreligious processes like nervous breakdown, and rooted in comparable personal histories of uncertainty and stress. Indeed, the two crucial factors in the classic conversion scenario—extreme suggestibility and, as a kind of emotional turbo-booster, the actual experience of paranormal "visions"—are characteristic of entry into all wings of Christian, and even secular, belief systems, as I hope the following pages make plain.

All of this applies, equally, to the broader social environment from which such belief systems spring; for there, too, the macro causal factors transcend the differing traditions. Key among these is surely a macro version of that same quality so crucial at the micro, individual level—stress and uncertainty. For if there has been one social ingredient always present at the various periods of religious revivalism, whether in the millenarianisms of the late-medieval period, the Wesleyan conversions of the early industrial revolution, or the "burned-over-district" conversions of the economically turbulent, 1830s' East-Coast America—it has been uncertainty, cultural and economic, supplying critical psychological fuel. And never has there been uncertainty like now. To take just one example, employment: in the United States corporations are getting rid of 2 million jobs annually. In the United Kingdom one recent estimate reckoned a staggering 60 percent of the workforce no longer had "proper" jobs. If employed at all, they were self-employed or on short-term contracts, insecure, uncertain, with minimal benefits.

As the millennium approaches, the technological revolution will be propelling us toward question marks over wealth distribution, and thus social cohesiveness, unprecedented since the onset of the industrial age. As Canadian neuroscientist Michael Persinger points out in chapter 12, social uncertainty can merge with individual stress to produce brain events that are only now beginning to be understood: the beliefs thus entered into can be of almost any complexion at all, including, of course, the various fundamentalisms of quite different religions in quite different societies around the world—Islamic, Hindu, even Buddhist, as seen with the recent gas attacks in Tokyo.

Add to this the possibility, in the West, that our neo-Romantic, postindustrial sensibility may itself facilitate increased mysticism and you have a heady brew indeed. This is why I take Peter Drucker very seriously when he says, in his 1959 *Landmarks of Tomorrow*: "The historian a century hence—should there be one to record our survival—may well judge the return to religion to have been the most significant event of our century and the turning point in the transition from the modern age."

Unlikely? Well, that was what they said when Drucker predicted the "discontinuities" of modern business back in the Sixties, and when McLuhan (also a predictor, by the way, of Western religious revival) in the same decade announced the imminent collapse of "Gutenberg" or rationalist, desacrilized, production-line civilization.

Time will tell.

Prologue

The first time Lloyd Kuehl went to England, it was to raise the dead.

He'd never set foot outside the States before, except while in the military, nor even got himself a passport until that trip of Summer 1991 But then Lloyd is hardly the kind of worldly-wise fellow one associates with Eighties, globetrotting Evangelism. Tall, ruggedly homespun in his checked shirt and jeans, belt buckle in the shape of a cross and mystic, middle-distance gaze in his eyes, Lloyd looks, and is, stone innocent. For years he's lived in Bellingham, Washington state, a U.S. port on the North-West coast, and before that in North Pole, Alaska: a wilderness man, a dreamer of dreams, with a genuine commitment to life in the raw.

His "personal relationship" with Jesus had begun with a thirty-minute mystic experience, climaxing in the bathroom. It happened shortly after his wife left home. His ceramic tile business had collapsed in the recession, leaving the fifty-year-old family man and father of five in tough circumstances. Still, ever since his conversion he'd been taking the homeless into his own house.

In Spring 1991 Lloyd got a phone call from Susan, a half-Haitian lady he knew a little through his local church in Bellingham. Susan said a friend of hers in England, Mary Ellen, had a husband on the verge of death from liver cancer. Could Lloyd help? Susan had met Mary through the Charismatic grapevine when she'd stayed in England previously. Like so many leading lights of the New Christian movement, Lloyd had no official position in any church; and yet he had a string of cures to his credit—including a reputed cancer cure—and he had healed Susan herself of open throat ulcers in just twenty-four hours. To Susan, the evidence was clear: this man had gifts.

There was a chance that Mary's construction manager husband, 42-year-old John, might no longer be alive should Lloyd finally make it to Blackstone, Yorkshire, where the Ellen family lived. But Lloyd spoke with God about that, while out back mowing the lawn. And there came this voice, clear as a bell: *I will raise from the dead,* the voice said—"I" being God. John may have died when I arrive, mused Lloyd, but the Lord's will is clear. I'll go anyway.

Lloyd and Susan headed off, independently, for the U.K. in early June 1991. Lloyd flew late one Saturday night, and another friend, Sandy, phoned Yorkshire to say he was in the air. This was welcome news in Blackstone, because John Ellen was deteriorating fast. "You wouldn't believe the effect that phone call had" said Susan. "Lloyd on his way at last—in the nick of time, we felt—and there were people praying for John everywhere, we heard, why, people were even praying in North Pole. So we felt this incredible rush of joy! And we told John! And he looked better, instantly! And he said, *I feel better*! And we had this sudden sense that the worst was over, that a corner had been turned, and Mary and I went downstairs for a coffee, and we were saying, Thank you Lord, thank you, *thank you.*

"Then suddenly, after about ten minutes, there was this dreadful thump. Mary sped upstairs: John had got out of bed, and he'd had this fall. And now he was in terrible pain and the doctor came round and gave him this painkiller. Then the doctor had to go on another call and around two in the morning—I was downstairs at the time—I suddenly heard Mary's voice:

" 'John, John, come back—in the name of Jesus, Spirit of Death, I bind you!' And I cried: 'Mary, what's happening?' and she said: 'He's gone!' "

This was the situation Lloyd flew into on Sunday morning. He was picked up from Heathrow by Alan Roberts, a member —like Mary and John before they'd moved north months earlier—of the Oxford New Testament Church, a fifty-strong Charismatic congregation in the University's industrial suburbs. Alan and Lloyd rang Blackstone, and heard John had died. "Come anyway!" said Blackstone. So off they went. Late that afternoon, they reached a household in shock. "The first thing we'd had to do that morning was tell the children," said Susan, "one by one, as they woke up." It was all the harder, said Mary, because the children had been expecting their father to recover. First up was two-year-old Jenny: "Mary just took her on her lap," said Susan "and said, 'Daddy has left us to be with the Lord,' and Jenny burst into tears."

Mary then "showed this unbelievable strength," burying herself in all the practical things: but what these did not include was contacting the undertakers, "because," said Susan, "we continued to live in expectation of a cure. We expected John to come walking down the stairs." When Lloyd and Alan arrived later that evening, Lloyd went straight to John's room and prayed, on his own, for three-quarters of an hour.

"I've never felt so alone," said Lloyd. Unlike other healing moments Lloyd had experienced—such as when he cured the woman of cancer and felt "this burning down through my head, and through my hands"—there were "no manifestations of the Holy Spirit" at all. After forty-five minutes of command and prayer, "I had to admit: I had attempted to raise John from the dead and failed."

It was a terrible disappointment, but no one gave up. Indeed, over the next few days the community at 7 York Lane hit a certain stride. Alan Roberts slept on the sofa downstairs.

Susan stayed with neighbors, coming over every day. Lloyd put up with the local Congregationalist pastor, James Freeman (on coming to Blackstone, Mary and John had joined James's congregation) and did the ten-minute stroll over from his house every morning. The children, except for Jenny, went to school. A daily routine emerged: plenty of worship and invocation, but nothing too formal: "We would be sitting together, just talking, perhaps, and suddenly we would drop, spontaneously, into prayer, or maybe sing." And all the while, John lay upstairs, right there in the bed where he had died. "Our continuing faith," said Lloyd, "was he would rise." As Susan recalled: "We had this amazing sense of expectancy"—so much so that Mary put out a glass of water by John's bed for that first sip. Susan waggishly suggested it should be sherry.

But John did not return: day followed day and he remained firmly in his bed. The little community continued to meet and pray; they celebrated communion together; neighbors discreetly left cakes and even money on the doorstep; but gradually, faith, not to say nerves, were getting frayed. "I suppose," said Mary, "we'd got into a bit of a thing about the time—four days after the death —you know, the Lazarus thing." Added to which, there were those around who were not entirely in step: one of them was the local undertaker, who happened to be in James Freeman's congregation. Unaware of the expectations at York Lane, he couldn't understand why they didn't fix anything up.

By the middle of the week, the time to draw stumps had well and truly arrived. The funeral was arranged for Thursday, in James's Congregationalist chapel. "To be honest, even at that stage we hoped John might rise," said Susan, "yes, right there in the chapel!" There was even a last glimmer of hope *after* the funeral, when the body was taken down to the crematorium, "Although once the body had been burnt that did look like the end," said Alan.

So that was it. Mary was a widow, the kids were fatherless. Lloyd's intercontinental intervention had been in vain and all that heady, four-day faith in John's return was now pure history. There was nothing left except grief, anti-climax and the need, perhaps, to salvage some compensatory sense of purpose from the wreck.

Lloyd had already met other Christians in the Blackstone neighborhood, and before he went back to the States he met still more, with Alan: they were so impressed by Lloyd that he and Alan began to wonder whether God hadn't *really* meant, in his message on the lawn that day, that Lloyd's mission had been to resurrect God's *church* rather than John. Whereas Susan and Mary wondered whether everybody's expectations during those four days, however (seemingly) misplaced, might not have been God's way of temporarily softening the pain.

While James Freeman, reflecting in his turn months later, wondered whether John and Mary's brief sojourn among his flock—a sojourn which might have seemed so short as to be pointless, given Mary's return to Oxford shortly after—could not have been God's way of injecting a new spiritual vigor into his little congregation—solid enough Yorkshire believers, certainly, but scarcely aflame.

This is something Charismatics have in common: however confusing events may seem at first, a divine pattern always seems to emerge at last, given thought.

1

The Coming of the New Christians

Ours is a time of sudden deviations and unpredictable change—a "discontinuous" age. But of all the tumultuous surprises of the last thirty years, none can match the grand revanche of irrationalism, which seems so contrary to the deepest instincts of the West. Yet it is happening today, and Lloyd, Susan and Mary, bizarre though their doings may seem, are at the heart of it. For if there is one quality which marks out the new Evangelical/Charismatic Christianity, it is its rediscovery of the supernatural: of miracles, healings, divine intervention, not to mention the (putative) raising of the dead.

I'd first met Lloyd Kuehl at a Charismatic meeting in Austin, Texas, in January 1992, and it was there—in talks with Lloyd and with other Charismatics—that I first began to grasp just how utterly extraordinary was their new-look, late twentieth-century Christianity, and to understand that they are part of a major, worldwide religious revival with three key characteristics, still not widely recognized.

First of all there is the kind of reinvented supernaturalism witnessed in Blackstone. The new Charismatic Christians really do believe God intervenes on a daily basis, heals the sick, helps out believers, raises the dead. (One reason Lloyd went to Yorkshire was that he'd heard of the nineteenth-century Yorkshire plumber, Smith Wigglesworth, who had reputedly resurrected no less than fourteen people in the neighborhood. Wigglesworth had also offered his dead wife the chance to come back, added Lloyd, but she'd turned him down.) Equally, the Charismatics believe in the immediate, life-transforming power of prayer: a soldier told me how God had saved his life in Northern Ireland; a builder explained how God had found him an especially scarce set of tiles.

The second characteristic of the movement is its sheer scope. Far from being on the fringe, Evangelicals are currently taking over the mainstream. There are, today, at least 400 million Charismatics worldwide, their numbers having doubled in ten years. Today Evangelical/Charismatics represent 25 percent of the world Christian communion (In 1906 they were less than 1 percent), and by the year 2000 it's been estimated that the proportion will be over 30 percent—almost one in three.

Finally, this is a truly international movement, a genuine prototype of the global culture envisaged for the twenty-first century, a network linked by computer, jet and fax. The organization which prompted my visit to Austin, for instance —the annual, international March For Jesus,—is part-sponsored by Ichthus, the British chain of New Churches to which the Ellen family's Oxford New Testament Church, in turn, belongs. Thus Lloyd, before he even met the Ellens, was connected to them via two international organizations; that his visit to Blackstone was inspired by his faith is typical. Between Europe, North America, South America, Africa, Russia, Korea, Australia, and even, come the mid-Nineties, mainland China, there flows a constant stream of leaders and Evangelists, of information and ideas. The result is global Christianity, a new-look, high-tech spirituality of unprecedented drive and clout.

Of these three, growth is the most striking. Take the one-day Charismatic street festival called March For Jesus. Back in 1987, when a series of local British Charismatic marches first coalesced into a large "Anti-Materialism" gathering around the City of London,

15,000 marched. Next year, the occasion was repeated: 50,000 marched. By 1992, numbers had soared to 200,000 Europe-wide. By now, the March had gone international, with gatherings in more than thirty countries. In the U.S., in particular, the March's growth took on the parabola of a space-shot: 1,200 marched in Austin in 1990; 22,000 marched in Austin and Houston in 1991; 300,000, nationwide, in 1992; and by June 1994, an estimated 1.5 million marched in over 550 cities throughout the United States, and over ten million worldwide.

And yet this is routine, it turns out, for the growth of virtually any Evangelical/Charismatic gathering, from the great prayer and worship meetings known as Spring Harvest in the U.K. (2,700 in 1978, 80,000 by 1993) to the explosive growth of the British "house church" movement ("house" meaning, originally, the homes of denominationally dissatisfied Christians, but later rented premises like school halls), which numbered 100 in 1970, perhaps 120,000 today, and probably 200,000 by the end of the century. The Seventh-Day Adventists in the United States (of which a breakaway sect is Branch Davidian, of Waco fame) have grown from 365,000 to 666,000 members since the mid-Sixties, the Jehovah's Witnesses from 330,000 to 752,000. The Assemblies of God have quadrupled from 572,000 to 2.1 million, while the more mainstream American Fundamentalist Southern Baptists have 15 million members and are now the largest Protestant denomination in the U.S.A.

Such statistics are remarkable, but the really extraordinary figures are global. Take Latin America: as the British academic David Martin showed in his seminal book *Tongues of Fire,* this bulwark of traditional Catholicism has seen a dramatic swing towards Evangelical/Charismatic Protestantism, their numbers having soared eightfold from 5 million to at least 40 million since the late Sixties. South Korean Protestantism tripled between 1940 and 1961, doubled between 1961 and 1971 and tripled again in the following decade, until in the early 1980s Protestants accounted for 41 percent of the population. In Zaire, the Evangelical Church is growing at 7 percent annually. In the Philippines, Evangelicals are averaging 10 percent growth annually—and thus should more than double in ten years. At least 30 percent of the former Soviet Union's 280 million people are now believers, according to estimates by Sovietologist Paul Lucey. Small wonder that in 1989 Gorbachev announced his baptism. All but nine of the world's 223 nations were due to take part in March For Jesus (MFJ) 1994— indeed, the expansion even includes countries such as Japan and India, which are also seeing fundamentalist revivals of indigenous religions.

This is such a remarkable transformation that it is worth taking a step back for perspective. In 1900, for instance, the northern hemisphere had 83 percent of the world's total Christian population, while the south had 17 percent; but by 1980, the south had nearly half the world's total. Or, as the theological historian Howard Snyder points out, today Christians number more than half of the population in two thirds of the world's 223 nations. Snyder sums up: "Christianity has become a global faith, the most universal faith in history."

Clearly we are living through the fastest expansion of Christianity ever; and it may be that this is part of a much broader transformation of Western culture. Perhaps the century that began with Freud's discovery of the unconscious is now heading for a climax in which irrationalism expands as faith in logic and science is in decline. Indeed, if the essence of Western culture can be defined as a combination of skepticism and faith in step-by-step rationality, then assuredly the Decline of the West —at this late-twentieth-century moment of Western "triumph"— is already fact.

The indications that a religious revival was afoot have been in the air for some time. There was, for instance, a special degree of noise around Billy Graham's U.K. visit in 1989—it seemed as if half the cars in London, that autumn, had "Life" stickers in the back window. Then there was the born-again conversion of media mogul Rupert Murdoch, who further declared, in interview, that a religious revival was the world's next big media story. Then there was the rampant paranormalism of the New Age movement—our local pub started "psychic nights" and got instant, standing-room-only crowds.

In late 1989, a TV magazine program did a short piece describing an Evangelical church in Bracknell, Surrey. This church had raised 2 million pounds for a new church building; its members showed a wild, arm-waving enthusiasm more American than British. I was intrigued. So I rang the pastor, went to see him, listened to him talk for two hours and came away with the sense of a totally self-contained, self-sufficient world: of a network, local and global, of people who shared like ideas of worship, morality, music, even clothes. Here were people with dramatic, if surprising beliefs; with elaborate, high-technology organizational systems; with an utter determination to persuade everyone in the world to their point of view. Here was a movement, a "trend,"—and one that seemed to fit into something wider still: a change of *Zeitgeist*. For in 1989 the high materialism of the Eighties had palpably peaked, and was in the process of turning into something different—and that something came to be characterized, in all its various forms, under the umbrella term "spirituality."

The particular manifestations of spirituality being discussed here need definition. The "Evangelical" part of the "Evangelical/Charismatic" nexus is plain enough—as the *Oxford English Dictionary* puts it, "From the 18th century applied to that school of Protestants which maintains that the essence of the Gospel consists in the doctrine of salvation by faith in the atoning death of Christ and denies that either good works or the sacraments have any saving efficacy." To which one might add: an unshakable belief in fundamentals like original sin and the sanctity of family life, plus an intense need to convey such principles to the man next door.

But Charisma? The noted Church statistician Donald Barrett (responsible for some of the statistics quoted above) reckons that, in traditional Charismatic groups like Elim and the Assemblies of God, it means Christians who "seek a postconversion experience called baptism in the Holy Spirit," and—as John Capon paraphrased Barrett in the *Baptist Times* in 1991—"recognize that a Spirit-based believer may receive one or more of the supernatural gifts known in the early church." Barrett has identified these "gifts" as: "instantaneous sanctification, the ability to prophesy, to practice divine healing through prayer, to speak in tongues, interpret tongues, sing in tongues, sing in the spirit, pray with upraised hands, experience dreams, visions, discernment of spirits, words of wisdom, words of knowledge, emphasis on miracles, exorcisms, resuscitations, deliverances, and signs and wonders . . ." And that's just to get you started. Nevertheless, one gets the feel. The Church, like society at large, has its Romantic and its Classical modes; and it is natural, clearly, for Charisma, as one cutting edge of the great, if largely unrecognized, Romantic revival of the last thirty years (a key interpretation, incidentally, of the so-called "Counterculture") to major on such "experience"—with its emphasis on signs, wonders, shrieks and swoonings—and we already know what "resuscitations" means. Now: is this Romantic or is this Romantic?

A more descriptive definition of the Evangelical/Charismatic movement might just as well concentrate on language, dress, and music. Despite the different places Charisma turns up—and there are New Christian claques inside almost all the denominations, from Evangelical Anglicans to Charismatic Catholics—it is, nevertheless, a style you recognize the moment it enters a room. I remember well the very first Charismatic service I ever went to—held in a school hall in Cobham, Surrey (New Church groups regularly hire their own premises) by the Cobham Christian Fellowship, leader Gerald Coates. By early evening the place was packed. Glam girls with glittering teeth gave out programs; old men in Paisley shirts smiled benevolently on;

fraught couples with flailing kids, young blokes with rings in their ears, best-behavior eight-year-olds, infinitely wobbly grandmas —all burst uproariously, come the start of the service, into the first of the evening's Charismatic hymns, "Shine Jesus Shine," written by Ichthus member Graham Kendrick (a key quality of all Charismatic services is the extent to which they sing their own, specially written music). Like most Charismatic hymns, this song has a feel somewhere between the new-look Labour Party and the Eurovision Song Contest.

The hands were up, the forefingers pointing, the congregation swaying in a kind of third cousin of the twist; the noise, helped on by a ten-piece band, was quite startling, until the end of the evening when Gerald Coates, microphone in hand, launched into an end-of-service winder-downer, and the band played moody, low-key music in the background. Gerald's theme was the struggle for Christian expression behind the then-still-extant Iron Curtain: the congregation's special guest that evening had been pastor Petru Dugulescu from Romania. "In nineteen sixty-five a man called Petru," crooned Gerald, in a Reaganesque rumination over Petru's speech, "a man of twenty years of age . . . came under the influence of God . . . we have the video of Timisoara Square . . . Lord, I love you . . ." Quite suddenly, Gerald's voice began to quiver and then break. Moments later I realized that Gerald was dissolving into tears.

This event established a style for all the Charismatic services I saw, in every denomination, during the next four years. The tears, especially, are a common feature, for an extreme emotional lability is characteristic of all Charisma. But just as typical was the organizational background of those Cobham services. Gerald Coates' Cobham Christian Fellowship, one of the earliest and most visible (around ten thousand members) of the New Churches, had started in the early Seventies, literally in Gerald's own front room. The break with the old denominations had come about because Coates and his fellow worshippers felt that the traditional churches had lost all genuine moral conviction—not to mention all sense of the supernatural power of God. An outsider might find the notion of "resuscitations" bizarre, but to a New Christian it is, if anything, rather easier to take than the notion of an all-powerful God who isn't all-powerful. Healing the sick, raising a corpse even—these are minor accomplishments for a God who made the universe in seven days. Hence, perhaps, the difficulty such groups have with notions like moral relativity, or the complex debate around abortion, or the interpretation of the Adam and Eve story as "beautiful legend." What is surprising is that they felt they had to do something about it. Fifty years ago, they would have *known* it was not their place. But in the late Sixties, erupting spontaneously all over the U.K. (and, as emerged later, all over the Western world) these little groups began, in the spirit of the times, to "do their own thing." It just so happened that their particular thing was neither sex, nor drugs, nor rock and roll: it was religion.

They launched their own services, they hired their own halls, they expanded a thousand fold. More significantly, their influence has been out of all proportion to their size, because they have colonized the traditional churches. It is in the attendance at a Charismatic-led inter-denominational event like the Marches For Jesus (a sevenfold increase between 1993 and 1994) that you get a true sense of what such influence really means. Most participants are from the traditional denominations rather than New Churches, yet it is the "Evangelical/Charismatic" style of worship that dominates the day. Anglicans, Catholics, Methodists, Baptists, the Salvation Army, even—they're all there, engaging with the full New Church supernatural agenda, shouting, dancing, bursting into tears.

March For Jesus started in the late Eighties as a one-day Christian praise march, organized by British New Church leaders; but as its protagonists worldwide point out, it is a great deal more than just a march. For one thing, it is a year-round organization —with offices and staff—because it takes that long to organize the events. For another, it has inevitably become a network of like-minded believers who have very quickly started thinking beyond marches: social work, housing, helping the sick. But above all, MFJ is a highly visible international symbol of the sheer power of the new Christianity—out there on the streets, noisy, enthusiastic, citizen-led, "bottom-up" as the sociologists say, congregation-driven.

Critical, also, is the movement's instinct for boundary crossing—a tame enough notion on the surface, yet actually one of the deepest, most subversive ideas of the twentieth century. From E. M. Forster's "only connect" in 1912 via the measurer-defines-the-measured thought-forms of quantum physics to cross-departmental "holism" in modern business, a strand of postreductionist thinking has been running counter to our 300-year-old belief in separation (the step-by-step production line, for instance) and specialization. Thus, the inter-denominational "holism" of March For Jesus is right in tune with the incoming all-embracing, postsegmentation world view of the Nineties. So too is that most popular of New Church tenets, "the priesthood of every believer." In the New Churches people declare themselves, in effect, their own pastors—and you would be hard put to find a specialization with a more specific and particular history than the priesthood.

In a word, such thinking is "gestalt": the form of thought in which a thing—or person, or business—is defined above all by its relationship with the circumstances in which it operates, so that the boundaries between the two are blurred and crossed. Whether it's a psychotherapist's patient defined by the family whence he/she came, or a light wave/particle defined by the scientist's questions about it, or a Nineties business re-engineered by its relationship with its environment, or the New Churches encouraging the old denominations to sink their differences, break down their boundaries, and march together—in all cases, a belief in the inter-relatedness of all things is evident, as is an approach which suggests that you cannot understand the parts without at least appreciating the whole.

The final, and perhaps most surprising, aspect of the New Church is its politics. As the Nineties have gradually got into their stride, center and left have come to ever-increasing prominence in New Church culture—which is the more remarkable because in both the U.S. and the U.K. fundamentalist culture has for so long been dominated by the right. This rediscovered radicalism is especially marked among the U.K. churches, and it has helped to make them a role model for the world.

March For Jesus was born here, and its principles, if not exactly left wing, are profoundly post-Eighties: community, feminism, inter-church co-operation on behalf of the poor. Ichthus, the London-based chain of churches which was one of the prime movers behind March For Jesus, is the U.K.'s community-oriented church *par excellence*: its members live in some of the poorest parts of London, they run schools, playgroups, a non-alcohol pub, employment schemes. Such activities hark bark to basic Christian virtues—the notion, for instance, that if I have two coats and you have none, then it makes sense for me to let you have one I'm not using.

Not that there is anything predictable about this Christian revival, especially given the movement's wrap-round, all-pervasive supernaturalism. Consider, for instance, the popularity in New Church circles of the word "Anabaptists," which is used as a shorthand for Christian traditions one might try to emulate. Yet the Anabaptists—especially the Anabaptist groups of, say, Holland and Germany in the sixteenth-century—were not so much Christian socialists as Christian communists, or even Christian anarchists. Prone to a brand of wild, roller-coaster millenarianism, the Anabaptists had whole cities in medieval Germany, for instance, getting hold of the idea that Christ had returned among them, declaring UDI, going from communism to free love to fascism within months—

all in one beautiful, psychologically faultless swallow dive of free-fall zeal.

And for those who "know" such shenanigans could never happen today, perhaps one should recall just three names: Manson, Koresh and Jim Jones. Not only were all three "Christians" (Manson, surprisingly enough, thought he was Jesus) but Jim Jones—in a phase of his career which had less publicity than the mass-suicide of his followers in Guyana in 1978—was, in the mid-Seventies the paid-up *socialist* chairman of the San Francisco housing authority. Our fears should suit the times. We are so used to right-wing fundamentalism as the language of Christianity gone wrong that we've clean forgotten the other fundamentalisms that have been just as characteristic of Christianity in the past. As the millennium draws nearer, and as the mass unemployment of the information age kicks in, a populist, post-"Prosperity" left-wing fundamentalism could be quite as threatening as anything cooked up by the right.

There have been many Christian upsurges of one kind or another throughout history, but they do share certain things in common.

The twilight of the Roman Empire, when Christianity was born; the Christian revivalism of expansionist, twelfth-century Europe; the Reformation, with its doppelgänger, the Renaissance; the rise of Wesleyanism amid the first stirrings of the Industrial Revolution; the Second Great Awakening in the U.S., amid the economic turmoil of 1830s' New England; and, perhaps the most suggestive tale of all in Norman Cohn's 1970 classic *The Pursuit of the Millennium,* those uniquely wild-side Anabaptist activities of medieval Europe. What, pondered the learned professor, plodding dustily around the shelves of a thousand European libraries, would make a whole city, a whole region, simultaneously flip? What connected the rise of millenarianism in Belgium and Northern France between the eleventh and fourteenth centuries, with similar manifestations in southern and central Germany from the thirteenth century down to the Reformation? Or comparable events in Holland? Or Westphalia? Or London?

It was by no means, reckoned Cohn, the worst off materially who were most liable to convert, even though in every medieval village there were many who lived at or near subsistence level, and a bad harvest often meant mass famine. Nor was it the worst abused, even though for centuries whole areas were repeatedly thrown into confusion by wars between feuding barons. Cohn stresses that "to an extent which can hardly be exaggerated, peasant life was shaped and sustained by custom and communal routine." Quite simply, "It was not often that settled peasants could be induced to embark on the pursuit of the Millennium." *Settled* peasants, mark you. By contrast, millenarianism found its most fertile breeding ground in the areas of new European prosperity: the nascent market economy, where the impact of rapid social change was making itself felt. The new freelance weavers, say, torn from the soil, the first stirrings of a rootless urban proletariat . . . Self-employment . . . Change . . . Insecurity . . .

In 1958, the *Journal of Experimental Analysis of Behavior* published a stress study on a couple of monkeys. They found that the one given ways of controlling whether it received an electric shock or not—that is, the one capable of affecting the outcome by making a "correct" decision—suffered more stress than the one which got just as many shocks, but was spared the agony of choice. *Uncertainty*—that, for Cohn, was the keyword. Worse even to suffer uncertainty than to know things would continue to be be dire.

In the conclusion to his book, Cohn makes the obvious connections with our own "Age of Uncertainty." He, of course, was writing in the late Sixties, well before the information revolution, as we now know it, got under way—before mass computerization, before the microchip, before the great recessions of the Seventies, early Eighties and now Nineties; before—to quote another book title of the late Seventies—*The Collapse of Work.*

In short, very arguably, there have been few times in history so ripe for a religious revival, and even for the extremes of millennialism, as right now.

At the end of one of the many Charismatic conventions I sat in on, thirty of the delegates came forward from the floor to pray. It was a moment of pure Charisma, of instinctive, inspirational prayer. They weren't praying about any world crisis, but were offering their leaders a blessing for the eighteen-hour days, the months of schlepp and trauma to come. So they stood there, in a cluster, in traditional—but to an outsider, quite extraordinary—Charismatic poses: arms stretched out wide; arms stretched forward in benediction; one arm resting on a leader's shoulder, the other arm stretched skyward, like a Sunday School picture of Christ.

This strange, medieval tableau seemed to convey a feeling of intense pain, even anguish, counterbalanced by this anxious, clinging, almost desperate faith. For a moment, you could feel how a society assailed by unemployment, nuclear terror, environmental Apocalypse and collapsing communities, and rendered rudderless by the seeming impossibility, ever, of being sure of anything at all for more than six months ahead—you could feel how such a society could turn to the time-honored way of achieving serenity, the option known familiarly as: religious conversion.

2

How Green Is My Vicarage

> But the defining thing in the Modernist mode is not so much
> that things fall apart but that they fall *together* . . . The threat
> to (conventional) order comes not from the break-down of a
> planetary system but from the repudiation of a filing system,
> where order derives as much from keeping separate as from
> holding together, with dockets and folders and pigeon-holes
> to distinguish and hold things apart.
>
> James McFarlane, "The Mind of Modernism"
> in *Modernism,* ed. Bradbury and McFarlane, 1976

But that wasn't how the New Churches saw it at the start.

Take 50-year-old Gerald Coates, whose Sunday service we
looked at earlier. His Pioneer organization currently links a chain
of eighty like-minded Charismatic churches around the South
East, while the local Cobham, Surrey, congregation he founded,
home base for the movement, has gone from nought to 650 in
just twenty years: indeed it's doubled since 1990.

Back in the late Sixties, Gerald Coates was just another aspirant
clothes shop manager in Epsom, outer London; and just another
ordinary, everyday member of his local Brethren Church in nearby
Cobham. He wasn't even a pastor. Nor was he (nor is he still)
within light years of the counterculture of the Sixties, visually:
Gerald is the sort of chap who wears club ties with diagonal stripes

and means it, who uses words like "product" and "upmarket"; his feel is more Epsom Chamber of Commerce's Retailer Most Likely To Succeed (1970) than New Age. What Gerald did have in common with the counterculture, however, was an ever-intensifying sense of the paranormal. In his autobiography, *An Intelligent Fire,* he describes, memorably, how he first "talked in tongues"—that crucial Charismatic experience in which believers, spirit-filled, start crying out ecstatically in words which bear no relation to their own language—or any other, usually.

To win more time for his religious activities, Gerald had landed himself a job as as a postman—starting at 4:30 A.M., but finishing at around 2:00 P.M.

> One day, cycling through Cobham, I began to sing one of Charles Wesley's hymns:
>
>> Finish then thy new creation;
>> Pure and spotless let us be;
>> Let us see our whole salvation
>> Perfectly secured by thee
>> Keyarunda—Sadavoostoo!
>
> Heavens above—I thought to myself—that's not in the hymn book!

He was talking in tongues! On the postal round! Needless to say, this and similar metaphysical experiences were just the kind of thing his local Brethren Church had difficulty with. "You must renounce this," they told him. But then came the moment of sociological breakthrough, the moment when Gerald became, unknowingly, a late-twentieth-century hero: for instead of accepting the Brethren line, knowing his place, swallowing his dissatisfactions and leaving it to the specialists, Gerald decided to hold his own services, in his own way, in his own home.

Do-it-yourself!

Crossing the boundaries, in fact . . . He had three like-minded friends in Cobham, and along with his wife they formed his initial nucleus, otherwise known as "network." As Gerald puts it: "Eventually I decided to gather the five one Sunday morning. The coffee table was placed in the center of the room, a white tablecloth covered it and a plate was placed on one side with some bread. Ribena was diluted in a glass. . . . I stood in the doorway of the front room, which measured twelve by fourteen. 'God in heaven—what am I doing?' . . . I'd transferred the Gospel Hall into my front room."

No young man brought up on a council estate (as Gerald was) in his father's time would have had the gall to set up his own system in quite this way; and, most especially—for this was the truly novel touch—in his own front room. And yet years later, Gerald would discover that all over the U.K. in the early Seventies, other, like-minded Charismatics were doing the same thing— quite unbeknown to each other. To borrow Rupert Sheldrake's phrase, a "morphic resonance," a pattern of thought, evolving like a biological form, can, at the right moment, resonate right across society. The early Seventies saw the first stirrings of the home education movement, of home health care and home births, and of home employment (now known as "telecommuting")—not to mention more familiar forms of do-it-yourself like home carpentry and home decoration. Boundaries were broken down.

Much of it was plain dissatisfaction with the established churches, notably the Church of England. By the late Sixties, the Church of England was burnt out whichever way you looked at it. Belief in the supernatural? Hard to imagine one of those kindly, twinkly, old-time vicars doing a little light ghost-busting, say. Moral absolutes? Here were bishops explaining that it was not what you did, rather the spirit in which you did it. Style of worship, liturgy? Here was the one area where the established church really did have identity still, even genuine beauty. Yet while it was undeniable that choral evensong in a cathedral was a profound celebration of *something*, exactly what was not so clear. The chaste, poetic spirit of Englishness? What Churchill called "our Famous History"? (Those military banners). Whatever it was, it felt utterly remote to thrusting, ex-working class aspirants like Gerald, of whom, by the early Seventies, there were a very great many in the U.K. (they later voted for Mrs. Thatcher). The term they used, curiously enough, to dismiss that alien C of E atmosphere was "religiosity"; and yet, quite as much, they were plainly talking class.

I remember meeting Gerald Coates in 1990, at his offices in Esher, West London, just down the road from Cobham. By then he part-owned a Georgian house on Esher High Street, and his offices were converted out of the stables, just a stroll across the yard. Low-slung settee, matte black wood, tubular steel, photograph on Gerald's desk of him with Cliff Richard . . . But the detail that reverberates in the mind was just in front of the office door, on the wall: a cluster of framed covers of Gerald's 'my-life-as-a-pastor publications. Just as a club owner displays his snaps of visiting royalty, or a record producer lines the corridor with golden discs, Gerald was showing off his books-in-print. As a showbiz interior, in fact, Gerald's office was unexceptional (if ten years passé). As the visual vocabulary of any kind of religious pastor, by the standards of middle England it was bizarre. For the plain modernity—well, near-modernity—of it stood out. In twentieth-century Britain the whole notion of God's Majesty had got so hopelessly mixed up with Her Majesty and the established way that mainstream religion, however unconsciously, had by now become utterly antipathetic, architecturally or organizationally, to the new. Perhaps this suggests why such dramatically new religious forms appeared, specifically, in the U.K. First into the Industrial Revolution and first out of it, bankrupted by war and at the end of Empire, Britain had, by the Seventies, come to the very end of one cultural road—and what could be more archetypical, culturally, than the Church?

Time for green shoots. Gerald's hesitant initiative, and those of others like him, struck gold. People wanted, simultaneously, the solid certainties of doctrine and the fluid outpourings of Charisma —and they were getting neither from the C of E. By 1972, thirty people were bursting out of Gerald's front room; by the mid-Seventies, more than a hundred were meeting in Cobham's Ralph Bell Hall. Gerald went on to wages—£25 a month at first —from offerings taken up weekly by his congregation; and as the Seventies wore on, those like-minded groups countrywide started linking up. The networking began.

It has been estimated that by the late Eighties there were around 109,000 house church members in the U.K.—up from 81,000 in 1985 and 44,000 in 1979—whose congregations are members of a whole series of New Church groups across the country: Coates' eighty-strong Pioneer organization in Surrey, Roger Forster's Ichthus in South East London, Terry Virgo's New Frontiers in Sussex, Harvestime (covenanted ministries) in West Yorkshire— according to the Evangelical Alliance there are many hundreds of them. There is no clear national structure, and the picture is complicated by the swelling floodtide of revivalists still within the denominations—Evangelical Anglicans, Charismatic Catholics, you name it. The Evangelical Alliance (EA), headquartered in London, does form a kind of umbrella body (Ichthus member Clive Calver is the Director General) but in no sense are any of the groups "under" the EA.

Such national structure as exists mainly shows itself in national events, and whether the events are established (like Spring Harvest, or March For Jesus) or new-hatched (like the first Dawn 2000 church-planting conference in Birmingham, in February 1992), the same leaders tend to turn up at the different venues. Gerald Coates, Roger Forster, Lynn Green of Youth With a Mission, Clive Calver of the Alliance—all these, and fifty others, gather regularly on an endless stream of platforms around the country. But the combination is different each time, and what brings them together is not a permanent structure, but the varying demands of each separate event. Each time, a different group of people is in charge. So the movement is, above all—in the current business jargon—task-oriented, with teams rather than hierarchies, capable of coming together and splitting apart in new forms each time, amoebalike, fluid. Aquarian, you could say, because that water image is more curiously apposite for our age than the heads who coined it could ever have dreamed. The revival's weird resonance with modern business structures ("tight-loose" is another bit of recent management-speak that fits New Church culture) is only one of many ways in which this most conservative (in some ways) movement reflects the most progressive (in other ways) developments of our time.

The other classic resonance is the revival's instinct for decentralization and all things "local"—as manifested, for instance, by Pioneer, in a string of Cobham community initiatives including the local youth club (taken over from the Council), a hostel for the homeless (with two more planned), several "outreaches" for the elderly that include work in local hospitals, plus innumerable social and support groups for Pioneer members. The result of such instinctive local focus has been that New Churches like Pioneer are sliding imperceptibly into the vacuum left by the imploding welfare state. Thus they are, in their own way, part of the only current growth area of Western political awareness: community politics.

This is especially true of the other prominent group in March For Jesus, London's Ichthus—the church which most fascinates the North Americans. For where Pioneer's emphasis has, inevitably, given its location, been on the kinder, leafier lifestyle of an outer-London suburb, Ichthus is positioned at the cutting edge of Western decline—the inner cities.

Founded in Peckham, London, in September 1974 (a little later than Pioneer), Ichthus grew to number around four hundred members in the early Eighties. Today there are forty-two congregations in London and its South-East suburbs, with around 2,100 adults and several hundred children in Sunday morning congregation meetings—plus another five communities in the Middle East and one in France.

The list of Ichthus community projects is heroic—focussed, in the best traditions of local-oriented movements, on the heart of its original catchment area, Peckham, home to some of the most intractable and desperate "underclass" estates in the U.K., and with male unemployment running at around 30 percent.

In the last five years, Ichthus projects have included an alcohol-free pub, The Brown Bear; a launderette and community center on the Gloucester Grove Estate; two nurseries and a primary school; a pregnancy counselling service; an "outreach" group to help prostitutes; help and housing for the homeless; a scheme to support housing estate residents' bid for self-management—not to mention innumerable instances of "Jesus action," which may include anything from buffet suppers for the elderly to reading for the blind.

But perhaps Ichthus' most remarkable Peckham commitment is an interdenominational employment project known as Pecan, headquartered in an old Baptist church hall just off the Gloucester Grove Estate. From there a staff of twenty-six—most, but not all, Ichthus members—make contact with the huge reservoir of long-term unemployed on estates like Gloucester Grove, aiming to knock on each door in their 8,000-household catchment area at least three times a year.

The results are striking. "Positive outcomes"—defined as clients placed either on courses or in jobs—were running, in 1995, at 75 percent, among the highest for comparable schemes in the entire country. (Although definitions vary, the figure for the local Training and Enterprise Council, for instance, is around 28 percent.) But then such fruits, in turn, reflect a distinctive office culture: everyone works in the same open plan office; everyone from the managing director to the crèche lady earns the same

£13,400 a year; and in 1993, Pecan was the first company in South-East London to win one of the government's "Investor in People" awards. Furthermore, Pecan workers live in and around the estate themselves, thereby removing the geographical distance which usually separates social workers from their clients.

Small wonder that the word "holistic" turns up rather often in the vocabulary of Ichthus founder, sixty-two-year-old Roger Forster —rather a New Agey word, perhaps, for an Evangelical Christian, but it does convey the instinct for inclusion, rather than separation, which is critical to the New Church world-view. As Roger puts it: "Our mission is for the whole body of believers, not a specialized section." Or, as he also believes, it is *every* Christian's duty to evangelize, not just a few elite shock troops of, say, the missionary societies. Inclusion, connection, involvement—this very holistic spirit, Roger argues, was precisely that of the early Church, before the decline, before miracles "died out" (or were ruled out), before a sense of Christian community was superseded, before the Church was subsumed into the Roman Empire and began its centuries-old identification with the state. "That's why our church's symbol is the fish rather than the cross," says Roger. "Because the fish— *ichthus* in Greek—was *the* early church symbol. The cross came centuries later."

He's quite a patriarch, these days, is Roger. He has plumped for the moustache-and-beard grizzled farmer look, earthy, home-on-the-range, and it is curious to be addressing Ichthus's agenda with someone who looks so traditional. The young Roger, however, was something of a pioneer. In his own Charismatic-Christian way, he seems to have been one of those "beat" Fifties precursors of the mystic Sixties: a kind of Evangelical Ginsberg, Maslow or Huxley. Indeed, his career kicked off with the seeing of a vision while at Cambridge.

"I was reading this attack on Christianity, *hee-hee,*" says Roger, who has a way of chuckling as he talks, "when suddenly this inner voice said 'Roger Forster, do you love me?' 'How can I answer you,' I replied, 'Me a little scrap of dust, *hee, hee*?' " Nevertheless, says Roger, this unusual exchange was accompanied with the sense that the whole room—table, chairs everything—was transfigured, momentarily: veritably awash with God.

The experience was profound enough to have fuelled Roger through all the long, uphill slog that followed—through the RAF years, when Roger preached to fellow National Service-men, through the time when Roger worked as a roving speaker, addressing other pastors' congregations on invitation, "living by faith." Back then, Roger's supernatural inclinations were, to put it mildly, marginal. "People forget just how very secular the Fifties were," he says. "This really was the era of the triumph of science." And then came the Sixties, and things got worse: "sex, pornography, collapse of standards—then the Beatles came along and snapped up a whole generation." A traumatic time.

And yet, amazingly, those same Sixties spawned a rebirth of that very spirituality which had been so marginalized in Roger's youth. "I noticed it in my own father," says Roger. "He was a liberal methodist, a good man, but he'd never really related to the supernatural. Yet towards the end of his life—he died in 1959—he began to pray again."

Slowly but surely, more and more people became receptive to Roger's supernatural word. Students, in particular, seemed to jump at it. When, in the Seventies, a further impulse developed in Roger—to "root himself" as he puts it, "locally," and thus to launch Ichthus—his constituency was ready made. The typically New-Church feel of Ichthus proved irresistible, both in the fostering of Charisma, and in the practicalities of day-to-day organization.

The Spirit and the Word . . . Or *Reason and Faith,* as one of Roger's book titles has it. A combination of the mystical and the practical, as expressed in community activism, camaraderie, a new-found sense of one global church rather than feuding, schismatic denominations; and feminism, something novel in any church; and congregations made up of active participants rather than passive observers—perhaps the essence of Ichthus's appeal (and of groups like it) is the breadth of needs they meet, both spiritual and physical. This may also explain, in turn, how March For Jesus became such a powerful symbol for the movement as a whole, because MFJ, too, is above all about breadth, about the reconnection of the separate. In that symbolic, marchers' determination to be off and doing, MFJ also shows the practicality of the movement. And the paranormal element is there, too, because the march is about "winning territory for Jesus" (the geographical school of spiritual warfare), whereby an area—be it a college, red-light district, whole city, even—can be won back from Satan by the physical presence of Christians. (This was the thinking behind the decision to hold that first 1987 march around the "demonic" City of London.) Most of all, perhaps, MFJ expresses a very 1990s feeling, transcending society as a whole: a postconservative, post-Eighties sense that a mind-set is ending, that fences are down, chains broken, restraints released; a whole floodtide of pent-up, strapped-down, locked-in emotions are swarming, suddenly, into an open place, "taking the walls of the church," as American MFJ puts it, "for the world to see."

An open place—a global place, indeed. The 1994 march took place in every capital city in every time zone in the world; and yet each individual march remained very much part of the community that spawned it. This direct link between global and local, regional and international, brings to mind the Green slogan, "Think globally, act locally." For like the movement as a whole, MFJ is shot through with this sense that things seemingly opposite are natural bedfellows, albeit in tension.

One might legitimately ask how all this forward-thinking holism squares with some of the more outlandish beliefs and doctrines of the Evangelical/Charismatic movement. Less born-again than born-yesterday, aren't the Elect engaged, culturally, in one single-minded, Gadarene rush for the door marked Exit?

Again, the answer seems to lie in the fact that the movement as a whole is itself a manifestation of a union of opposites held in tension: that is precisely why the Evangelical/Charismatics have attracted their two-headed title. It is rooted in the feeling that the two parts of the movement really are at opposite ends of the spectrum, and if you leave out either of them you miss the point of both.

Hang on to your "/"; you'll need it. Because on the one hand,—the left side, as it were, of the "/"—Evangelical Christianity—does indeed contain the most adamantine rigidities. On abortion they are unequivocally, wholeheartedly "pro-life." Sex is unthinkable—un-Biblical! before marriage. Sin is original, inevitable and ingrained. Satan, otherwise "the Enemy," is alive and plotting—he black, we white. The Apocalypse? Revelation was right.

And should two or three such notions gather together in one place, then things can *really* move: witness those U.S. Evangelicals who convinced themselves in the early Eighties, that (a) the Soviets were Demonic, (b) the Apocalypse meant nuclear Armageddon, and (c) this was by no means all bad, as Armageddon was but an inevitable step toward Christ's rule.

Certainty. Sternness. Inflexibility. Law and Order. This is the traditional Puritan agenda, the kind of masculine, reason-driven (in form if not content) mental process that Edward de Bono calls "rock logic." Plus, critically, the Evangelical love-affair with the text of the Bible. In revival circles, to carry around some huge old family tome, highlighted with arcane notes, is the height of chic. This, of course, is the very stuff of the Reformation: no intercessors, priestly or otherwise, shall come between us believers and God's law.

On the Charismatic side of the equation, it's another country. Instead of grid-like rigidity we have the go-with-the-flow attitude which de Bono characterizes as "water logic." Instead of reason and order, we have instinct, vision, the Holy Ghost. Instead of step-by-step, linear progression, we have the all-at-once, the miraculous. Instead of the verbal architecture of the sermon, we have the pre-verbal instinctiveness of "tongues." This is the distinctively modern end of the movement, where change, fluidity, uncertainty and flexible boundaries are paramount. The Chinese use the concept of Tao to embrace such principles—the very word Fritjof Capra alighted on as he struggled to describe the "oriental" quality of late-twentieth-century atomic theory in his book *The Tao of Physics*.

Marshall McLuhan described the step-by-step, rationalist culture of print as "The Gutenberg Galaxy." That was by contrast with the culture he thought was superseding it—the new holistic, instinctive "all-at-once" culture of electricity. "Oral/Tactile" was what he called it, pointing out that the adoption of such a culture would involve rediscovering modes of perception more medieval than modern, more Eastern (he talked, for instance, about the great "oral" civilization of India) than anything we were used to in the West.

From McLuhan's perspective, we are now going through a kind of hi-tech Romantic revival, with society as a whole eschewing the "cognitive" in favor of the "experiential." The "experiential" religious revival (which was another of McLuhan's predictions) may be part and parcel of that process. Such a revival might need to embrace both the rocky, backward-looking mode and the watery, rollercoaster mode in a grand union-of-opposites—the love affair with solidity being a reaction to the experience of the fluid, a compensation for the terrors that inevitably go along with all that flux.

For what seemed like the five hundred and fortieth time, I was listening to the honeydew tones of Graham Kendrick's "Shine Jesus Shine":

> Shine, Jesus, shine,
> Fill this land with the Father's glory . . .

Flow, river, flow,
Flood the nations with grace
And mercy . . .

Very water logic, very Taoist . . . It was April 1992, and the
scene was the first U.K. meet of yet another Charismatic initiative,
the international church-planting conference Dawn 2000 in
Birmingham. Not only was there the routine line-up of U.K.
Charismatics—Roger Forster, Gerald Coates, Lynn Green et al.
—but a fair turn-out of internationals, too: Wolfgang Fernandez,
Dawn's European coordinator; Ule Haldeman from Switzerland;
Peter Wagner, church-plant whiz from Fuller Theological Semi-
nary, California—all had flown in for the launch. The objective: no
less than 20,000 New Churches in the U.K. by the year 2000. There
was much talk of the next focal point, the grand international
Dawn 2000 meeting scheduled for Seoul, Korea, in June 1994,
timed to coincide with that year's March For Jesus.

There were chirpy thirty-year-olds in Fairisle sweaters and
common-sense slacks, moody eighteen-year-olds with dangly hair
and crosses in their ears, florid fifty-year-olds, fluffy OAPS—all
smiled amiably on as, come the hymns, a line of Salvation Army
officers in the middle of the hall broke into the twist. One of the
things about dancing as you sing is that hymn books can be a
bit cumbersome—hence the Charismatic tradition of projecting
hymns onto a screen in front of the congregation, the better to act
out those experiential motions. Far preferable, this, to old-style,
hedged-in, hymn-book-in-hand Gutenberg because Touch is not
limited to the tame injunction, "Now turn to the person next
to you and give the Sign of Peace" (that is, shake hands). Arms
are thrown around shoulders, caresses, embraces, even kisses are
exchanged. For the exceptionally distressed, there are "love hugs,"
a kind of heavy-duty kiss-and-caress combo. It all fits McLuhan's
expectations of an oral/tactile culture. But such events also have
a startling capacity to swing from one end of the spectrum to the

other, combining a sometimes alarming expressiveness with a level of analysis one would have thought impossible in the same hall.

Most prominent of those in cognitive gear was the American Peter Wagner. He has satin-smooth, snow-white hair and that same moustache-and-beard option as Roger Forster though he favors the distinguished-professor-of-art variant. His first talk that Thursday morning began with more facts, statistics and measurements generally than you would have thought possible, and they just kept on coming. Launch costs for a Presbyterian church, U.S.A.: $500,000. Launch costs, Assemblies of God: $2,500. Presbyterian decline, Northern U.S.A., 1964–74: 50,000 members a year. Current growth projection, Assemblies of God? 5,000 new churches . . . The ordered, rational, superbly classical grid of Wagner's concepts crept out like a net across the conference so that whenever he and others like him were talking, it was unthinkable that anything remotely immeasurable or instinctive would ever happen in that hall again.

Nonetheless, during the first real celebration meeting of the conference, there occurred a moment of purest, most exemplary Charisma. One of the ways Charismatics facilitate the emotional content of a service is by running three or four hymns together one after another, seamlessly, into a kind of emotional ski-run uninterrupted by any sermonizing or rationality. That Thursday evening we had just such a troika on the trot, two jolly hymns, one moody—until we arrived, duly mellowed, at one of the few traditional hymns Charismatics still sing, "When I Survey the Wondrous Cross." As we swung through the slow, stately verses more and more emotional momentum built up until, after the very last note, there was silence . . . and the silence went on . . . thirty seconds . . . a minute . . . and the hall stayed silent . . . two minutes . . . Then a voice in the corner of the room spontaneously started yet another hymn—"Be Still for the Presence of the Lord" —and gradually the whole room joined in. As the song, and the mood, swelled up again the room was full of the most intense tenderness, gentleness and peace. You could almost sense people nestling, palpably, on the downy-soft breast of the Lord.

Which was why what followed was so especially strange: within minutes, Gerald Coates was speaking—his subject, Satanic child abuse. In a breathtaking emotional U-turn, the atmosphere was transformed. The audience's anger, its curses, its outrage poured out on the heads of the abusers—climaxing in a mass of Christians trying to exorcise the Devil right there in the very hall, arms up, faces contorted with ruinous imprecation.

You were left wondering, aghast, about the relationship between such tenderness and such wrath. Both Lamb and Beast had been invoked at once—with only the Elect, as the Congregation saw it, standing between the Lamb and its violation. All were Christian soldiers, Horatios on the bridge.

From gentle Jesus to *Dies Irae* in thirty minutes! 180 degrees without a skid mark. It was the wildest, most vertiginous Charismatic rollercoaster I had ever seen. Appalled, I shot out of the hall—and there, in an anteroom downstairs, I found a group of delegates who had already left the sound and fury of the room upstairs because they wanted privacy and quiet to read their Bibles. Silence. Calm. Order. That anteroom fulfilled the same function every day.

There, in one building, you could see the Evangelical/Charismatic movement in both modes: separated not, as is more usual, by time (as in the reason-emotion-reason sequence of one of those meetings), but by space: upstairs, the Charisma; downstairs, the Evangelical. Upstairs, Aquarius; downstairs, Gutenberg. Upstairs, the Spirit; downstairs, the Word. But both in the same building. And both in the same head.

Evangelical . . . / . . . Charismatic!

3

The Mystic West

It is perhaps possible for us to make some guess already as to these forms [of anticipated Western religious revival] which [it is self-evident] must lead back to certain elements of Gothic Christianity. Be that as it may, what is quite certain is that they will not be the product of any literary taste for Late-Indian or Late-Chinese speculation, but something of the type, for example, of Adventism and suchlike sects.

Oswald Spengler, *The Decline of the West,* vol. 11, 1922

The Waco cult . . . a mutation of an earlier Adventist splinter group . . .

Time, March 1993

The economic historian Karl Polanyi pointed out that the really dramatic changes in economic or cultural history tend to arrive, almost by definition, by surprise. In 1795, for instance, with the British Industrial Revolution already rolling, "Capitalism arrived unannounced . . . For some time England had actually been expecting a permanent recession of foreign trade when the dam burst, and the old world was swept away in one indomitable surge toward a planetary economy." The great revanche of the irrational in the late twentieth century is another example. Indeed, you could have been forgiven, during the Enlightenment's last stand

29

in the Seventies and Eighties, for predicting the polar opposite
of what we have seen—a never ending expansion of common
sensical, computer-driven automatism. Further, the breathtaking
expansion of what one might call "supernatural Christianity" has
been accompanied by a far more public decline in attendance at
traditional, conventional-style churches.

In the twenty years from 1970, for instance, the major denominations in the U.K. lost 1.5 million members—a million in the Seventies
and another half-million in the Eighties. In the U.S. between 1965 and
1988, the Episcopal Church declined from 3.4 million to 2.5 million,
the Presbyterians from almost 4 million to 3 million, and the United
Methodists from 11 million to 9.2 million. If conventional, formal-
istic Christianity is indeed dying on its feet, the link with the rise of
the New Church movement is clear: inspirational, rollercoaster Christianity seems to be what is now required.

Or as that great intuitive Tom Wolfe put it, in his prescient
"The Me Decade" (1976):

> Today it is precisely the most rational, intellectual, secu-
> larized, modernized, updated, relevant religions—all the
> brave, forward-looking Ethical Culture, Unitarian and
> Swedenborgian movements of only yesterday—that are
> finished, gasping, breathing their last. What the Urban
> Young People want from religion is a little . . . HALLE-
> LUJAH! . . . and TALKING IN TONGUES! . . . PRAISE
> GOD! Precisely that! In the most prestigious divinity schools
> today, Catholic, Presbyterian and Episcopal, the avant-garde
> movement—the leading edge—is "Charismatic Christianity"
> . . . featuring talking in tongues, ululalia, visions, holy-
> rolling, and other non-rational, even anti-rational practices.

From the hindsight of the Nineties, one might add in here the good
old Church of England, cantering gamely up in the rear. Figures
indicate that more than half of new Anglican ordinands now regard

themselves as Evangelicals, with the result, as the Reverend John Moore, director of the Anglican Church Pastoral Aid Society puts it, that "as only a thousand of the ten thousand Anglican livings currently have Evangelical trustees, four out of five of these ordinands are going to go into non-Evangelical positions."

No one, however, could possibly have grasped the immensity of what has been happening by keeping in touch with public consciousness via the usual channels. The American media had a good run in the Eighties with what was routinely described as "right-wing fundamentalism," tying it all up (quite correctly, as far as it went) with Eighties materialism, Evil Empire rhetoric and the Reagan backlash. In particular, a spectacular demolition job was done on "televangelists" like Jimmy Swaggart, the Bakkers and Oral Roberts. By the early Nineties, the European media, too, had grasped that some kind of weird Christian revivalism was in the air—a touch belatedly, one might think, given that a major source of U.S. inspiration has been the U.K. Snaps appeared in the papers of Charismatics waving their arms, the more enterprising documentary crews filmed exorcisms in the suburbs, and an endless parade of rather pallid-looking believers recited ever more repetitive visionary experiences on TV.

Not a bad story, and yet there was still a sense that all this was essentially marginal, fringe, a manifestation of the paranoid right to match that other Eighties phenomenon, the "Loony Left": both were held to be way out there in sociological limbo. The musical aesthetics of the movements didn't help. Dominated by the output of publishing house Make Way Music (which is very big on the work of songwriter and Ichthus member Graham Kendrick) the hymns being sung made it sound as if the whole revival was going transcendental to the theme tune from "Neighbours."

Nevertheless, the real denial, as they say, went deeper and had to do with prevailing attitudes towards the supernatural. A whole generation born between the wars, come to power in the Fifties, still there (just about) in the Eighties—with a consciousness that

stretches right across the political persuasions—is utterly dedicated
to the classical scientism of the European Enlightenment, and
remains wedded to such notions as scientific management,
scientific socialism, social engineering and making the desert
bloom. To this generation, the final exorcism of the superstitions
and grotesque Victorianisms of their parents—fictions in great
measure responsible, after all, for both wars *and* for Auschwitz—
has been a virtual crusade.

Against such a background, the return of irrationalism and
the supernatural—coming so soon after the brief efflorescence
of like-minded gobbledegook in the Sixties had been seen off—
was hardly going to be welcome. Helped on by certain visual aids
like short haircuts, power watches and rectangular briefcases, life
was supposed to have settled down again to the sure, square beat
of reason and the marketplace. Typical of the shock troops of
this reaction was the American scientists' organization CSICOP,
born out of a symposium held in Buffalo, New York, in the late
Seventies entitled "The New Irrationalisms: Antiscience and Pseu-
doscience." CSICOP consisted of an "international group of
prominent philosophers, psychologists, physical and biological scientists," whose early hit-list included Uri Geller, king of the fork-
benders, who CSICOP reckoned, after their rationalist attentions,
would never bend fork convincingly again. Similar attitudes were
prevalent in the work done by the Healthwatch Group in the U.K.
to "expose" attempts to cure cancer by nonconventional means;
and in the fall from grace of neomystic psychiatrist R. D. Laing, the
Sixties guru whose case histories included a woman who allegedly
cured herself by turning herself into a hound and back again in one
three-day episode from Good Friday to Easter Monday, and whose
reputation, by the mid-Eighties, rationalists felt had been well
kicked into touch.

By the late Eighties one could plausibly convince oneself that
the Enlightenment had quite won back its tottering throne
(a 1986 Channel Four book and-series package, "The New

Enlightenment," was typical), and the American writer Michael D'Antonio was only expressing the consensus when he declared in his 1989 round-up of Eighties fundamentalism *Fall from Grace, The Failed Crusade of the Christian Right*:

> In the end . . . the Christian Right crusade of the 1980s could be seen as America's longing look backward at religious absolutism. It was, it seems, only a pause in the secularizing process that has been underway since the turn of the century. The failure of the Christian Right crusade demonstrated that the born-again construct of a Christian America is no longer possible.

Which settled it, surely? Yet Tom Wolfe had finished up his essay "The Me Decade" with this ringing pronunciamento: "We are now, in the Me Decade, seeing the upward roll (and not yet the crest, by any means) of the third great religious wave in American history—" The first, by this count, occurring in the 1740s, the second between 1825 and 1850—"one that historians will very likely term the Third Great Awakening." In the early Nineties, an unrepentant Mr. Wolfe was running around the lecture circuit telling anyone who would listen that the "next" hot trend would be a religious revival . . .

But hadn't that already happened? And wasn't it now over? Or were we still in danger, as science writer and CSICOP supporter Isaac Asimov had earlier warned, of plunging back (unspeakable horror!) into an irrationalist "Dark Age"?

One of Wolfe's bull points was the connection he made between the "counterculture" and the new religiosity. In the Nineties, the counterculture, despite the heroic efforts of Eighties conservatism, is not merely surviving, it is—in its son-of-counterculture mode, New Age—running rampant. Indeed there are traditionalists who define the Clinton-Gore presidency of the U.S.A. as "the counterculture come to power." Even so, Wolfe's countercultural-

Charismatic connection might seem a touch surprising, inasmuch as your routine hippy and your regular Evangelical are not necessarily the first folks one thinks of as bedfellows.

Nevertheless, as Wolfe puts it:

Very few people went into the hippy life with religious intentions, but many came out of it absolutely RIGHTEOUS. The sheer power of the drug LSD is not to be underestimated. It was quite easy for an LSD experience to take the form of a religious vision . . . without knowing it, many heads were re-living the religious fervor of their grandparents or great-grandparents.

Norman Cohn, likewise struck by similarities between modern acid culture and his medieval millennialists, wrote: "Self-divinization—which some try to realize with the help of psychedelic drugs—can be recognized already in that deviant form of medieval mysticism." Or as John Passmore put it: "The word 'beat' in the phrase 'the beat generation' " has little to do with music; rather, "it is an abbreviation for the 'beatific,' those who have experienced the beatific vision."

The argument broadens. As the historian of Evangelicalism David Bebbington writes:

The [Charismatic] movement was rooted ultimately in the changed mood of the early twentieth century that gave rise to non-representational art, stream-of-consciousness literature and a pre-occupation with the non-rational in all its forms. [By the Sixties] an avant-garde outlook confined before the war to a small number had created . . . an extensive counter-culture. The ideas of the few had reached a mass audience . . . the attitudes clustered around Expressionism early in the century had by the Sixties become an "Expressive Revolution." [A religious movement with such ideas] was

likely to grow, and, as the counter-culture was assimilated to
the mainstream culture during the 1970s, to become a major
force in popular Christianity . . . Charismatics succeeded . . .
because their time had come.

Nevertheless, Norman Cohn's thesis that *uncertainty* is the key
merits a further look. One extraordinary quality of the late
twentieth century has been the range of insecurities (or "choices,"
or "changes") available: uncertainty has become the norm. 1,700
maverick nuclear warheads in the Ukraine, for instance, following
the dismemberment of the USSR—itself an unprecedentedly
destabilizing geopolitical event; or more specifically, in the West,
the long-term, ever more precipitous decline of the middle class
(British university professors earned eight times the national
average in 1914, but by the mid-Seventies earned less than some
unskilled workers); or the even more catastrophic decline of the
once "working"class, now the class least likely to work. Then add on
the daily floodtide of doomwatch statistics: third-world debt in the
late Eighties, 1 trillion dollars; world population in the early Nineties, 5 billion, set to double by 2054; annual species loss worldwide
(virtually nil in 1800), pushing 100,000 a year by 1992; level of
CO_2 in the atmosphere set to double its 1990 figure (after milliards
of relative constancy) in just fifty years. Consider also the effects
of revolution, the gender revolution, the geriatric revolution (by
the mid-twenty-first century there will be an estimated 1 million
people aged a hundred or over in the U.S. alone), AIDS . . .

   The illustrations to a book such as U.S. Vice President Al Gore's
Earth in the Balance (itself a quite unprecedented piece of writing
for a senior U.S. politician) are instructive. The graphs showing
population, species extinction, temperature, pollution and so on
all tootle along quite happily for hundreds, sometimes thousands
of years. Then suddenly they hit today, and we have lift off . . .
To say they "rise steeply" just doesn't get it. They're vertical. They
bear no relationship to anything that has gone before. Back in

1970, Alvin Toffler predicted "future shock" for a world which, even then, was changing inconceivably fast; by the early Nineties, arguably, "future shock" (Reaganite conservatism and the British return to supposed "Victorian values" were all part of it) was something we were already in.

At the domestic level, too, unpredictable change has become the norm. 1973 was, indeed, the "break" year, the hinge moment when the Western middle classes were alerted to the fact that nothing could be taken for granted any more. Take U.S. median family income, for instance between 1973 and 1989: after falling off a cliff in 1973, and again between 1978 and 1982, by 1989 it had just about clawed its way back to where it had been sixteen years earlier. Or take U.S. average real earnings: after climbing precipitously since the Second World War, they tumble steadily after 1973, so that by 1989 they are back to the levels of 1961. Indeed, whatever the issue, current predictions seem designed to promote anxiety. Old age? There are currently only three U.S. workers per pensioner, and that figure is set to drop to two by 2045. Housing? By the late Eighties in many U.S. metropolitan areas, housing costs were swallowing up half the income of a two-job family, double the proportion twenty years earlier. Crime? "Half nation fears to go out at night" according to a Home Office survey trumpeted in the *Observer* in January 1994, as a phenomenon once assumed to be a North American problem spread remorselessly into Europe.

But in all this swirling blizzard of economic and cultural confusion, it is the question of employment which hurts most. In the early Nineties, California—which had so recently boasted a wealth sufficient to have placed it among the half-dozen top nations in the world—needed to generate 250,000 extra jobs a year just to maintain current levels of employment, yet in 1991 it lost 330,000. As for the much-vaunted 13 million-plus new U.S. jobs created during the Reagan years, such statistics—as with similar figures bandied around in Europe—beg the question, "What is a job?" A steady income, a structure to one's life, a way of building a home, a family, a future? By the early Nineties, for an increasing proportion of the workforce in both Europe and the U.S. (one estimate put it as high as two out of three), such jobs meant nothing of the sort: short-term contracts, part-time positions outside the protection of employment law, de-unionized shop floors. Too often these "new" jobs have proved wonderfully convenient for hard-pressed, cash-strapped employers, but desperate, stopgap measures for the "employed." In the face of the new information technology, the old stand-off between capital and labor seems to have finally broken down; and in 1991, U.K. business guru Professor Charles Handy estimated that "less than half of the workforce in the industrialized world will be in 'proper' full-time jobs in organizations by the beginning of the 21st century." Or as the sociologist David Bouchier put it in a prescient *Zeitgeist* piece written in 1987 (pre-crash and pre-1990s global recession):

> In Truffaut's film classic "Les Quatre Cent Coups," the small protagonist Antoine is reduced to a pitiful state of *uncertainty* [my italics] by the piling-up of one unhappiness after another. Each problem, individually manageable, all together add up to a crushing weight of *uncertainty* and fear. Something like this has happened to the ordinary people of America in the 1980s.

Loss of faith in the primacy of the rational, and the collapse of the certainties which have shaped life in the West are two key causes of the current religious revival; but as with all great historical developments, there are others, too.

Daniel Bell, the key popularizer of the term "postindustrialism," predicted in 1975 that the collapse of work which would cause such instability among the erstwhile middle and working classes would also lead to a moral crisis. With the decline of overt religion in the West, work, come the industrial revolution, had largely taken its place: as Weber and others had long before pointed out, for the heroic, neo-Puritan capitalist, "work, as a calling or vocation, was a translation of religion into a 'this-worldly attachment'—a proof through personal effort, of one's own goodness and worth." But with the postindustrial decline of work, "one comes back, in a more serious way, to the problem of what modes of attachment are possible, in a world in which nature has been excluded, work has lost meaning, culture has become empty . . ." Finally, Bell decided, "in a curious way, one comes back, in an unfashionable way, to religion."

If "work" was one Western secularization of religion, science was another. And in the late twentieth century that, too, has suffered a steady decline—if not in influence, then in prestige. The post-1945 nightmares of nuclear power (both civil and military), and the rash of overt, public illustrations of fallibility—disasters like *Challenger* and Chernobyl, incapacity in the face of evolving viruses, especially AIDS—these have been accompanied by something most nineteenth-century positivists would have regarded as pure romance: post-Newtonian physics. Absolute time? Dead. Absolute space? Gone. Abstract measurement? A fiction. The relationship between cause and effect? Enter the "Uncertainty Principle."

Work declining, science on the rack—and then, with the end of the Cold War, yet another of the secularizations of religious experience vanished as the "Evil Empire" collapsed. (Somehow Saddam never quite hacked it as a substitute.) If history abhors a vacuum, what value-systems would swarm in to fill the bill?

At the start of the century (a period in which many of the arational "expressionist" impulses were first gestating, later to trickle down into the counterculture) Richard Maurice Bucke published his *Cosmic Consciousness,* announcing that once "in contact with the flux of cosmic consciousness" (a higher state of man he felt would evolve with the new century) "all religions known and named today will be melted down. The human soul will be revolutionized. Religion will absolutely dominate the race." One of the curiosities of Bucke's thesis was that this remarkable outcome would, he felt, be largely promoted by the coming technology of "aerial navigation" (this was two years before the Wright brothers' first flight), before which "national boundaries, tariffs and perhaps distinctions of language would fade away." A thrice-blessed world in which "old things will be done away with and all will become new" would take shape under the influence of such jet determinism.

Technological determinism of a different kind was critical to another who predicted a religious revival, Marshall McLuhan. As already mentioned, McLuhan's preferred technological trigger was electricity (above all "the media")—set to usher in not merely his familiar "global village," but a whole new psychology too. (McLuhan intuited, in fact, a great deal of what a very few years later emerged as the left-brain/right-brain thesis.) Part of McLuhan's analysis was his announcement of a New Age of religion largely impelled, he felt, by the instantaneous interconnection of human nervous systems by the electric technologies: a kind of neurological global church to go along with his global village. More, this revival had already happened: "The computer promises, in short, by technology, a Pentecostal condition of universal understanding and unity." Our age "is probably the most religious that has ever existed. We are already there." McLuhan added, more prosaically, that new communications systems would collapse conventional religious, as well as all other, institutions (enter the bottom-up, decentralizing Coates, Ichthus, MFJ et al.), and that Christianity in its "centralized, administrative, bureaucratic form" would become increasingly "irrelevant."

Perhaps the most remarkable prophet of all was Oswald Spengler, author of *Decline of the West* (1918–1922), predictor of "Caesarism" (or Hitlerism), de-urbanization, and the decline of Western science—just for a start—and author of a cyclical theory of history which predated the Green movement by seventy years in its penchant for biological metaphors: cultural flowerings, "springtimes," autumns, and so forth.

Delving down into the depths of his Teutonic scholarship, comparing such far-flung cultures, in space and time, as the Classical, the Egyptian, and the Chinese, this noble-browed patriarch dreamed up his grand theory of "second Religiousness." In the last phase of any culture's "autumn," he argued, you could predict a return to the green shoots of its "springtime," albeit in shadowy, somewhat parodied form. And as all cultures are, even if they no longer know it, deeply rooted in their religion (from cult to culture, as D. H. Lawrence put it) you could expect, in their last phase, a return to the forms of their religious springtime —hence "second Religiousness." There was no shortage of examples (there never is, with Spengler): the deep piety that so impressed Herodotus among the "late" Egyptians; the Shi-hwang-ti revival in ancient China; the late-classical, Roman religious revival under Augustus, that noble revanche of the Roman spirit which was foreshadowed in the great quasi-religious works of both Horace and Virgil.

For, declares Spengler: "The material of the Second Religiousness is simply that of the first, genuine, young religiousness—only otherwise experienced and expressed. It starts with Rationalism's fading out in helplessness, then the forms of Springtime become visible, and finally the whole world of the primitive religion, which had receded before the grand forms of the early faith, returns to the foreground."

That it should have been "intuitives" like the prose-poetical Spengler, the mystic Bucke, and the "unscientific" McLuhan who made this particular prediction is perhaps to be expected. It may take a paradoxical rather than a scientific mind to predict anything as "discontinuous" as an a-rational revival in history's most scientific age.

In a highly suggestive footnote, Spengler added:

"It is perhaps possible for us to make some guess as to these forms, which (it is self-evident) must lead back to certain elements of Gothic Christianity. But be this as it may, what is quite certain is that they will not be the product of any literary taste for Late-Indian or Late-Chinese speculation, but something of the type, for example, of Adventism and suchlike sects."

At the time of Spengler's writing, as we have seen, what he called "Adventists" numbered little more than 1 percent of the Christian communion; that figure is expected to rise to 30 percent by the year 2000.

Most people could probably identify the connection between the religious revival and those irrationalisms which began to unfold in the Sixties and extended into the Seventies. It wasn't just Tom Wolfe who saw the counterculture as an essentially religious phenomenon. Others noticed how strange it was that these "revolutionaries" seemed utterly uninterested in political power— seemed obsessed, rather, with an all-embracing change of values. But in what sense were the Eighties, of all God-forsaken decades, a "religious" time?

For whatever had been the mystic shenanigans of the dreaded Sixties, it was entirely plain to all sensible, businesslike minds by the Eighties (and *all* minds, by then, were sensible and businesslike, if only on the surface) that reason, common sense, the market, science—the whole square ideology of specialist, segmented Victorian liberalism—had quite won back its cultural crown. Why, even the young thought so! Indeed the young, if anything, were even more keen on it than the middle aged. "Real men" appeared and wouldn't eat quiche. "Girls" emerged from erstwhile feminism and announced they Just Wanted To Have Fun. More perverse still, a dire prediction in Germaine Greer's *The Female Eunuch* of one possible misdirection of feminism— "the Omnipotent Administrator in frilly knickers"—became Prime Minister of the U.K., and oversaw such "common-sense foreign policy" (the vogue phrase) as the 6,000-miles-distant Falklands War. Most emblematically of all, a Material Girl announced that

she, and others like her, did all the horrible things they did because
the whole lot of us now lived in this unredeemably Material World
. . . While on campus walls kids scrawled things like, "He who dies
with the most toys, wins." Now was this religious?

It all seemed common-sensical and square enough, as long
as you approached it with no sense of paradox or, as the
Freudians say, of "reaction-formation." Yet the first thing one
should notice about this "common sense" decade was the chill,
fearful, very un-common-sensical wind that blew through it,
a mere whisper beneath the glitz. As David Bouchier put it,
again pre-crash, in his piece "The great greed of 1987": "Greed
is driven by a fearful sense that there may not be much time.
Slow accumulation, long-term strategy and forward planning
are relics from an earlier age of innocence. The sense of
economic doom which hangs over the country [U.S.A.] is almost
palpable."

Eat drink and be merry, for tomorrow . . . consider the Eighties love affair with black—not merely the color of business, but
also the color, throughout the centuries, of death, depression
and ascetic self-denial. Check the magazines in 1984 and black
is everywhere, not just in the clothes. Typical was a British
pro-birth-control (read anti-AIDS) poster from the mid-Eighties:
jet black from top to bottom, nothing else, just the color alone—
pure Apocalypse, total doom, and in the middle, simply the one
word: "NO."

As for all that "common sense" . . . The Australian political
psychologist Graham Little, in his 1988 study of Reagan,
Thatcher and the Australian Malcolm Fraser entitled *Strong
Leadership,* reminds us that just because political leaders say
they are acting rationally, that doesn't mean they are. Indeed, not
only were the heroic simplicities of Reaganism and Thatcherism
profoundly reminiscent of the rock-like, adamantine tendency in
the Evangelical/Charismatic nexus, but their own much-talked-
about "Charisma" was demonstrably first cousin to avowedly

religious Charisma, and at times their religiosity became quite overt. Mrs. Thatcher once told a rally, "The Old Testament Prophets did not say, 'Brothers I want consensus.' They said, 'This is my faith and vision. This is what I passionately believe.' " As for Reagan, Paul Erikson examined his rhetoric in his book *Reagan Speaks,* and described his speeches as "sermons." The Bible, in Reaganspeak, legitimized America's divine mission, just as it showed the Soviets to be the anti-Christ; and lest things should get a bit dull, there remained, hovering around in the background, nothing less than "Armageddon." Reagan's subliminal message was to offer America, in a period of profound denial, a magic-carpet, back-to-the-future ticket to the dreamworld of a child: a world in which childlike, "at-a-stroke" solutions—from Star Wars to the sacking of the air-traffic controllers—to modern complexities were instantly to hand. One is reminded of Anne O'Hare McCormick's line on that other avoidant period, the Twenties: "We were," she said, "in the mood for magic."

The rhetoric matched the mood—from Reagan's "Evil Empire," to Mrs. Thatcher's "enemy within" as she notoriously called Britain's striking miners, in a phrase which originated with Evangelicalism—meaning, quite simply, the Devil. The stark, Manichean division of the world into the acceptable and the damned was a profound social impulse of the time: something that Thatcher and Reagan reflected, or gave a voice to, quite as much as they promoted it themselves. Thatcher may have introduced the notion of governmental "wets" and "dries," of "one of us" and the rest, but such distinctions were rampant, equally, in society at large.

Characteristic was the famous *Times* leader of 20 May 1982, "The Still Small Voice of Truth," reacting to the Argentinian invasion of the Falklands, in which the leader writer managed to repeat the word "evil" no less than ten times within one five-hundred-word piece. Indeed, the diatribe declared (with emotion more evident than grammar):

An individual becomes more complete within himself by a conscious act of understanding the forces of disorder which rage within him, and by reference to some constant source of morality, an evaluation of the immense power of evil in the world, and the fact that mankind as a whole—nations, societies and groups—are all capable of becoming merely instruments of that evil, is part of that understanding; and part of that morality.

Anthony Barnett quotes the passage in his book on the Falklands War, *Iron Britannia,* and comments: "What raging force lay behind the composition of that sentence?"

The mind-set being described here is a secularization of something central to WASP religiosity for three centuries: good old, black-and-white, me-blessed, you-damned Puritanism. But how does that square with another cultural driving force of the Eighties, materialism? The anthropologist Jean Liedloff, who spent several years in the hunter-gatherer culture of the South American Yequana Indians, once declared: "The trouble with the West is not, in fact, its 'materialism'—it's that it's not materialist *enough.*" Or, putting it another way, if only your serious New York advertising executive truly enjoyed the carness of his car, or the painterliness of his Monets, or the rollingness of his acres, he'd be better off. His problem—indeed, the driving force of so many acquisitive Western lives—is that the car, the picture and the estate per se are the last things on his mind. What concerns him, rather, is all these material items as symbols. Symbols of how he is placed socially; symbols of how he is valued by his firm; symbols, above all, of his own sense of his worth—there to convince him, the heroic executive, of his value as a human being.

The psychotherapist Janov (of the primal scream) also divided behavior into "symbolic" (Janov's word for neurotic) and "real," and felt that Western civilization, as a whole, was utterly neurotic, dissociated, and "symbolic." To late-twentieth-century Westerners sold on the notion that the work-and-consumption, consumption-and-work cycle is, above all, "practical," this may sound strange. Yet such "spiritual" interpretations of materialism have, in fact, been around for years. Martin Luther is an example, as Norman O. Brown relates in his psyche-history of capitalism, *Life Against Death*: "All around him Luther felt the irresistible attraction and power of capitalism, and interpreted it as the Devil's final seizure of power in this world, therefore overshadowing Christ's Second Coming and the Devil's final overthrow."

By the seventeenth century, in one of the shock U-turns of ethical history, acquisitiveness had become the outward and visible evidence of Western virtue rather than vice; nevertheless, the spiritual angle, the transcendental interpretation of matters "material," remained. Indeed, by the nineteenth century it was routine for someone like Bishop Lawrence to pronounce: "In the long run, it is only to the man of morality that wealth comes. Godliness is in league with riches. Material prosperity makes the national character sweeter, more Christlike." Small wonder that the corollary of this position came galloping close behind: as Henry Ward Beecher told his New York congregation in the 1870s: "No man in this land suffers from poverty unless it be more than his fault—unless it be his *sin*."

As for the twentieth century, not only have we had Max Weber showing how the Calvinists reckoned God signalled a man's virtue, or lack of it, by his net worth and Freud pitching in with uncomfortable insights into the nature of wealth-worship, but by the Fifties we had Norman O. Brown arguing that consumption itself, not merely wealth creation, was a religious act. For what is conspicuous consumption anyway, argued Brown, but the public parading of society's surplus; and to what purpose has the surplus been devoted historically (the temples, the cathedrals, the maintenance of a priestly or regal elite) but the celebration of all society holds sacred? We may not consciously see the surplus, in its modern form, as "sacred," but certainly all the trappings of worship are there. As Brown put it: "We no longer give the surplus to God; the process of producing an ever-expanding surplus is itself our God."

In the U.K. at least, the mind-set characteristic of the Eighties finally imploded with the departure of Mrs. Thatcher in November 1990; at this point too, religion's great contemporary rival, the casino culture, commenced terminal decline. In Ferdinand Zweig's book *The British Worker,* an anonymous bus conductor articulates the three great "dreams" of the ordinary British citizen as "religion, socialism or gambling." By 1990, socialism (at least as defined by its opponents) seemed dead indeed; and gambling looked finished, too—no more magical wins on the stock or housing or insurance markets. Which left religion.

As the Eighties folded, all that battened-down irrationalism came bursting to the fore. There was, for instance, a rash of ever-more-overtly millennial books: Naisbitt and Aburdene's *Megatrends 2000*; William Rees-Mogg and James Dale Davidson's *Blood in the Streets,* followed by their even more millennial *The Great Reckoning*; Tom Wolfe's *Bonfire of the Vanities*; Peter Jay and Michael Stewart's *Apocalypse 2000*; all those "End-of" books, *The End of Ideology, The End of History* . . .

Suddenly the New Age movement ("New Age" is another of those phrases, like "self-improvement," which has an overt history in the Evangelical movement) was everywhere: "alternative" and occult practitioners boomed, the U.K.'s "Pagan Front" issued statements to the press, and Hollywood stars publicly thanked their "channels" when accepting a Hollywood prize. By the end of the decade, various New Age groups embraced an estimated 20 million highly educated adherents in the U.S.A. alone. Eighteen-year-olds threw away their power shoulder pads and went hippy; fashion editors did spreads on the New Religiousness; the last vestiges of all that rationalist, gridiron Eighties design vanished from the TV and magazine scene and was replaced by the wildest, weirdest most surreal water shapes a computer graphics package could generate. One of the great media cackles of 1990 was the moment when sports commentator David Icke flipped—that same David Icke who had been one of the Green Party's most rationalist, statistics-orientated spokesmen—and appeared in a purple track suit to inform the media he had been contacted by a thirteenth-century Chinese Mandarin, one Wang Yee Lee, and also by Socrates. They had explained that he had been chosen, up the top, to save the world.

It was as if all the pent-up countercultural arationalisms that had been building since the Sixties suddenly came flooding through. Simultaneously, the British media cottoned on to the Charismatic phenomenon in its overtly religious form. No longer was this the exclusive province of sociologists like Naisbitt and Aburdene: now even venerables like Lord Rees-Mogg, ex-editor of that not entirely New Age journal the London *Times*, were predicting the coming "Revival of Religion." The spiritual renaissance was becoming the hottest number in town.

Whereas in the "materialist" era the smart thing had been to find the business angle on everything (on-yer-bike minister Norman Tebbit, typically, wrote articles advocating managerial clear-outs in the Church of England), in the Nineties the vogue was to find the religious angle on all things previously assumed lay. Not only did the Weber-Veblen-Brown notion of the mysticism of capitalism start infiltrating the once militantly rationalist social science journals—"The sacred and profane in consumer behavior" was one title in the *Journal of Consumer Research*— but suddenly a hip theologian like California's Matthew Fox was turning up everywhere, and finding "original sin" at the bottom of consumerism. Fox argued, "Consumer society has, I believe, built its entire advertising edifice on the fall/redemption theology . . . It offers us wares with the implicit and often explicit promise that 'here lies perfection.' "

That renowned hot-house of paranormal Evangelicalism, the *Harvard Business Review,* had this to say about Michael Milken in an article by William Taylor in its January 1992 issue:

> In his own way, Michael Milken was a monk. And in the Beverly Hills office of Drexel Burnham Lambert, he created his own version of a monastery. Only in his monastery, money itself became the abstraction, the ideal around which all activity was organized. Milken and his followers were obsessed with money. Not for what it could buy, not even for what it could do, but for what it *represented.* . . .
>
> Ultimately, my concern with Michael Milken is not that he was too driven by the pursuit of wealth. My concern is that he was *not driven enough* by the pursuit of wealth.

As for Naomi Wolf, she came cresting through on a new feminist wave which was itself a further symptom of the post-Eighties mind-set, and devoted a whole chapter of *The Beauty Myth* to beauty-as-religion—"The Church of Beauty." "What has not yet been realized," she wrote, "is the extent to which the rituals of the beauty backlash do not simply mimic traditional religion but *functionally supplant it.* They are literally re-constituting out of old faiths a new one, to affect women's minds as sweepingly as any past evangelical wave." And she is talking of such "holy oils" (her phrase) as perfumes.

The early Nineties had religion on the brain in much the same way as the early Eighties had business. A "mystery" hit in the English pop charts in summer 1992 consisted of the taped voice of a genuine tramp, plus New Age orchestral backing, singing over and over again the line "Jesus blood never failed me yet"—just that. The decade was beginning to shape up with a feel you could almost personalize—as, say, one of those new, archangel-lookalike Nineties male models with reinvented long hair: Sixties clones at first glance, and yet, on closer inspection, infinitely more ardent.

Most emblematic of all was the moment in 1992 when the Forever People, a California-based paranormal group, turned up on British TV. Here was the authentic spirit of the Nineties. The Forever People weren't peddling any fuddy-duddy nonsense about life after death, or miracle-working, or vision-seeing. No, this lot's —undeniably unique—claim was they were *never going to die at all*. Immortal now, immortal they would remain (some members had already died). They really didn't see, they informed chat show host Terry Wogan, how any of this was any harder to believe than, say, such Christian stories as the resurrection of Jesus Christ.

For all such eccentricities, the religious revival does seem to have a central role in the wider culture of postindustrialism. It was not so much *what* the movement's supporters said or did or thought that mattered: it was—as with all late-twentieth-century developments—the *way* they said, did and thought it. And more literally than one might have thought possible, that way is one manifestation of a "quantum thinking" revolution in society as a whole.

Take the Evangelical/Charismatic tag, for instance. As already noted, the term seems to express the conjunction of opposites— and the oblique that separates the two poles is suggestive. Since the 1960s, the oblique has become a veritable linguistic phenomenon. Even twenty years ago, magazines like *Time Out* had almost as many obliques in them as they had words. If a man/woman wanted a job/vocation that would give them bread/health/fulfillment, then they would naturally put an ad somewhere like *Time Out*'s Therapy/Personal Growth Section. You would have got a very blank/uncomprehending reaction from your local head had you mentioned the word "quantum" in this regard in 1975; and yet the real reason why it felt hip to place an ad like that was a muzzy-headed feeling that this both/and way of thinking expressed something important and new. To this extent, the "/" represented the instinctive projection into everyday language of one of quantum culture's most essential forms of thought: the notion of "indeterminacy," of being not merely unsure "what" something is, but of strongly suspecting that it might turn out to be (at least) two quite opposite things at once.

Behind this suspicion lies the early-twentieth-century answer to the grandest of physics conundrums, the question of whether light is a particle or a wave—the answer being that light turns out to be both particle and wave, depending on how you measure it. "A particle on Tuesdays, a wave on Thursdays"—neither one thing nor the other, because both/and. Yet indeterminacy, whether in Evangelical/Charismatic or universal terms, is just one quantum form of thought among many: all, as one would hope of anything quantum, interrelated. There is the associated sense of inter-connection—the obverse of all those neo-Newtonian notions of segmentation, division and separation—which seems to represent a return to an almost medieval feel for gestalt, for "holism." The particular parallel with quantum physics lies in the idea that indeterminacy has been arrived at because of the interconnection of the observer and the observed. Whether light is a particle or a wave depends on the questions asked—and who's asking them: the observed and the observer are no longer seen as capable of separate definition. Exit the Newtonian world of "separate"; enter the quantum world of "connect."

The Green movement, to take the most obvious example. (Anyone who thinks *that* was "imposed," "top-down," hasn't doorstepped the council estates.) Now here was a fine instance of applied "gestalt" thinking, the sense of an entity, or an industry, not just in itself, but in relation to its surrounds; the very opposite of old-time industrialist, drop-the-portcullis, produce-and-be-damned separatism.

There are legions of manifestations of this shift. Interactive museums, equally, end the separation between artifact and visitor. Interactive theater rejects the proscenium arch and aims to bridge the gap between watcher and performer (a theater group like

Interaction crossed still more boundaries, inasmuch as it was, quite consciously, a social-work as well as a theater group.) New Age groups like Zoo Check in the U.K. state their intention to break down the "rights" barrier between animals and human beings. In industry, specialization is eschewed in favor of "skill-sharing" in task-oriented, inter-disciplinary teams. Business training videos, such as those presented by comedian John Cleese, now urge corporate apparatchiks to break out of their narrow, Newtonian heads and indulge in a little "creativity in business," as Cleese's title ran. The very open-plan design of offices; the very clothes people wore to work (gym shoes, jeans); the very furniture (dart boards on the wall); work/play boundaries, now, being broken down . . .

In the Nineties, indeed, there seems to be a counterculture whichever way you look. Schools? Home education. Policing? Neighborhood Watch. Law? Private prosecutions. Cancer? "Systems" cures exploiting the mind/body gestalt, as opposed to treatment by Newtonian surgery, or "separation" of the tumor from the patient. Shopping? Car boot sales . . . The collapse of specialization has even extended to mental health: not only is the separation of the mentally ill from the community—as represented by mental hospitals (and dating back, as Foucault showed, to the separatist Puritan/Cartesian spirit of the seventeenth century)— seen as unhealthy, but that everyday specialization known as "crazy" seems increasingly under threat. For now, with post-Laingian psychiatry, we are all—doctors, patients, nurses—at one point or another on the same mental health continuum.

Early in the century scientists used to talk about "getting into the spirit" of quantum theory. In the Nineties, you can get into the spirit of quantum culture, too. And at the heart of it lies that experiential, small-within-big-is-beautiful, both/and, Evangelical/Charismatic revival.

4

Ichthus

The post-Eighties mood which is so characteristic of the movement at large was evident at the very first Ichthus celebration
meeting I went to at Warwick Park School in Peckham, South-
East London. The dress code spoke volumes. It was strictly one
layer-T-shirts, jeans, sagging trousers worn with trainers, the pale,
bland colors of the disenfranchised and poor. About 150 people
were present, many of them children, teenagers and blacks.

In some ways this was a familiar enough Charismatic scene.
There were the roof-threatening, percussive hymns. There was
one of those obscure and quite extraordinarily lengthy sermons,
making a deeply felt, if elusive, Old Testament point all mulched
in with tales of Locusts and Retribution and Mighty Hosts, not to
mention dogs licking up backsliders' very vitals. Then there were
reams of local organizational notices, as the Charismatic gathering
inhaled and exhaled the data crucial for community.

But there was something else, too: something light years
distant, in flavor, from "right-wing fundamentalism," a kind
of dignity and gravitas, so that despite the percussive hymns it
was possible, for a moment, to feel as if you were surrounded by
seventeenth-century Puritans—not least because poverty, however
painful, does gel with the Gospel rather better than Armani. The
leaders were different, too. Whatever might be said against Roger
Forster, he is no Jim Bakker; and there was another leader at that

meeting, a young man of about thirty, slim, bearded, modest, very grave. He led hymns and prayers with a seriousness I'd not seen before among Charismatics, a far cry from both the exuberance of the Americans and the M25 razzmatazz of Cobham. When the service was over, Roger Forster introduced us. Mike Pears lived locally, on the Gloucester Grove Estate. If I wanted to get a feel for Ichthus as a community, maybe I should get to know him. We fixed a date.

Shortly after I set out for the first of many visits to North Peckham, threading my way off rackety old Peckham High Street to what seems, as you walk towards it, an oasis of calm surrounded by open spaces, parkland, trees. Yet as the estate enfolds you it becomes something else: great slabs of egg-box flats stacked one on top of the other like wannabe castle walls, interspersed here and there with these tall, windowless, mystery brick towers, the kind of edifice any thinking urban guerrilla would instantly use as a machine-gun post. All 1,200 households are linked together by seven miles of roofed-in walkways—a great notion, doubtless, back in the Seventies, to enable people to walk anywhere on the estate without getting wet, but somewhat of a disaster by the early Nineties, because today they are uniformly dark, stark, graffiti-ridden and soaked through with a wrap-round all-in all-pervading urine stink.

In one corner, just opposite a little green, was the three-bedroom flat that Mike Pears was renting off Southwark council for £270 a month. His wife Helen answered the door, looking wary—routine for Charismatics on first meeting—and Mike and I sat down in the sitting room, Mike in blue jeans, sweater, gold-rim glasses, grave. Helen bustled in and out dusting, common-sensical in red rubber gloves. Mike did the talking.

They had been living there with their two children aged five and six for five years, having moved in (the typical New Church way) to plant a church. There's another Ichthus group a mile down the road—Ichthus won't normally leapfrog any further than that, otherwise it's difficult to maintain inter-group relations. It was "what we call a resurrection job," said Mike. "There was this old Baptist church just down the road with eight members and money difficulties. So we came to this agreement whereby they kept their membership and we supplied new blood—and new money. The idea was to maintain the identity of both groups—hence our title, 'The Ichthus Wells Way Baptist Church,' although we're not really into labels." At first it was just the Baptists plus twenty Ichthus immigrants; now, after seven energetic years, the congregation had grown to sixty. Not, it is fair to say, without some difficulty. "The locals mistrust everyone," said Mike. "They mistrust strangers, they mistrust institutions and, above all, they mistrust politicians—with very good reason: politicians round here treat locals like pawns."

And they mistrust Evangelicals—which is why Mike and co. have always advanced the Word with discretion and tact—much in the mode of that inter-denominational back-to-work group Pecan, mentioned earlier, which is just down the road and very much part of Mike's patch. "Pecan's first thing is to offer a service," said Mike, "the most useful service, arguably, you could offer round here—help with getting a job. It's only secondarily, so to speak, that they offer Christianity."

The problems, locally, are gargantuan indeed. It's not just the unemployment; nor is it just those doomwatch Gloucester Grove buildings, although they are notoriously infested with ants and cockroaches, and British Telecom engineers have been known to refuse to do repairs because of the rats. It is something less specific, yet probably more crucial—a mood, a psychology, a perception both on the part of people who live here and people who don't. It's there, for instance, in the dogs all over the estate: Rottweilers, Alsatians, pit bulls. They are there, ostensibly, to protect their owners from attacks and break-ins, but to other residents they are simply a further threat. It's there in the sense tenants get of this opaque, unmentionable wall between them and the local council, with everyone on the tenants' side of it invisible to those on the other—a sense best illustrated by the story about how the council once bricked up a ground-floor area to improve the environment and never even noticed that they'd bricked in two residents' cars. It's there, most poignantly, in the sign outside one flat that reads: *Dear burglar, we've been burgled three times already, we've nothing of value left, but if you must break in again, please don't mess the place up too much.*

A mood, an atmosphere—or as Mike Pears puts it, "a spirit. We do believe that diabolic powers can dominate, even take control of, physical space. And yes, we do believe such powers are active right here, right now, on this estate." At such a moment you remember just how much quiet-spoken Mike parts company with folks he'd otherwise resemble to a T: few social workers, after all, take quite *that* perspective on Gloucester Grove. Sober, solid Mike also has available as many facts, figures, files, and action programs generally as the most advanced and rational secular outreach could crave. But there's no avoiding the Ichthus view that at bottom the local difficulties are just plain Satanic—the work of man's most ancient and indomitable foe, Old Nick.

In familiar Evangelical mode, a whole battery of weapons have been arrayed against him. First off, there's that amoebic, bottom-up structure so characteristic of the New Church movement.

"We get together at three levels," said Mike, "house group, congregation and celebration." Each different type facilitates a different quality of experience. "We have, for a start, three house groups, each of them meeting, say, once a week: prayer, intimate dialogue, support. Then we have a weekly congregation meeting every Sunday at Wells Baptist Church: maybe sixty of us this time, hymn-singing, prayer, community notices: those same house groups brought together again here, but in another gear now. Less low-key, you might say, more extrovert. Then, finally, on a Sunday evening, we have our celebration meeting—the kind of thing you came to at Warwick Park School—and that's in yet another gear again: utterly extrovert this time, sometimes several congregations combining together, a joyful, noisy, exuberant expression of our collective love of the Lord."

Onto this skeleton are tacked innumerable adjuncts, both tactical and strategic. There are, for instance, the whole range of community projects. Ichthus runs a nursery for estate children in the same church buildings that house the Sunday services and Pecan. There's another nursery, too, and an Ichthus primary school. Add to this the launderette, also just down the road from Mike, in the opposite direction from Wells Church: a survey done on the estate by Pecan in 1990 found that only half the households on the estate owned a washing machine and many people had to walk over half a mile to the nearest launderette. Launched in partnership with local resident Alan Wisniewski as part of Pecan's program to encourage local people to open up their own businesses the launderette sold sweets, tea and coffee along with its laundry services, and became a social center.

Then there are "works" projects such as Pecan; and beyond that, more broad, human applications of Christian doctrine, which are critical to a "relationship"-based organization like Ichthus. Jesus Action, coordinated from the Ichthus head office, does anything from buying an old lady's shopping to putting in a new kitchen for a young couple. Ichthus runs programs for teenagers on drugs. And it arranges one-off events, such as the march and pray-in at the center of Gloucester Grove Estate (a touch surprisingly, perhaps, local tenants said they enjoyed it), or the night the church transformed the Baptist building into a restaurant, charging locals just £3 for a posh meal complete with waiters and waitresses (they were packed out). Plus socials, barn dances, barbecues . . .

"One thing we did early," Mike told me, "was hire a bus one evening and lay on a tour of London. Because a lot of people round here, would you believe, have never been to the center, even though it's only three miles away. Indeed, many won't even go anywhere that means crossing major roads—it's part apathy, part old-time local patriotism."

All this is relationship—and community-building, but Ichthus's local agenda stretches to broader issues, too. There is their concern with law and order as evidenced by their support for the campaign to catch the so-called Stockwell Strangler. "People will interpret this as they will," said Mike, "but the bald fact is we prayed on the Saturday night and, come the following Monday, he was arrested." Some of their activism is, in effect, political —for instance, their support for a local black who was, the campaign argued, wrongly sent down for assault with attempted robbery.

It all adds up to an agenda which is, on many issues, about as far from conventionally perceived fundamentalism as could be. But then it is easy to forget (understandably, given the conservative record of recent fundamentalist activity) in how many different guises Christian ideology has been enacted in the past—how various, in fact, have been the interpretations put on the Word.

Mike is, in fact, just the kind of Christian who has been influenced by the Anabaptists; but then he also talks with approval of the Jewish tradition, recorded in the Old Testament, of "The Year of Jubilee" every fifty years, when all debts would be cancelled and all slaves released. He talks, too, about his sense of a Heaven based on *authority* rather than hierarchy; and, coming back to Gloucester Grove, about how the underclass may be mixed up in all manner of wrong, but that should never make us forget that Jesus said blessed are the poor—not just passable, or alright, or forgiven, but *blessed*. And why? For they shall inherit the earth!

It is not medieval millennialism we are witnessing here (not yet, anyhow), nor, come to that, is it old-time Christian socialism (despite some common ground): rather, it is an inner-city version of that same spirit we detected in Gerald Coates: do-it-yourself, "the priesthood of all believers." There is a profound sense that the way to address life, whether spiritually or materially, is quite simply, to get out there and . . . address it. Don't wait for a general election, don't hang on a council vote, don't put it all on the back burner till next year's funding comes through, but, like Rubin said back in the Sixties, Do it. Hold the service, start the business, launch the school. And do it on your own terms, even on a shoestring; and do it to your own taste and your own design.

"The priesthood of all believers." The "inner-directedness" of all citizens, whether born-again or lay. The collapse of all inappropriate reverence for every form of specialist and arbitrary separation. Once again, the "quantum" language of early Nineties, stumbled on by people separated by huge gulfs of geography and culture, is indicative of the centrality of this movement. You find the same terms in the title of a new postmodern television series, "Without Walls," as, four thousand miles away, in the language happened on by one Mary Peoples, way down there at the bottom of *The Tennessean* newspaper's report on Nashville's 1993 March For Jesus. "Denominational walls separate us," declared this scion of Tennesee's Born Again Church. "But this is a day when the walls are coming down!"

At Peckham, notably, certain phrases would keep recurring. I remember a congregation meeting at Wells Way church where the address was given by a woman whose theme turned out to be—no surprises here—"crossing barriers." She was majoring on two particular texts: Ephesians 2:11–22, on Christ's demolition of the "barriers" between Gentile and Jew, and Mark 7:25–30, about the time a young Greek woman approached Jesus to get him to cast a devil out of her daughter. Here, as the preacher pointed out, you had two boundaries crossed: the breaking down of the Jew-Gentile divide (by virtue of the woman's nationality), and a little late-Classical gender-busting too, for few first-century women would have dared approached a man publicly in this way. This woman, too, "broke barriers."

It was appropriate that the service included a notice announcing a new Wells Way Ichthus "Justice Group," because this project also crossed boundaries—Ichthus's own barriers, in this case, because some felt they tended to limit "justice" issues to neighborhood rather than international contexts. The move was towards thinking globally, in fact, to match all that acting locally. Typically, the prime mover of the group, twenty-six-year-old Richard Wells, was not at the time in the Ichthus leadership: the impetus was coming from the bottom up rather than the top down.

I joined the newly formed "Justice Group" one evening at a house shared by some Ichthus members just a few streets from Mike's. There was Gareth, an accountant, neat in a polo shirt, the sort of guy you might bump into down the local squash club. There was Richard Wells himself, broad shouldered, balding, new leftish, John Pilger fan. There was Carol, long flowery dress, no make-up, posh: there were women like her all over London twenty years ago, answering phones saying things like "Mile End Road Red Ladder People's Collective." Superlative vowels. And then there was Sonya. Or was it Sandra? Or was it Sam? It was in fact, I finally twigged, Psalm—her parents were missionaries. She was twenty-two, dishy, beads, patched trousers, serious boots, psychedelic top: I eyed her carefully, throughout that evening, from top to toe, from toe to outasight top, and not once did I find one single detail, visually, to set her apart from a full-blown, turned-on, tuned-in late-Sixties hippy.

Richard served. The thing that struck him, he said, was that there was this whole range of international issues just waiting to be addressed—the sort of thing John Pilger raised in *Distant Voices,* or Noam Chomsky in *Deterring Democracy.* U.S. foreign policy, in particular, concerned him, especially with regard to South America. There was the further question of the worldwide abuse of Christians, especially in Africa. Absolutely, said Psalm. Civil war in the Sudan for ten years! It was terrible, it had to be stopped. Why, there was a TV program about it all that very evening, right after the meeting; we were all very welcome to stay on afterwards and watch it. And then there were the problems in China, added Carol, kicking off her shoes. Christians being beaten and abused by the Chinese authorities. Not forgetting, said Gareth, Islamic tyranny in Pakistan—there was one case in particular, a man who'd been sentenced to death for insulting Allah. Nor, going domestic for a moment, said Richard, should they ignore the upcoming sleep-out week to help the homeless, due in June. Here was an absolutely outrageous piece of British injustice, right under their very noses. It was utterly immoral. Some Christian answer must be found!

So they began to pray about it—quite ordered prayer at first, led on by Richard; then, slowly, seamlessly, they moved into that floaty, dream-frippery way of Charisma (one of the curiosities of the process is how readily adepts can drop into this mode)— muttering, murmuring, almost singing, with little spontaneous surges coming from each participant as the spirit moved them, rising steadily in intensity until the climax, cries and rolling trills and whirrs as they went into "tongues." By then the spontaneity was coming thick and fast. Psalm, for instance, who is "into visualization," shared how she'd had this image of a dragon, lowering, threatening, and also of a rat gnawing away at a dog's tail. Richard, in turn, called on the Lord to put "holy fear" into the Chinese police. "Smite them!" cried Psalm climactically . . . And the moment passed.

They resolved to lobby the appropriate governments, and our parliament, and do the demos; but all of that, of course, was just a start: the key was the follow-up work, the meetings to plan activities with real push. So, dates:

"Eighth any good?"wondered Richard.

"Sorry, no."

"Tenth?"

"Afraid not."

Eighteenth? No. Nineteenth? No. Twenty-first? Ah! Everyone could do it . . . except Carol. Twenty-second? Yes! Everyone could do it . . . except Psalm. The twenty-fifth? Now Psalm could do it, but not Carol.

"Oh dear," said Psalm, "evenings really are a dead loss." It was true. For all that earlier spontaneity, the reality of these Ichthus folks' lives is a series of locked-in preconceived grids of organization—marches, meetings, worship, celebration—stretching weeks ahead, so that to actually fit anything in you need a sledgehammer. It was like that Dawn 2000 conference moment in reverse: there, we'd had our dose of rationality first, then moved into Charisma; here it had been Charisma first, now this overwhelming surge of "reason."

Something was figured out eventually, but it took twenty minutes. Psalm turned to me with one of the jolly, nice-to-the-new-boy grins she'd been shooting me all evening.

"It's dreadful, isn't it," she said. "Look at us—a church of workaholics!"

This work ethic is one of the qualities which sets one thinking of old-time Puritans.

> A servant with this clause
> Makes drudgery divine;
> Who sweeps a room as for thy laws
> Makes that and the action fine

It is also one of the main characteristics that differentiate today's Charismatics from those of the immediate past. Not for nothing is Clive Calver, the Ichthus member who is General Director of the Evangelical Alliance, constantly harrying Evangelicals to rediscover the world-view of socially conscious, activist nineteenth-century Evangelicals like Shaftesbury, Wilberforce and Booth. For Charisma in particular (at the best of times more inward looking than Evangelicalism) went through a period of exceptional introspection at the start of the century; now, however, just as Evangelicalism is discovering a new intensity of inner life, Charisma is developing an ever-widening relationship with the outer world.

I met Richard Wells, who works as a local authority Senior Housing Officer, a couple of days later round at his flat. It is fair to say that his home, though comfortable, was not quite what is evoked by the word "prosperity": red-brick Edwardian working-class flats off Coldharbour Lane in Camberwell, doomwatch corridors, world-weary common parts, Victorian values wallpaper. But as Richard pointed out, it all depends on your priorities.

"I personally believe the church has three main themes," he said, fixing me with a wide, pellucid, gaze. "The Evangelistic, the Charismatic and the social." He agreed that it was significant that he tucked "social" in there with the others. "Because for years we had this thing of separation from the world. The inner cities, in particular, were virtually abandoned by the Church for a hundred years. But that's over now. We're connecting again, both inter-denominationally and socially, and Ichthus is at the forefront of what's going on." In Richard's mind, certainly, the connecting process takes a global as well as local form. "Internationalism like mine is still quite new in the movement," he said, "but it's spreading."

Richard's views are fuelled by a reading list which sounds more new left summer school than Evangelical. "I got into Pilger about a year ago," he said. "Now, what I like about him is that he writes with *passion*—just that very passion and engagement, in fact, that other journalists slag him off for. I like the way he highlights things others ignore—the quite extraordinary, and unforgivable policies of the West in places like Cambodia, the genocidal treatment of Australian aborigines. Without people like him we'd never hear such things." Then, in a natural progression sideways—Pilger being one of Chomsky's fans—Richard's reading moved on to Noam Chomsky, enlarging his concerns to include El Salvador, Guatemala, South America generally. "I can't believe the *detail* of Chomsky's research! He systematically demonstrates the Third World's subjugation by the West—appalling."

Which set Richard thinking further. ("The place I have to

avoid is Books For Change in Charing Cross Road—*every-thing* in there looks interesting.") Soon he was off and away, he said, into the Matrix Churchill affair—reading Kenneth Timmerman's *The Death Lobby: How the West Armed Iraq,* and then *Betrayed* by David Leigh. Richard flicked though a copy of *New Internationalist* lying open on the coffee table. "I mean, there we were trading with the enemy. It's incredible."

Political labels can be misleading with the likes of Richard Wells. "I'm not a socialist," he told me, "because socialism denies man's fallen nature and exalts, even deifies, the State. Yet man's sinfulness is the very reason, as the twentieth century has surely demonstrated, why socialism won't work. But I'm not a Conservative, either—because the Conservatives, who *do* believe in man's fallen nature, use that knowledge to exploit, and encourage, their fellow-citizens' selfishness and greed. What I *do* believe in is the individual—and genuine choice. Indeed in that way I'm to the left of Labour—because I reject their fixation on state power."

Yet Richard rejects the left wing stance on abortion. "I'm absolutely against it. But though some would see such a position as anti-choice, to me it's based on the same reverence for life that makes me a fan of Noam Chomsky."

If any label fits at all, Richard shapes up as some kind of radical liberal—or, if you throw in his environmentalism, a Green. But it is hard to put him in any political compartment. Even so: "I suppose there are two areas where my position has pretty much firmed up," he said. "One is my growing concern for justice *internationally.*" And the other? His firmest look that day. "Community politics."

This, at least, is predictable, given the supreme instinct Ichthus has for local organization and activism. What is less obvious though, is that there is a quality to the theology of a group like Ichthus which also fuels that New Church spirit of do-it-yourself. For in the pantheon of Protestant theology, Ichthus has always been Arminian rather than Calvinist—and what that means, in turn, is a downgrading of Calvinist determinism and an upgrading of choice. "Everything we do in Ichthus," said Richard, "focuses around this notion of free will, that we have a choice." As Charles Reich said in that countercultural bible of the Seventies, *The Greening of America*: "The central fact about Consciousness III [i.e., countercultural consciousness] is its assertion of the power to choose a way of life . . . the power of choice, the power to transcend . . . the supreme act is the act of choice."

An appropriate theology to drive a religious group which shares that most basic of countercultural beliefs: a vastly extended notion of personal responsibility for the world (the environment, world peace, relationships generally) and thus faith in one's personal capacity to force change. You can change, because you choose your environment. Small wonder that Eighties conservativism peddled its own, reductionist style of "choice"—limiting it to consumer choice—as an instinctive and largely unconscious attempt to contain this dangerous creed. And small wonder that a religious movement with a wider sense of the meaning of the word has set about transforming religious services, housing, employment prospects and educational systems.

The precise distribution of the Evangelical/Charismatic balance clearly varies both within and between individuals. There is a world of difference, for example, between Richard Wells and Psalm, though they work happily in the same group. What is striking about Richard's mind is above all its order: clear, pellucid constructs as clear and pellucid as that gaze; well-oiled grammar, statistics, logic. (He has though, experienced Charisma: he described how at the age of sixteen a spiritual "waterfall" drenched him from head to toe, and he converted.) Nevertheless, with Richard it is reason that is prominent. Whereas with Psalm it is Charisma: intuition, inspiration, instinct.

And yet Psalm, like Richard, is into "works"—as is Carol, the other (posh) girl at the Justice Group meeting. Indeed Psalm and Carol were working together at an Evangelical hostel for the homeless just round the corner from their shared house. As well as all those Ichthus meetings, working groups and celebrations, Psalm and Carol had enormously punishing schedules at the hostel. "We work an eight-day shift system, which means for seven days we work an average of around nine hours in every twenty-four, sometimes during the day, sometimes at night. Then, on the eighth day, we work twenty-five hours—then get two days off." The work is extremely demanding: they had twenty-two clients at the hostel, aged between sixteen and twenty-two, seven female, fifteen male, all homeless, all desperately trying to sort their lives out. "The only words I can think of to describe it are opposites," said Psalm. "Dreadful, wonderful, enjoyable, exhausting." And for that she was paid £25 a week, plus free accommodation (in the shared house) plus £15 for food—and you can knock £4 a week off that straight away because both Psalm and Carol, like other Ichthus members, give 10 percent of their income—the immemorial Christian tithe—to the Church. You can live on £46 a week, of course, especially when you're twenty-two, but it means that —like a lot of Ichthus members—you live in a certain way.

It means, for instance, that there is no way either Psalm or Carol will own a car. "My problem is affording a *bike*," said Psalm. "Having said that, I do use public transport sometimes, expensive though it is—bike riding's dangerous." And as for food, intelligent bulk-buying is one trick. "I go to Kwik Save, Iceland, and get things like mincemeat, chicken in bulk. I make mince and onion, chopped tomato in pita bread."

As for clothes, it's amazing what can be done if, like Psalm, you're really into frugality. "My parents were missionaries in Madagascar, and not only did they have little money themselves, but we were surrounded by real poverty." So, as with food, Psalm does very well on very little—although when she has time off, it does mean car boot sales and street markets loom rather large in her leisure profile. In such circumstances, neo-hippydom pays dividends, since the aesthetic demands heavily mended, loose-fitting clothes, rather than smartly tailored chic. "These trousers, for instance"—the red ones with the patch—"were two pounds in a car boot sale." Psalm added the patch. "And as for the boots"—knitted, South American ethnic—"I got them from Oxfam for just 50p."

The whole ethos is reminiscent of the "voluntary simplicity" of the Greens. The *Evening Standard,* in the late Eighties, did a feature showing that a couple needed £60,000 a year in London even to scrape by, but here are Psalm and co. batting along quite happily on forty pounds a week. She even manages to bump her second-hand basics up with the odd shrewdly calculated new purchase: "Take that tie-dyed top of mine," she said. "Now that I did buy retail—cost me twelve pounds from Covent Garden." If Psalm goes to the cinema, it'll probably be cheap night (£2) at the Elephant and Castle; while a typical night off for Carol is a quiet evening in with her boyfriend—she writing letters, he, a music student, twanging the old guitar.

Having said all that, there is, to put it mildly, a whole other dimension to Carol and Psalm's lives. Psalm, in particular, lives out Charisma in its most intense and passionate form (those visualization moments—the dragon, the gnawing rat—during the Justice Group session were typical, and paranormal experience, of one sort and another, is an everyday part of her life). Not that she was always like that. Her particular missionary background was much more Evangelical/Baptist than Charismatic; and although her parents, in their early fifties now, were always pretty open-minded, one can detect a generation gap there, as in society at large. For Psalm herself, Charisma—when she first came across it on her return to Britain in 1990—was something new.

"My parents had helped set up this fellowship in the South London suburbs—Cheam, Surrey—before they went abroad," she said, "so I picked up the threads there on my return." Although she was, at that stage, still coming out of several years of rebellion and unbelief, Psalm was impressed by how "real" the faith there was—especially among the young. Things at Cheam had taken a distinctly Charismatic turn. "I mean, *real* healings, real signs from God." Plus real excitement in the services —with her Evangelical background, Psalm had never seen worship quite like this. "I'd never realized God would actually speak to me. But we'd have these worship sessions and people would experience these incredible moments, they'd say God was moving and so on, and I found you could actually communicate directly, personally with God. I thought, Wow!" (Psalm's taken on certain of the verbals as well as visuals of hippydom.)

The dynamics of prayer were different, too: "Prayer as I'd known it, Evangelical prayer, was always such a drag, a discipline, and it was, too, something you listened to passively, you *received*. But here we were producing prayer ourselves, as the Holy Spirit led us. Sometimes it would develop into a kind of ministry, we'd be encouraging each other. Sometimes we'd just sing. But sometimes, too, there'd be this other experience I'd never encountered before, this thing of pictures, receiving messages visually from God—the sort of thing, in fact, I was describing at the justice meeting."

There were a string of instances of this, said Psalm. There was the time one of the congregation there, Alan, described precisely —down to the the last detail—the little house where another of the congregation, Becky, had lived in Cheltenham. A house he'd never been near. Then there was the time when the congregation got into exploring the idea of occult objects, and Alan visualized a little ornament Psalm had bought at a car boot sale, a little ship. That certainly was beneficial because she'd had bad vibes about it, as it happened, from the start. She decided it was occult and threw it away. Good riddance.

Above all there was the time when Becky had this long word from the Lord for Connie, a friend of Psalm's from Madagascar. Even though Connie wasn't a Christian, this mighty power developed in the room and Becky began speaking in the first person. "I see this terrible loneliness," she said. Psalm knew just how spot on this was. Becky had got Connie's feelings precisely, and Psalm was sitting there, thinking, Wow, this is amazing! As for Connie, she was so touched, she said it was like God speaking directly to her, and in the end she came to the Lord.

"So finally I'd wanted to speak in tongues for ages," said Psalm, "and I asked these congregation members to pray with me and to my surprise and shock I received tongues and I thought, Wow! So at that point I got baptized in the Holy Spirit."

It is a bit difficult to relate such experiences to the prosaic, Evangelical schedule which is Psalm's everyday life. Yet plainly Charisma is a wonderful source of the energy such a schedule demands; and it was Charisma, not logic, which inspired the change in values which brought her to her present circumstances. Because spiritual though Psalm is now, she wasn't always thus. "I mentioned that period of rebellion" said Psalm. "Well, when I was fifteen, in the mid-Eighties, I was *well* into all that materialism thing—like everyone else, come to think of it, at that time. My idol was Madonna! I had fitted jackets, I had shoulder pads you wouldn't believe. It sounds funny, but I used to have this phrase in my head in those days, it kind of summed up my values . . . *I'm ruling the world.* Curiously enough, it coincided with the most insecure patch of my life so far. Anyway, come the Nineties—like an awful lot of people I know—my value system turned upside down. And yes, the first evidence of it someone sees, the thing that strikes you visually, is, I suppose, my dress."

As it is, indeed, with Psalm's fiancé, Ian, who turned up at that moment. For if Psalm looks quintessential spirit-of-1972, twenty-six-year-old Ian (also an Evangelical Christian, though not in Ichthus) feels earlier still: very Paris Riots of 1968, is Ian: wispy beard, long hair, denim jacket, jeans. Ian had, in those heady Eighties days, been way out on the opposite pole of the hippy-yuppy nexus. While Psalm was Material-Girling in the Third World, Ian was spending six months a year travelling with the Peace Convoy—that most outrageous caravanserai of heads, reds, Greens, spleen, and New Age ideology generally, not forgetting the presence of every last lingering noxious substance body or brain could dream of.

"I suppose," said Ian thoughtfully, "I was out of my head about nineteen hours a day." Yet now, since his conversion to Christianity (an LSD conversion, appropriately enough) he's eschewed drugs and become, like Psalm, a social worker—at a hostel for homeless men. Despite the seeming polarity of their lifestyles back in the Eighties, Ian and Psalm are now at one in Evangelicalism and social concern—Nineties people with a Sixties feel.

"That's how it is with young Christians these days," said Ian. "The wheel has turned full circle. Socialism's hip."

"Hip" is another bit of counterculture-speak you find knocking about the Charismatic movement these days, and the old divide between "hip" and "square" is reminiscent of the distinction between Charismatic and Evangelical. Having said that, despite the marked crossover between Charismatic Christianity and hip's heir apparent, New Age (a crossover denied with equal vehemence by both sides), the differences, too, are marked: it's complicated.

Take that most central twentieth-century phenomenon—what the psychologist Norman O. Brown, in an apt phrase, called "the Resurrection of the Body." Both New Age and New Christians are very big on making the body-and-mind (or soul) (or unconscious) reconnection apropos of healing. And in the case of New Christianity this process is unquestionably part of a broader promotion of the body from its traditional, lowly Christian status to something very much loftier. That hyperphysical hymn-singing, the new, more formal traditions of "liturgical dance," the touchy-feely "love hugs" at the Dawn Conference, the young women in Gerald Coates's congregation, happily presenting their sexuality, visually, in church—all suggest a new balance of power between body and soul. Attitudes to sex, however, remain rock-logic firm, notwithstanding all that Taoist fluidity.

Psalm and Ian, for instance, despite their engagement, will

not have sex before marriage. ("Holy, spirit-filled sex afterward," said Ian, "absolutely.") Twenty-two-year-old Ichthus member Jean Fair, an ex-Green voter, is also engaged, but she and her fiancé are both virgins, says Jean, and they will not have sex before marriage either. Carol, Psalm's co-worker, says the same. The prohibition can even work retrospectively: where a couple were having sex before their conversion, afterwards they will remain celibate until they tie the knot. Carol adds, with feeling, that of all Christian rubrics she finds this one the hardest to keep.

There are other areas in which the old, adamantine Evangelical certainties have fluidified. Take the traditional Evangelical attitudes to child-care which, in their assumption of the innate wickedness of babies and thus of parents' divine duty to break a baby's will, could mean that an old-time Evangelical upbringing was indistinguishable, in extreme cases, from child abuse. Typical of the movement today are the views of pony-tailed Philip Stokes, a thirty-three-year-old congregation leader who is married with two children aged seven and five. Phil's sense is that children are essentially good, albeit they need discipline. He quotes Jesus' words: "Unless ye become as little children, ye shall not enter into the Kingdom of Heaven." Children should be punished sparingly. As for the Old Testament notion of original sin that so alarmed the old Evangelicals like John Wesley's mother—re-enter the Ichthus theology of choice. Phil doesn't believe in the innate sinfulness of kids any more than he believes in their innate sinlessness. What he does believe is that children evolve, steadily, into ever greater accountability as they grow up. Or as he summarizes it: "I take Jesus' view. I believe children are in the kingdom unless and until they choose to opt out."

Once again, as gentle (hip) Jesus moves foreground and adamantine (square) Jehovah steps back, you get a sense of the overlap between New Christianity and New Age—a sense you often get when looking at the relationships (as opposed to the doctrine) of this most relationship-based New Christian movement. Consider another slogan from the Sixties, "The personal is political." The

Nineties version of this is that, just as the movement looks for a "personal relationship with Jesus," so groups like Ichthus identify with the belief that individuals can make a difference, that personal action has meaning in the communities they foster.

Mike Pears, for instance was given much of the furniture in his house. Phil Stokes was given £1,700 toward a new car. Ichthus as a whole gave a couple, both Ichthus members, £3,500 for the deposit on their new home. As Richard Wells put it: "I have people to stay in my flat, I lend out my car, I lent my tape deck out for a year, but this is all just routine, everyday stuff, par for the course. The word I'd use to describe it is the New Testament word *Koene*—fellowship. Or, if you like, the notion of extending family relationships to the community at large." The overall feel, certainly, is of a genuine commonality of goods, a constant, steady, quietly revolving, communal pass-the-parcel of settees, fridges, cots, ironing boards, cutlery, hoovers, even cars.

While this combination of communal self-help and frugality can indeed do wonders with household costs, what about household income—especially for those married members who need rather more than, say, Psalm or Carol? Mike Pears and his wife, both self-employed, get a pretty regular £400 a month from Ichthus for their fellowship work (Helen helped set up the Ichthus schools). On top of that, Mike does a fair bit of freelance lecturing and teaching, which might earn him another £100 a month; and there are gifts from well-wishers, including anonymous gifts— Mike calls this "the supernatural brown envelope syndrome." One month, for instance, Mike earned £150 from teaching and received £80 in gifts. So Mike and Helen are looking, each month, at a joint income of around £1,000—less than sumptuous, but surprisingly adequate given those traditions of communality and frugality.

So knock off £270 a month rent, £120 a month for food, maybe another £70 a month in bills and you begin to see why, despite the simplicity of their lifestyle, Mike still feels they can buy new—if Marks and Spencer—clothes for their children, can go out for the odd restaurant meal at about a tenner a head and have even committed themselves to paying £200 a month for an almost-new car. Indeed, they don't even take housing benefit—though they're entitled to it—and housing benefit, in other Christian budgets, is the mystery factor that makes otherwise impossible sums add up. Phil Stokes, for instance, pays rent on his house of .£500 a month and has a joint income, with his wife, of around £850 a month, including £70 a month in child benefit; his perfectly adequate lifestyle remains a puzzle, until you realize that because he gets £300 a month housing benefit, his real monthly rent works out at just £200.

What this seems to boil down to is that while it is indeed wonderful how easily one can spend £60,000 a year living in London, it is no less wonderful how easily one can survive on quite a lot less—if, like these Ichthus members, you know your way around the benefit system and, above all, if some really intelligent budgeting is applied. The budgetary adroitness of Ichthus is crucial. Mike, as a congregation leader, has a car, but the working rubric in Ichthus is one car per five members, which pans out just fine in a community where people actually do give each other lifts. Mike and Helen have two bank accounts—one current, one deposit—but never overdraw or use credit cards; their car is one carefully thought out exception, but in general they avoid the considerable sums many people spend on interest. Their food, too, is carefully budgeted for: not only do they avoid the more obviously cost-inefficient, ready prepared items, but when, for instance, they found out one month that they'd overspent, they promptly went on a vegetarian diet for six weeks to recoup.

Their religious commitment has other implications too. Certain monthly commitments many self-employed people would think were vital, they simply ignore: health insurance, potentially costing £40 or £50 a month? Why pay that when, if you're sick, your fellow Christians will provide? A pension, at perhaps £50 or £100 a month? Mike Pears reckons he may have to think about that eventually, but for now, there's a sense that God will provide.

When it comes to the family holiday, the networking internationalism of the New Christians comes good. Mike Pears was planning a lecture trip to Italy, with Helen and the kids—their accommodation paid for by local Christians, their fares subsidized by Ichthus. While another Ichthus couple, Dave Winter and his wife, were planning to spend over a month in Uganda. They were paying their own fares, true, but had also fixed up cheap accommodation via the international New Christian network.

There is nothing very spontaneous about such lifestyles, and we are well over at the planned, thought-out end of the Evangelical/Charismatic continuum. But should one be looking for any examples of "living by faith" (as the Charismatics have it), there's no shortage around Ichthus—and one would be hard put to come up with someone who's doing it to quite the level of twenty-five-year-old Carol Bond, a member of the Wells Way congregation who lives at the south end of the catchment area, almost in North Dulwich. Carol is Romantic with a very large R indeed—as was evident the moment I stepped into her large, dark bedsitter on the ground floor of the vast, clapped out semi she shared with five other Christians.

Fed up with order? Overdosed on Square? Try Carol—you'll never, ever, see an interior quite like this. Maverick strewings, heaps of paper, long-lost biros, piles of fluff; that sweet dust smell that every student knows; giddy, swaying heaps of books jutting up amid it all, like desert rock formations in cowboy films; more books, papers, clothes, shoes, flung in Dionysian abandon on the unmade bed; a table inches deep in wall-to-wall junk, plugs, cups, shoes, a coin, lunch, tea, supper, breakfast, poetry books, tickets, hangers—and, the climax, a wardrobe in the corner of the room, not merely stuffed full, but actually spilling forth clothes like a Bernini fountain, bursting, erupting, in an exquisitely sculpted arc across the room. This is no ordinary mess. This is mess with a mission, mess with a message.

In the middle of it all, sitting on the floor, is black-eyed, lustrous

Carol, like a great glowing gypsy. She's talking about how much she loves this Christian drama course she's on, and how she did an English and drama degree at Goldsmith's, and how her favorite poet is John Donne, no, not the love poetry, more—a lustrous look—his Divine Sonnets! Their passion, their enormity of feeling . . . She also adores those intense nineteenth-century writers like Coleridge, George Eliot, Alfred Lord Tennyson!

When Carol moves on to the nuts and bolts of making it without an income, living by faith, it's less than surprising that, for her, such specifics have a very metaphysical dimension indeed.

"True, I have no other income" she says. "But then that's intentional. True, I did use to take the dole at one stage—but I gave it up voluntarily and when I signed off I felt God telling me not to claim housing benefit either. Because, you see, I want to have no income because I want to put myself to this ultimate test of faith—to prove that it is possible to survive purely by putting myself in the hands of the Lord. Also, this is a very good way of jolting oneself out of any lingering materialism—any fantasies that you control where money comes from, whereas in reality, of course, only God does that." The actual mechanics of Carol's living by faith are quite ordered. "I budget things just like other people," she says. "The difference is, I employ prayer—rather than, say, work—to get the money for them. But I'm quite organized: I keep an account in the back of my diary of how it's coming in."

She showed me. On a back page of the diary was a list of items in a column:

Clothes

Jacket

Jumper

Make-up

Rent

Gas

Poll tax

And on another page, more specifically:

Shopping: £20
Gas bill: £50
School fees: £70

Carol tut-tuts. "It's been a bad month , she says. "I've had to pay for the gas, the electricity, the phone bill, school fees and thirty pounds for a photo session for my course. And now I've a trip coming up to to Plymouth, that means I've got to pray in some train fare, that's another thirty pounds."

Most days, like many Charismatics, Carol prays for an hour first thing in the morning—and then again on her return from college in the afternoon. As for her sources of money, there have been some short spates of actual work, but most of it comes in one form or another of a gift: "Christian well-wishers, friends . . . One day I was desperate for three hundred pounds for the rent and, after I prayed, this friend from outside London said, look, I've just had this tax rebate, take it. It was for three hundred pounds."

Carol explains that the whole point of this lifestyle is that she sees it as part of her wider, ongoing dialogue with God. This is only one aspect of that dialogue, for, as with Psalm, God also speaks to her in "pictures." So far as the specifically financial aspect of her life is concerned, she is, she says, quite "firm" with God. "Because, unlike some, I'm taking Him at His word. After all, Jesus paid with his life so we could have these rights! So I'm quite out front about it all—I say to Him look, rent, food, clothes, these are my *rights*. I demand them, God!"

On Carol's figures, it seems to work out rather well. When I met her she'd been living by faith "properly," she said, for around six months. During that time she must have "prayed in," as they say, around £3,000.

5

Jobs for God's Boys

The abstemiousness practiced by Carol Bond, and others like her, was not usually voluntary. The recession which began in the late Eighties enforced poverty on the inner cities, and meant still more of that hopelessness endemic even in the boom, so that the demand for social projects like those run by Ichthus was growing all the time. To get a closer look at these projects, I decided to spend some time at the launderette, the nursery school, and other Ichthus venues. In each the feel was much the same: young, fresh, optimistic faces, a touch bland; bright minds (many Ichthus members are graduates) touched by a curious naiveté; overall, an atmosphere that again owed more to gentle Jesus than to stern Jehovah. In Ichthus's nursery school, the Evangelical aspect is low-key indeed: as the children watch their puppet shows, play with their letters and color in their pictures, there's very little overt proselytizing going on at all.

But as the unemployment figures marched steadily upwards there was one project which stood out above all others—and that was, of course, Pecan. The back-to-work scheme with the remarkable success rate was the more interesting because it was a classic example of that inter-denominational co-operation so crucial to the revival. For while 60 percent of Pecan's staff were indeed members of Ichthus, the other 40 percent included denominations as diverse as Baptists, Pentecostalists, even Church of England. So one day Mike Pears walked me the hundred yards down the road from his house to the Pecan offices at Cottage Green, and there I met Pecan's Managing Director, thirty-three-year-old Ichthus member Simon Pellew.

Green sweater, rueful manner (Simon was, he says, bullied as a child)—he could have been a Maths teacher at a public school, sitting there hitting a computer in one corner of an open-plan office converted out of the Wells Road Baptist Church. Next door is the former church hall where the local Ichthus group now hold their services. Here, in the ex-Church building itself, there are half a dozen desks, some word processors, a copying machine and four other Pecan employees in track suits and jeans. Not that there is anything unprofessional about Pecan, least of all Simon. Indeed, with his geology degree and his MSC in Energy Policy and his fashionable business argot (along with British Gas, earlier jobs included a stint with the environmental organization the International Institute for Environment and Development) he could fit seamlessly onto any bond desk in the City. You can see why he's given himself this "Managing Director" tag—by no means the label you'd expect among a bunch of social workers.

"What we're really trying to do," said Simon, "is take the good things about business practice—efficiency, cost consciousness, proper planning etcetera—you know, Tom Peters' *In Search of Excellence*—and make them the practical expression of something many might think utterly different: our own spiritual commitment and beliefs. And why *not* combine the two? There's no law I know of that says Christians must be inefficient."

Yet more interesting is how Simon proposes to go about it. After all, what Pecan does, essentially, is match around 800 unemployed "clients" a year—10 percent of the unemployed population of North Peckham—to the twenty courses run by its staff and volunteers: clearly rather different from running, say, a factory. Yet there is overlap.

"Take our equal pay policy, our flat £13,400 a year. Sure, many argue management must be paid more if you're going to get good people and yes, it's true that I, and others here, could earn much more elsewhere. But I don't buy this fiction that you've got to pay people huge sums to get results. Let's face it, whenever anyone does a job motivation survey, pay's about the seventh thing people mention, way down there after feeling valued, enjoying the work they do, etcetera.

"Whereas with the symbolism of our pay system, hopefully, the person running the crêche actually *feels* the work to be as vital as the M.D.'s. And if each job's that vital, whatever it is, then clearly we've each of us got to give each task the very best shot we can."

There is similar thinking behind the open-plan Pecan office: that's all about, "flat hierarchy and accessibility, Charles Handy, *Understanding Organizations*"—as it is, too, about that most bedrock Pecan ethic of all, cross-fertilization: whether between individuals, denominations or office teams. The associated notion of flexibility between grades, so that anyone from the M.D. to a trainer may, in an emergency, lick stamps, is important, too, as is Pecan's lack of pressure to put in hours—what Simon calls "high trust and low control." A pattern emerges here, and it is similar to the "tight-loose" structures of the Evangelical/Charismatic movement as a whole: "task orientation" is the key. As Simon summed it up: "I simply don't *care* how *long* people work at something, or who does it, or how. What I do care about are the *results*."

All of which is impeccable modern management, with the particular flavor of what has been called the "feminization" of business. Academics such as those Harvard Business School feminists Shoshana Zuboff (*In the Age of the Smart Machine*) and Rosabeth Moss Kantor (*When Giants Learn to Dance*) would love all this (once they have got over the fact that these folks are "fundamentalists," that is). And yet, despite Simon's reading, the greater part of Pecan's ethos, apparently, just "evolved." Nor should the effect of the spiritual impetus behind the endeavor be forgotten. "Put it this way," said Simon, "you call it business practice, I call it Christianity. It's surprising how much our interpretation of the Gospel leads us into just the kind of business practices you've seen. In Ichthus, in particular, we really *do* believe in mutual accountability."

The heroic moment for Pecan, the moment when they really start doing things other agencies don't, comes when they go recruiting, knocking on eight thousand estate doors to find "contacts," which they do three times a year. The results speak for themselves. A third of all contacts actually come along to their courses, and it's among these that there is that remarkable success rate.

I went out door-knocking with the recruiters: with Nadia Banoub Mitri, a raven-haired doctor from Egypt who had actually joined an Ichthus off-shoot back at home (it's always that much easier, she reminded me, for a Middle-Easterner to come to terms with Ichthus's supernaturalism than someone from the West); with Dutchman Paul Van der Hagen, feline, swivel-hipped, leery of the estate dogs, like a slightly feminine, high-sobriety, seventeenth-century Calvinist; and, most memorably of all, with two of Pecan's regular recruiters, twenty-five-year-old Dave Winter and twenty-nine-year-old Patrick Anderson, a couple who'd been an item as a recruiting team for months. (For mutual security, Pecan recruiters always work in pairs.) Come the sunny spring Monday when Dave and Patrick and I headed off for the Gloucester Grove Estate, they made quite a pair: Patrick Anderson, black Pentecostalist, short, streetwise, who described his crisis-conversion seven months earlier; Dave Winter, an engineering graduate, skinny legs, John Lennon sunglasses, ring hanging off one ear.

For anyone whose beliefs include Satanic "spirit of place," the Gloucester Grove's the ticket. It's the way it wraps round you, castle-like, intimidating, overshadowing, all dark, brute, lowering physical bulk. The tenants' own do-it-yourself fortifications don't help: grilles, grids, guard dogs—a big favorite is a picture of an

Alsation displayed on the front door, ears pricked, eager-looking, alert. One tenant, taking the fortification motif to its logical conclusion, has extended his dustbins and outhouse into a crazy, teetering fifteen-foot-deep outwork, quite separate from his neighbors. Defend that first, presumably, then fall back behind the front door for the last stand.

There are vast empty corridors, huge hundred-yard vistas, windy, rubbish-strewn, without ornament or shrub; with these hard, unkind, graffiti-stained surfaces everywhere, grey concrete, dirty brick, which make you feel that if you touch them you'll scrape off a layer of skin. Perversely, among all this mayhem, each walkway crossover looks just like all the others, so time and again you think you know exactly where you are and you're actually half a mile away, you're lost.

"Like a lot of recruiters, I just work a half week," said Patrick. "I don't think you could work the full week here, it'd be too mentally tiring."

After wading through all this for half a mile, we reached our first flat. Patrick knocked on the door. A pause. Mystery clunkings. And then, as if propelled by clockwork, came a sudden growling screeching shrieking rasping sound, with thumps, as if twenty-five Hounds of Hell were chasing the All Blacks round the hallway. More screechings; earth-traumatizing bangs; whatever it was, they had it on the ground now, and were homing in for the kill. . . . Then the door opened to reveal a small, mild, timid little man, looking scared. Plus one bull terrier, leashed. No, he was not interested actually, he said politely. Your lot have been round before. But he does think Pecan does very good work. And thanks very much for thinking of him, anyway. It's really good of us to go to all this trouble.

The next door the lady wouldn't open. The next door the bloke said to poke the leaflet through, he'd read it. The next door the lady was on the loo, which Patrick established via a shouted exchange through the letter box. No interest. The next door there was a teenager with a baby and mad eyes, and when Patrick started in on his spiel she got the giggles and slammed the door.

"I couldn't do this if I wasn't a Christian," said Patrick. And so it went on, down the corridor, through the morning, throughout the day; mild faces, mad faces, weary faces, dogs; men standing there uncertainly, blinking uncomprehendingly at Patrick's leaflets; women gazing suspiciously out of these little glowing oases of domesticity, babies on arm; everyone simultaneously lonely, curious and reluctant to chat. You could see why the recruiters worked short hours (ten till twelve in the mornings, two till four in the afternoons) and Patrick stuck to his half week. There's a limit, clearly, to how often you can psyche yourself up.

Not to mention, pointed out Patrick, the metaphysical dimension. There was one time, he explained, when this bloke came up in the corridors and started shouting at him—get out of here, leave me alone, this is my place. "Territorial demon, see," said Patrick. "Christ is Lord of all, but demons have these *local* powers. So they're very into their own particular space—and, as a Christian, I was threatening it."

By lunchtime, Patrick and Dave, by pulling every trick they knew, had managed roughly their one-third average response: a fair morning's work. "It's those opening moments that are hardest," said Patrick. "One scam is to introduce myself as 'Shirley'—by the time I've explained my woman's name, I'm in. Plus things like seeing they've got kids, and saying, 'We've got a crèche, you know.'" "You think on your feet," adds Dave. "No pre-cast theories—spontaneity."

Which I saw for myself that afternoon when, as the sunny day stretched out into one of those warm, dreamy, hanging-out kind of afternoons, we came down one walkway, aiming for a corridor a hundred yards on, and there on one of those lookalike crossways was a huddle of blacks, four boys, three teenage girls, two seven-year-olds bashing away at a lorry tyre. In their midst was a Jamaican bloke in his twenties, gold jewelry, heavy-lidded, soft drink in fist.

You couldn't find a worse place to sell something, really—zero intimacy, no chance to concentrate, people walking up and passing time and peeling off nonstop. But Patrick knew the bloke, Leslie was his name, so we stopped and soon we were chatting and next thing we were talking about Pecan, and Patrick asked Leslie if he'd ever thought of doing a course, and Leslie said: not interested.

More people wandered by and the kids knocked all hell out of the tire and Patrick asked Leslie what do you do, and Leslie said, I'm a chef, and Patrick asked if he'd ever thought of starting up on his own and now, at last, there was this tiny flicker of interest in Leslie's eyes. Any grants?

Then suddenly, *wham!* Dave Winter was in there, too—Dave who'd seemed a bit shy at first but now, dramatically, has been kick-started into action, and out flooded a white-hot stream of statistics and enthusiasm. Well no, Dave couldn't be too sure about grants, but look at the success rate on the course, 40 percent get jobs, 29 percent get training, 6 percent join the Job Club, really worth it, Leslie should really think about it. Leslie showed a bit more interest . . . then more still. . . . Until Leslie was finally, indubitably alight, hooked. By the end I realized that even in this warm, floaty half-hour's hanging-out, we'd had our own authentic little micro-moment of Charisma: first Patrick, then Dave had palpably shifted Leslie's mood (not to mention their own) right here on the second-floor walkway. A "positive contact."

Not a bad day, overall—and it all felt different, somehow, after that: positive responses, in fact, of around a third; fat Africans, harassed Englishwomen, heavy-lidded Jamaicans, all signing up to come in for a course. The high spot of the day came when some Nigerians asked us in and Patrick asked whether there was anything we could do for them, and they said, well we do have this problem with hay fever. And so, to get a really good crack at it, Dave and Patrick prayed for them in tongues.

It was weird, as ever, the way this spiritual dimension constantly intertwined with all that rationality. But then how could Dave and Patrick have done without it—or something like it? For their faith is surely the foundation of their tenacity, and tenacity is something, on this job, they need in cubes. As do their clients, to make a success of the training—which is where it helps should they happen (and they often do happen, of course) to convert. Come to that, during the days I was with Pecan, the staff on more than one occasion started praying for me. A first, in my experience, but not unappreciated.

Pecan is a prime example of how it's not what you do, but the spirit in which you do it. You'd hardly expect Patrick to say he actually liked the job—and yet he does: "It's wonderful," he told me, "like being a footballer. I really look forward to each day." He's not talking about the door knocking—not the hundreds of rejections, anyway. "It's the office atmosphere. I've done a lot of jobs—I'm a plasterer by trade—but what's new here is this sense that work can be nonthreatening, somewhere I feel at ease. We support each other. Sounds weird, I suppose, but when I think of the office, I only think of love."

This is not, it's fair to say, how all of us see our workplaces —yet it's a consistent tone among the Pecan staff. Twenty-four-year-old Alison, also a recruiter, said it is the "sense of community" that she values most—and she feels the symbolism of equal pay, and the sense of enhanced self-worth this gives everyone, is crucial. As for the "parenting" conventionally expected of the traditional, patriarchal boss, Simon's very good, but the truth is that everyone at Pecan parents everyone else. It need hardly be added that when Pecan hold a business meeting the preferred layout for the chairs is a circle.

Such countercultural instincts also extend to training relationships. Twenty-nine-year-old Jem Mackay is one of four Pecan trainers who put on the actual courses. Funky, bearded, raw-edged, he reckons the whole essence of Pecan's approach is to "open people up, set them free—not squeeze them, as some courses do, into a mold." Each course lasts about a month, working an approximate five-day week, and they do "all the practical things, sure—CVs, time management, the setting of goals. But the crux, we've found, is rebuilding clients' confidence.

"Classic example: we had one girl, really good-looking woman, had all the skills. She'd had a very good job, previously, supervising a team of twenty. Then she lost it, and when she came to us she'd been unemployed for a year. So in one of our exercises she drew a cartoon to show how she felt: devastated, crushed, flat out on the floor. A month later, at the end of her course, she drew us another. This time she was standing up, arms stretched out—raring to go. She'd *had* the skills, you see, and indeed she'd kept them—what she'd lost, over that year, were the intangibles. And that was what we helped her to win back.

"So that you could, in a way, sum up the difference between trainers and clients like this: the clients think they're joining a job club—the trainers know it's an encounter group."

A session may well head off in a very different direction than planned, if that's what the clients seem to want. As 24-year-old physics and biology graduate Ian Stedman, Job Club leader, put it: "Your typical training course tends to be very specific, aiming at particular skills, a particular job. We prefer to blur a little, fuzz around the edges—let people find their own way to what they need."

This can mean that someone may turn up with the obvious problem—no job—but in conversation it may quickly emerge that the underlying problem is debt, or family difficulties, or both. "It's not till you've teased all that out that you're in a position to have a serious crack at tackling employment. What it boils down to, in fact, is that we start, effectively, by facilitating a social club —and build from there."

All of which might sound a bit New Age, flaky even. Yet

those Positive Outcomes figures speak for themselves. As do the clients, indeed, of whom around 40 percent land actual jobs, with a further 35 percent getting on to courses, or doing further training or other development. Ushma Patel, for instance, was made redundant in the BCCI collapse, and joined a course in January 1993: the same day she got her job in marketing she got four other calls from interested companies. Goke Odunlami, a course member in May 1993, got a job out of the first interview after his course. Gill Keswick, made redundant after thirty years with the GLC, got a job with Roehampton Hospital while still on the course. Emma Heath, a course member in March 1993, explained: "The Pecan course helped me a lot as it showed me exactly where I was going wrong. Everybody took part and it was like being part of a team, encouraging one another and listening to other people's experience." A month after her course, Emma got a job.

Considerable interest in Pecan is shown by neighborhood businesses. The local Marks and Spencer, for instance, help out by putting Pecan clients through mock interviews at their Walworth Road store. Brian McCarthy, one of the store managers, commented: "The practical, hands-on approach adopted by the trainers to develop the individuals was amazing. I really sensed a genuine commitment in the group to achieve."

This glowing testimonial might, in turn, help explain how it is that companies assisting Pecan financially (as well as Marks and Spencer) include British Telecom, Barclays Bank, the Post Office, Shell U.K., Sainsbury's, Oxford University Press, Cambridge University Press, LWT, Boots, Rothschild and Sons plus a string of others—to the extent that of Pecan's £271,350 income in 1993, virtually all came from various forms of donations and grants.

However, Pecan is hardly unique in its South London patch; indeed, over fifty companies provide job training under the auspices of the local Training and Enterprise Council, many boasting a comparably "progressive" office culture. Nevertheless, for all the differences of statistical definitions, Pecan's results stand comparison with the very best (the average local Positive Outcomes figure, as we have seen, is 28 percent); while culturally, Pecan unquestionably has certain quite distinctive qualities, many traceable to its Christian roots. There is, for instance, its particular stress on client morale as opposed to skills, by no means shared by a training provider like Brixton's Baytree Centre, for example; but then Pecan's philosophy here is rooted in its peculiarly Christian sense of "spirituality." There is its Christian-populist, "bottom-up" sense that the client him/herself should be the mainspring of a project's energy; no "top-down," statist, coerciveness for Pecan, unlike some local job clubs. But, above all, there are the all-pervasive effects of those extraordinarily energizing supernatural beliefs, for all their obvious perils; something, after all, has to drive the recruiters along the corridors, the long-term unemployed through their course.

So it is the more curious that another quality differentiating Pecan from some local organizations is its relative easiness with modern business systems. Or as one social worker put it: "Some of the more right-on groups are, frankly, plain antibusiness." Whereas Pecan, arguably, tries to reinvent business to new ends.

The day after that door-knocking trip with Patrick and Dave, I joined them for one more afternoon, because this time their schedule included visiting a lady they reckoned might yet become a Christian—always a relevant consideration, even if employment was Pecan's main event. So round I went once more to the Pecan offices (once again, as I arrived, the staff were praying for me, led by Simon). Once again we headed off along the doomwatch corridors, past the graffiti, the dogs, the fortifications, until we ended up in front of the flat of the young woman concerned, Linda. "She's very sick," said Dave.

We knocked, and this time the door opened to reveal a

young cockney woman, ill-looking, pale, and Patrick said did she remember us, and would she like us to pray for her, and she said, well, obviously it wouldn't do any good, but come in anyway.

So in we went to this weary, messy flat, and Linda started talking about her illnesses, how she was on all these tablets, and having fits and blackouts, and how she'd been diagnosed as having cancer of the stomach, and also possibly, cancer of the bowel. In fact she'd had six different kinds of cancer in six years.

She collapsed into a chair and sat there looking half amused, half stunned, as Dave and Patrick settled themselves gingerly on the edge of their chairs. Did Linda mind their praying for her, they wondered?

"I don't mind," said Linda, sardonic, "but I know it won't do any good." There followed quite a debate about the advantages of religious as opposed to medical cures, and it turned out that Linda was due to have a stomach operation on the twenty-fourth of the month, and she was absolutely *certain*, she said, that this was what was going to cure her, none of this mystic pie-in-the-sky nonsense, no, not her!

"I tell you what I'll do!" she said suddenly. "If you cure me, I'll become"—a flourish—"a Born Again Christian! And you'll have won! But if you don't"—a leering grin—"why then I'll die, and you know what that will mean."

"What's that?" said Dave.

"*I've* won!" said Linda triumphantly.

Nothing abashed, Dave Winter started a prayer session in which he took the lead, with Patrick as support. Dave sat directly opposite Linda, a couple of feet from her, once more dropping effortlessly into that dominant alter ego that had appeared for Leslie on the crossway, but quieter now. He stared with this direct, clear gaze into Linda's eyes: firm, authoritative, sure.

"We say to the cancer in your stomach, go back, in Jesus' Name," said Dave. Putting heavy stress on the word "Jesus," with each "Jesus" coming at the end of a little rushing climax followed, in turn, by a backwash like the breaking and receding of a wave, he went on: "Thank you, Jesus . . . Yes . . . thank you, Jesus . . . thank you . . ." He was building, now, to the next crescendo: "For we BIND you here, we say to you, STOP GROWING, cancer, yes, in JESUS' name, we will prevent you, yes, go back! We bind you, yes! In JESUS' name!" Climax again followed by another backwash: "In Jesus' name, we thank you . . . thank you, Jesus . . . thank you, thank you . . . Jesus . . ."

Linda sat there looking sardonic, then giggly, then, quite suddenly, utterly fascinated, with great blue wondering eyes. Dave seemed to gather energy as he went along, and now he was heading off, finally, into this climactic skittering spiral of tongues

"RRRR shynawegocoskihokanwopoccorongosoccinawah!" cried Dave, those first Rs rolling, spinning like a jet revving up its engines, "RRRR segmumarotadiasotokekumamakowasetodecumasotomasundo, I bind you, in the name of Jesus I say I PREVENT you, you must stop growing, cancer, in JESUS' name I say, be bound, RRRRRR casotrosigmasenussissmo, cassastrsastrocassumaalumadoyingoccatawapesutrocuma!" Linda sat there, gazing.

"I don't know about all that," she said finally. "I'm still going to have that stomach operation on the twenty-fourth."

Such disappointments happen, on occasion, with even the most heartfelt proselytizing. "You know, the really strange thing about Linda," said Dave, as we wended our way back that afternoon, "is that despite all this atheism her own mother was Born Again. In fact, there have been times, in the past, when Linda herself has been intensely religious."

What struck me as strange, not unpredictably, was how our visit had plunged us back from the rational, computerized end of the Evangelical/Charismatic continuum to the movement's supernaturalism. By now I was getting quite dizzy with these

constant oscillations between the two psychological extremes—
one minute hyperrationalism, the next hyperintuitiveness, a
kind of strobe lighting of the soul. How did all that sober Ichthus
blandness relate to the moments we'd just acted out in the flat?

One clue lay in that very blandness. After all, there's something
spooky about wall-to-wall niceness—it seems remote from both joy
and anger and as, such, unreal. As one House Church member put
it, commenting on day-to-day emotional life among Charismatics:
"After a few months of it, I'd come to feel so isolated that I made a
stupid attempt at suicide. Now that wasn't the House Church's
fault, but I had become so very desperate—all I'd wanted was an
ordinary conversation, and I simply couldn't get it from those
people. They would rush up to you after a weekend retreat
and say, 'Oh, I think that I've made a real breakthrough into
true lovingness,' and you could be standing there going mad
with loneliness." Such depersonalization, abstracted from both
genuine pleasures and pains, begins to sound akin to the state
which underlies the most dramatic visionary experiences of all—
"dissociation."

Then there is the paranormalism itself. Yorkshire vicar and
long-term Charisma critic Peter Mullen says: "I have a file two
feet thick, full of letters from people who have been driven to the
edge of despair—and some beyond the edge—by this hocus pocus
. . . One of its worst aspects is a sort of cartoon supernaturalism:
Jenny driving me into York one day: 'Let us ask the Lord to show
us a parking place.' The Lord also showed us a traffic warden."
Nevertheless, argues Mullen, the reality is more serious: "A man
I know was exorcised at a Charismatic prayer group because he
said he didn't believe the Devil is a person. He ended up in the
psychiatric ward. A woman was told by a bunch of peripatetic
healers that God would cure her terminal cancer of the liver. She
died four days later, confusion worse confounded."

On the other hand, there is that measured sobriety of Mike
Pears; that day-by-day devoted, social endeavor of Philip Stokes,

Richard Wells, Psalm and Carol, Ian and Jem; there is all of that community-building of which the Pecan effort is just one part. Is Charismatic irrationalism so utterly unthinkable when it fuels such Niagaras of faith? Must everything—can everything—be thought out, measured, planned? Hasn't the whole story of the twentieth century been the gradual realization that virtually any belief system you can think of, including most "scientific" paradigms, are at bottom arbitrary, even arational? It depends, presumably, what "irrational" impulses we are talking about: not everything instinctive is antisocial.

The nineteenth-century British Prime Minster Lord Rosebery argued that if you really want to get things done, then "practical mystics"—those with reason *and* faith—represented the "most formidable of combinations" that he knew of.

Practical mystics—advancing the Union Jack through darkest Africa; reborn today in deepest Peckham.

6

Finding the Lord

New Church life in the inner cities is clearly a crucial element in the revival. But the key quality of Charisma is that it is rooted in personal, paranormal experience. What are the parallels between the "macro" processes in society at large, and the "micro" experience of the convert?

One common factor is by now familiar: uncertainty. One day I received a letter written by Gerald Coates in response to a note I had sent him about my book:

> A lady—a millionairess—looked at her business, wealth and the such and realized she was not fulfilled. She phoned the local Anglican vicar (I'd rather not say where!) and he said he'd phone back—but didn't! She then phoned the Roman Catholic priest and he promised to phone back— he didn't either! She then saw your piece in the Sunday Times Colour Supplement magazine—contacted our office, came to a meeting, gave her life to Christ at the very first meeting and her life has been quite transformed—almost to my astonishment I must confess.
>
> She came round to see me a few days ago, the day my autobiography was published. Took a book and went off to see one of the wealthiest women in the land! (Sorry about the number of exclamation marks in this letter!) As a result

the woman has asked to see me to discuss Christianity as she is totally disillusioned with some of the New Age perspectives and believes much of it is fraudulent having committed herself and her business to it for some time. So at the end of April we are having dinner with this lady and her husband—thanks to you.

All of this, if a touch coy, was intriguing. Who was the mystery millionairess? And who was her mystery friend? And would the threatened dinner party ever take place? And how on earth had my article been midwife to such a spiritual awakening?

As Gerald explained when we later spoke, another convert had joined Cobham as a direct result of my piece: a copper from the CID, with twenty years on the force. As the officer concerned put it in a letter to me: "A millionairess and a hard-nosed copper is not a bad score." By the time I finally made moves to get in touch with the (first) millionairess, a falling-out had occurred between her and the Cobham Christian Fellowship, and she had apparently gone down the road to join another local revival group, Millmead in Guildford. Nevertheless, she and I were eventually put in touch. She turned out to be a franchisee (six shops) of the Body Shop cosmetics chain; and the other disillusioned millionairess she had mentioned was none other than Ms. New Age Businesswoman herself, Anita Roddick: Body Shop boss, feminist, millionairess, networker, animals' friend. (She is just the example one might have given of the kind of franchise operator in mainstream business whose organization mirrors precisely the franchise operation which is, by one definition, March For Jesus. Both "franchises" have simultaneously colonized the United States—by June 1993 there were 133 Body Shops in the U.S., the first having opened in 1988 in New York.) The crossover here between New Christianity and New Age is especially appropriate when you recall that Anita Roddick— arch proselytizer for "values" in modern business, arch opponent of animal testing for cosmetic wares—is also, in her own way, distinctly Evangelical.

The first millionairess was called Pauline Rawle, and I met her at her long, low, red-brick farmhouse near Effingham, sleekest Surrey: sea-green meadows all around; brilliant flower beds, carefully worked; elaborate garage-cum-stable-cum-guest-bedroom outhouses; white Mercedes, turquoise pool, receding lawns.

Bustling through a cluster of cleaning ladies and shaking my hand was this little, bird-like blonde, Ms. Rawle. She was dressed all in white, with a red shoulder-padded jacket on top. Her sitting room, through the hallway, was white too, and adorned with white flowers; there were giant white artificial daisies, also, in the white loo along the corridor, their petals eyelash-like, their centers open wide like yearning eyes; little Aimée, Pauline's miniature poodle, was also white.

"Aimée, Aimée, you *know* you're not allowed on the chairs!" We sipped coffee in the sitting room and started in on this Aimée routine, which persisted throughout the visit. Aimée cocked her head on one side; toyed with obedience; found it boring; disobeyed. She jumped back onto my chair, tumultuous, affectionate, a chaos of licks.

"Aimée, AIMÉE!" pleaded Pauline. "So wilful, that dog—childlike! Well! If you'd told me a couple of years ago that I of all people would become a Christian, I'd have—Because the thing about *me*, you see, was that I wasn't just un-religious, agnostic, anything like that. I was, rather, a full-blown, out-and-out, *atheist*.

"Okay, so my mother was an Evangelical, true. But her faith was always so *childlike*. And me—I'd always taken the view that there were just two things that caused all the trouble in the world, and they were: nationalism and religion." Indeed, explained Pauline—talking in a high, breaking voice, as if constantly on the verge of tears—in the Eighties she'd been well into all that materialism. There'd been the Body Shops for a start: built the whole thing up from her first one, back in the early Eighties, and then added on this chain of accessory shops as well. At one stage she must have been pulling in a million a year profit. Her "conversion rate" (converting walk-ins to buyers, it turned out), she said, was especially good. But the high life had palled. Indeed, gradually it had sickened her. What was the meaning of it all? "Your hope is that all this success, owning all these beautiful things, will make people love you." But it didn't. Pauline felt there was something strangely removed about such materialism—it was all symbolic, somehow, rather than real. She'd met this chap on a cruise ship and he'd talked to her about his "nineteen homes." Now really— who needs nineteen homes?

Pauline fixed me with an eagle eye; she has a way of delivering sentences with gaps in between, the looks smoldering away there in the pauses.

"You see, it's always the next thing you're going to buy that will make you happy, the next million, the next home—but really you're using these things to stave off—deny—your spirituality. Because what you're really feeling, at bottom, is just, plain . . . well, lonely."

The conversation having taken this lurch, Pauline expanded further:

"I mean, look at me. *Lonely.* I had everything materially but nothing spiritually. My first marriage had broken up, then I broke up with my fiancé and then the business problems kicked in as the recession hit. I'd borrowed one and a third million to start the accessory chain: I used to wake up at night sweating. Eventually it got to the stage where there was simply too much pressure from too many different directions. I couldn't take it any more. I took this overdose."

Pauline was caught in time, fortunately, and rushed to hospital. "But I'd lost my husband-to-be, *and* my accessory chain, by then— half my businesses—even though I still had the Body Shops. But the problems were mounting there, too; and who, in all this time,

was around to give me consolation, support? No one. I remember
when I was in hospital I talked with this psychiatrist. He listened to
me for a while and then he said: "You don't need psychotherapy
—you need a friend."

"So when I moved here from north London, where me and my
fiancé had been living, my whole idea was this new start. New
location, new friends—but I suppose the moment when I realized
just how utterly *lonely* I was came shortly after I moved here and
went into hospital again for this minor op. And no one came to
visit me, not my children, not my fiancé, no one.

"So, how to make friends? There was the golf club, there was
bridge—and then I thought—what about the church? So I had
a look at the local C of E, but I didn't like it. So I contacted the
Catholics—they never phoned back.

"And then, one Sunday, I read your article! And I remember
what struck me most: you described this girl who said how friendly
she found the Christians, before she converted, when she first met
them in the pub. Friendly, welcoming. So I thought, I know what
I'll do—I'll get in touch with them."

Suffice it to say that Cobham, unlike the straight denominations, were round like a shot.

"So this woman came, and we talked, and she gave me some
stuff to read, but I still wasn't sure. I was pondering. My heart
was for it, but my head held back.

"But then God spoke to me: 'Don't try to do it all with
your intellect.' He said, 'Do it with faith.' Proverbs 3:5: *Trust
the Lord with all thy heart; and lean not unto thine own
understanding*."

Despite this exemplary Charismatic distinction between the
Spirit and the Word, Pauline didn't hear the actual voice of
God, she says, more "a thought in the head." On a visit to the
local Marks and Spencers, on the other hand, she had a more
overt Charismatic experience—a sign.

"Funnily enough, in the course of our chat the Cobham

Christian Fellowship lady had asked me, how did I like the neighborhood generally? And I said, 'Fine—but I do miss Marks and Spencers! I suppose the nearest is in Guildford?' 'No, there's one much nearer,' she said, 'at Tolworth. Excellent parking and a very nice selection of wines.' So as she left I said 'Thank you for everything you've told me today. You've really given me something to think about—especially Marks and Spencers!' "

"Well, after she left I started worrying and worrying about Christianity until this thought came into my mind: *Just ask God into your life and put him first. Just say the words!* And all that night I lay there tossing and turning, saying to myself. *Just say the words. Just say the words!*

"Anyway, the next morning I woke up and remembered Marks and Spencers and I thought—I'll try it. So off I drove and when I arrived, there was this one parking place left and I got straight into it. And as I walked in someone yelled, 'The sign is on fire!' And I looked up and yes, it was—the Marks and Spencers sign— and it was dropping this stuff right on my Mercedes, the symbol of my material success!"

Pauline shot me a look.

"So the Fire Brigade came and the store took my particulars and finally, after all that chaos, I got back into my car and I said: 'Okay God, I give up, come into my life.' And I phoned the Cobham Christian Fellowship girl. 'Do you think it was a sign, I asked?' 'Do *YOU* think it was?' she replied. 'Because if you think it was —it was!' "

Shortly afterward, Pauline got baptized.

As an entrepreneur, it wasn't long before Pauline was wondering what she could do, in an organizational way, for the movement.

"Come and look at my plans for the house," she told me. So we decamped from the sitting room and, pursued by an indefatigable Aimée, we found our way over to the stable wing I'd noticed on the way in.

"This," said Pauline, "is my real plan. This is what I was put on this earth to do. I'm going to turn this place into a refuge for the most victimized people in our society: abused children! I'll have bedrooms here," she indicated, "staff rooms over here, a playroom in that corner—because there is nothing, *nothing* more terrible —or more prevalent in our sick society today—than the sexual abuse of little innocents. One point two million a year!"

Indeed, said Pauline, as we settled ourselves back in the sitting room, she ought to know: "I abused my own children, although not sexually, because there's more than one kind of abuse: my thing was control. I simply couldn't let my children live their lives —if you do anything to anyone without their permission you're an abuser.

"It's plain why abuse victims are so often atheists. Who can believe in God, or anything at all, in a world where God has allowed the worst thing in the world to happen to you—child abuse? Your emotions are all locked up and you can't feel love— and if God is love, where does that put God? Yet only God can help an abuser, because an abuser is in *Hell*. Don't talk to me about curing an abuser—no human agency can do it. Only God!"

Pauline gathered pace. "Do you want to know the real reason why all this is happening? The real reason is that we are in the Last Days. Have you heard of Barry Smith?" No. "Barry Smith is this New Zealand prophet who reckons George Bush's New Order is actually the rule of Satan in the End Days. A big part of it, actually, is the insinuation of a one-world currency—that's what credit cards are all about, along with keeping tabs on— i.e., *control of*—what we're all doing. But then, as Barry points out, credit cards are only the beginning of it. There's computer barcodes too, they're all based on the Devil's number, six-six-six, and there are these plans to have these numbers engraved on everyone of us on this planet—Revelations, you know—the Mark of the Beast!"

This brisk exposition had lost me a little, but Pauline explained that she'd got it all from this "subculture of Christian books and tapes," any of which I was welcome to borrow. "I spend hours, these days, reading, viewing," she said.

Pauline smiled. "You know—in the old days I was such a bore, all I talked about was business. Now, all that's changed—all I talk about is Christianity."

Pauline's story is classic conversionism. Loneliness, pressure, emotional trauma, need for control: all these are characteristic of sudden religious conversions. Further, her instinct for the new, postindustrial organizational forms of Evangelical Christianity— so structurally similar to the "small-within-big-is-beautiful" Body Shop franchise system she already knew—and her development from materialism to spirituality combine to make her situation an intriguing micro version of the macro picture already described.

Nevertheless, I was surprised by Pauline's story. True, I'd long had a sense of the relationship between stress and Charismatic conversion—not least when I met those involved in that attempted "resuscitation" in Yorkshire. Like most, I was aware of the more familiar "crisis conversions" of recent history: that of Nixon sidekick Charles Colson, for instance, who went Charismatic at the height of Watergate: "Something began to flow into me —a kind of energy," Colson wrote, describing what happened to him as he drove away from a friend's house when the pressure was at its height.

> With my face in my hands, my head leaning forward against the wheel, I forgot about machismo, about pretense, about fear of being weak. Then came the strange sensation that water was not only running down my cheeks, but surging through my whole body as well, cleansing and cooling as it went. They weren't tears of sadness nor of joy, but tears of release. I repeated over and over again the words TAKE ME . . . something inside me was urging me to surrender.

Colson was later jailed, but became, and remains, an Evangelical Christian. The black activist Eldridge Cleaver was "born again" while in hiding from the U.S. justice system. "I was looking up at the moon," said Cleaver, "and I saw the man in the moon and it was my face. Then I saw the face was not mine but some of my old heroes. There was Fidel Castro, then there was Mao Tse-Tung . . . While I watched, the face turned to Jesus Christ, and I was very much surprised."

Not everyone who has studied such phenomena would have been quite as surprised as Cleaver. For simple intuition would suggest a relationship between conversion and intolerable stress; and, more soberly, a list of academic studies has drawn out such connections too: E. T. Clark's 1929 study *The Psychology of Religious Awakening* was one of the earliest and most influential. Clark found, *inter alia,* that 55 percent of sudden converts at a revival had suffered from a sense of sin, compared with 8.5 percent of all those converted.

Nevertheless, the intensity of the stress/conversion relationship in Pauline's case was extraordinary—that first meeting had only hinted at Pauline's real difficulties, the full extent of which emerged later. And when I went to meet the other convert sparked off by my *Sunday Times* piece—the CID policeman —and he too turned out to have a memorable tale of pain, the extent to which my two "personal" converts were living out the stress-conversion thesis seemed startling.

Not that forty-five-year-old Peter seemed, on the surface, to be under quite the same pressure as Pauline. His own sense of himself, as described in the letter he sent me, was that before his conversion he had been "the most cynical and hard of men."

However, since he had publicly announced for Jesus the previous summer (he'd been baptized by Gerald Coates in Pauline Rawle's swimming pool), it was "amazing to see the difference in me." His personal life had been radically reformed: for instance, any question of his sleeping with his forty-one-year-old fiancée Julie (who had also converted) before their marriage was a non-starter. His daily schedule was also new: up at 6 A.M. every morning—lately it had been more like 5:30—followed by a quiet time till at least 6:30, Bible reading, prayer, Christian contemplation; more quiet time on his return from work at 4:00 (Peter was working as a police lecturer, these days, doing youth and community work), a cup of tea, more Bible reading, prayer. Then, on a weekly basis, maybe a couple of Cobham Christian Fellowship meetings in the evening, including a prayer meeting once a month, and perhaps a supper party on the Saturday night with CCF members and other friends. "I like to cook." An ordered, sober, Christian existence. Peter also took part in more ambitious forms of Christian direct action: he had just come back from a CCF visit to Romania, where he and a team from Cobham had fitted a heating system in an orphanage. "Wonderful, really," said Peter. "The locals gave us this great party when we left. They were bowled over that people could come all this way and do such things for free."

Just the kind of thing, in fact, that the positive, works-orientated Puritans of old would have identified with. To look at Peter and Julie sitting there in Peter's little flat in Bookham, just a mile or two down the road from Pauline, all seemed rosy indeed: Peter is short, burly, mustached, soft-spoken, the kind of homely bloke who says "not a lot" a lot; Julie is relaxed and cheery: suburban bliss. And yet, as they chatted a little more about their lives, the sadnesses emerged.

There was Peter's own self-description of himself before the conversion: *cynical and hard*. Hard on himself, certainly: you don't spend your life around criminals by accident, whatever the rationalization. Both Julie and Peter also had failed marriages: when we met, Julie's divorce was just coming through, and very traumatic it had been.

Then there were Julie's illnesses—poor Julie's life was, it seemed, shot through with sickness. Her ex-husband had bowel cancer, and Julie had been nursing him. She herself had multiple sclerosis:

she'd had it nine years and yes, it was a progressive disease, she said, though mercifully slow. Nevertheless, it gave her this terrible fatigue—you'd do something like the ironing, say, and it would take you half an hour to recover.

Even so, said Julie brightly, there was good news about that since her conversion: in the last two months she'd been cured! She'd been "slain in the spirit" (i.e., suffered a temporary, therapeutic, ritual-induced collapse) at a Cobham Christian Fellowship healing meeting, and had not felt better for years.

There were more routine difficulties, too. Peter and Julie both needed to sell their homes into the property stump to get married. And . . . I had this strange sense there was something else as well, something ominous and unnamed that seemed to hover at the back of the conversation all evening. If so, it was never raised by either Peter or Julie, but there were two clues. One was their manner: despite all the tales of healing and euphoria, despite the enthusiasm, neither could quite get much of it into their eyes. The other was just—a word: a word, nevertheless, which kept recurring throughout the evening, repeated in all the talk about houses, relationships, the future generally, a word which Peter, in particular, used a lot: the word was, of course, "uncertainty."

I gradually began to realize that more linked Peter the policeman and Pauline the millionairess than just the Cobham Christian Fellowship. The layers revealed themselves only slowly, step by step, a dance of the seven veils. With Peter it was still, in part at least, a hunch. With Pauline, when next I met her some weeks later, it was fast becoming obvious. The clouds on the business front had palpably blackened, and as I arrived at Pauline's on a blistering May afternoon in early summer 1992, it was clear that quite a whirlwind was working up.

Pauline was sitting with her head in her hands. "I have *such* a headache," she said. "Like two knives. I don't know if it's demonic," she went on. "Could be, of course. Demons take hold of us in all manner of ways. There was a man I knew, had emphysema, kept going to this healer, couldn't get cured. Told the healer he'd given up smoking." Pauline shot me a look. "Turned out he'd been smoking all along. The demon Nick-O-Teen—"she separated out the syllables—"made him lie."

Pauline's view is routine among Charismatics—it is one of the qualities that make them seem quite medieval. The rationalist Peter Wagner, for instance, statistics whiz of the Dawn 2000 conference, caused quite a stir in the States when he reportedly suggested that travellers check their luggage on return from foreign parts. The danger, he explained, was that a visit to a Pagan temple (for instance) might mean demons in the bags— Demonic stowaways!

It was the demon discord who looked like Pauline's biggest problem. Indeed, he'd clearly been on overtime since that moment earlier in the year when Pauline so nearly hosted that Potsdam of New Christianity and New Age, the Gerald Coates-Anita Roddick dinner party. First Pauline had fallen out with Gerald: "He's so *controlling*," she complained. "He got to hear that as well as Anita and her husband Gordon I'd invited the local vicar. Next thing, Gerald's on the phone: 'I don't think that's a very good idea,' he says. How dare he!" said Pauline. "How *dare* he tell me who I should and shouldn't have as guests in my own home!" The icing on the cake was that it turned out at the last moment that Anita and Gordon couldn't make it anyway: apparently Anita had forgotten it was Gordon's birthday. "They do things like that," muttered Pauline darkly. What was also happening—the larger falling-out, it emerged, the one evidently giving Pauline the real grief—was the decline of her relationship with Anita and Gordon. This was the more hurtful, Pauline stressed, because it hadn't just been a business partnership, ever—it had been a friendship. Why, Pauline had been one of Anita's earliest franchisees!

There was also a money problem. "My companies' position has certainly deteriorated since Christmas," said Pauline. "The profit margin just isn't there any more and the banks are getting twitchy."

Nor was the support there from Body Shop. "Anita never used to be like that," said Pauline. "Success has changed her. These days it's all about *control*." (Although one couldn't help wondering how the Rawle-Roddick relationship could have avoided change, as Body Shop expanded.)

The mother of all battles, apparently, had taken place a couple of years back, when one of Pauline's shops had been prosecuted by the Trading Standards Officer. Pauline was found not guilty —but the Roddick-Rawle relationship, said Pauline, had never really recovered. In May 1992 she was called in to Body Shop headquarters to discuss what was wrong with her companies. "Anita herself wasn't due to be there but as I went in I bumped into her outside. 'What a lovely jacket you're wearing!' she said. She was sure everything could be sorted out—and when was I coming round to dinner?

"But the meeting itself was *dreadful*. The *tone* of it all. Did I realize, they asked me, that I was bringing Body Shop into disrepute? Well, if I'm such a dreadful person, I said, why don't you just buy me out? And they knew how much it would hurt me to lose my shops, like a child losing her candy. So I went home and the next day, Saturday, I just *cried*. And on the Monday I said, 'I'm going down to Devon and you can *have* the shops, and the house, I don't care.' And then they said, look, Anita will come to see you."

Pauline's eyes went wide.

"And do you know what? She *did* visit, and once again, she was coming on as sweet as pie, *of course* we can sort it all out, *of course* we'll find a way, no problem. In fact do you know what she suggested?"

Pauline's eyes went wider still.

"She asked if I wanted to go to the rainforest with her!"

At this juncture Aimée threw herself into the air and howled. There was someone at the door! Word came in from the hall— it was a courier, it turned out, hotfoot from Body Shop HQ

Pauline opened the letter. "Innocuous," she said, and put it aside. "You see, there's this documentary about Body Shop on the TV tonight and already their share price is dropping. So the last thing they want is to bring the row with me to a head right *now*.

"Not that anything's been settled," she pointed out. "Indeed, it's getting worse. I mean they refer here to the "deteriorating financial position" of my company. Well it would be deteriorating, wouldn't it, if I can't get credit." Pauline thumbed through some other post. "A County Court summons here from a supplier. Three thousand pounds."

True, said Pauline, there had been a possible solution, and that was that her fiancé, who already had one Body Shop, "should take over all of mine. I mean that was the way he proposed to me, actually."

He'd liked the fact that she was a strong woman, reckoned Pauline. He'd married a seventeen-year-old before, and now he wanted someone who would stand up to him. "But this is how it is with men, they either want total control themselves, and marry someone much weaker than them, or else they choose someone stronger, so they can be the child. No wonder it didn't work out. It's the eternal problem. Immaturity. Childishness. Refusal to grow up."

She gazed at me with these reproachful eyes, yearning, wounded, just like those yearning flowers down the corridor in the loo; her voice high like a little child's; her love life in ruins; her businesses collapsing around her. . . . And then slowly, with an emotional trajectory reminiscent of that Dawn 2000 meeting when the Christians U-turned against the abusers, her pain translated, gradually, into ever more furious and bitter wrath.

"I'll bet they're worried at Body Shop," she said. "Their share price is already dropping and after tonight's effort it will plummet. I bet they're worried about what's going to come out. And a good thing too—they are utterly rooted in witchcraft and control.

"But you can't look at these things in isolation. It's all tied up with the End Days, with the spirit of Satanic materialism and fear —that's why what Barry Smith is telling us is so important, that's why I'm bringing him over to do a lecture tour later this year. Control! First you understand what they're all trying to do to you, then you deal with it. . . . Control! Just you wait till tonight. They'll be shaking in their shoes! And so they should be! They deserve every last thing that's coming to them!"

Those eyes which had been so soulful were now flashing with vituperation and fury—indeed, for a moment there I felt Pauline had included me, too, in her Apocalypse.

Control! Comeuppance! Punishment! Revenge!

In the event (as so often is the case with Armageddons), the documentary on Body Shop, which did indeed go out that night, ended neither the world nor Roddick. Still, Body Shop's share price collapsed to nearly half its spring 1992 level by the autumn. The program's main allegations prompted Body Shop to initiate a law suit, which Body Shop later won. Nevertheless, reflecting on all this later, I found myself shaken. Pauline had exhibited a cluster of classical conversionary characteristics— that locked-in-childhood quality, that impossible stress, those chronic relationship problems. But there had also evolved this sterner stuff, typical of the angriest, most adamantine end of the Evangelical continuum. Pauline had shown a star- tling capacity for what psychologists call "projection," and a climactic explosion, finally, of no-holds-barred, may-they-rot-in- Hell fury.

But the real shocks were still to come.

Shortly after that discussion, the phone rang and it was Pauline Rawle. Since we'd met, she said, she'd been thinking about child abuse, and why there should be so much of it at this time. It was the Enemy: the more abuse, the more suggestible its victims became; the more suggestibility, the more believers He found for His lies and wicked designs.

So, Pauline went on, changing tack, had I been in touch with Peter at all?

"No, not lately."

"So you haven't heard?"

"Heard what?"

"His case came up—his police corruption case. Didn't he tell you? It's been pending for months. . . . He's been done for a data protection offense, they found him guilty and he's been chucked out of the force!"

So that was the cloud I'd sensed hanging over Peter—the pressures on him must have been even greater than I had thought. But there was an even more dramatic denouement to the tale of Pauline Rawle.

A few weeks later, wondering vaguely what had happened to Pauline (I'd failed to raise her on the phone), I picked up the *Daily Telegraph* and read the following caption opposite a picture of a distraught-looking Pauline. "Mrs Rawle: compared herself with God, said judge."

The story read:

BODY SHOP WINS COURT CURB ON EVANGELIST

Body Shop, the environment-friendly cosmetic chain, has won a High Court injunction preventing an evangelical Christian woman from operating six of their franchise shops because they say she tried to impose her beliefs on staff.

Mrs. Pauline Rawle, 50, who attended courses at the Hampstead-based Victory Church, "tried to compel her staff to take mystic violence courses run by the church," said Sir Peter Pain, granting the injunction yesterday.

Mrs. Rawle, who ran a £5 million a year franchise for six shops under the Body Shop name, later sacked or suspended 50 staff and failed to pay for goods worth more than £400,000, he said.

The shops, in Bromley, Maidstone, Canterbury, Romford, and two in Croydon, were closed, then reopened.

Body Shop, created by Mrs Anita Roddick in 1976, had gone to the High Court to prevent Mrs Rawle from operating under their name.

The judge ruled that Mrs Rawle, who lives in a seventeenth-century converted farmhouse in Effingham, Surrey, had dealt with staff in a "curious" way, and had expressed "great hostility" toward the Body Shop management.

He said: "She compared herself with God and the Body Shop with Satan." As her interest in the Victory Church increased earlier this year, she began taking more interest in the staff.

At one meeting she told staff they had all been sexually abused before they were three years of age, and many of them found this distressing.

He added: "I take the view that she should be stopped as soon as possible."

He ruled that she could no longer pass herself off as being associated with Body Shop. He refused her a stay pending a possible appeal.

Mr. Phil Talbot, a Body Shop International spokesman, said: "We are delighted with the verdict. It is important to stress this is a one-off. Our main priority now is to re-establish ourselves in those five towns which now do not have a Body Shop."

He said that several of the staff would be taking Mrs Rawle to a tribunal on claims of unfair dismissal.

Mrs Rawle, clearly distressed at the decision, said: "I was

hoping for justice, but this is not quite the justice I was hoping for."

A few weeks later the papers ran another story about Pauline Rawle.

She'd gone bust.

7

The Leap of Faith

Stress, or the "uncertainty" factor, is the ingredient which virtually everyone studying religious conversion has found crucial—from historians and psychologists to neuroscientists. This remarkable, interdisciplinary consensus had been reached, often, by people researching in ignorance of each others' work.

I had seen the evidence in my own interviews, too. Lloyd Kuehl's conversion, for instance, followed on the collapse of his business and then his wife's departure; and his childhood, too, had been unusually deprived. His father had died during the war; his relationship with his stepfather, he said, had been very difficult. Or take Mary, John Ellen's wife; her story included depression and psychiatric treatment at the age of seventeen. Mary's friend Susan's much-loved Dad died when she was six and a half, and her guardians promptly packed her and her sister off to boarding school; she married early, at twenty-one, in search of love; got divorced, and lost custody of the kids; found a new husband, much-loved, who started running around; desperate sadness, crisis. . . . Then, at the nadir, Susan heard a voice, felt this windlike swish, knew this "unbelievable joy," became a Charismatic. Or consider Carol Bond, the Ichthus lady with the stiff prayer schedule. Her mother's first marriage, to a husband sixteen years her senior, broke up when Carol was a child; Carol spent her teen years, she says, with "boy after boy," in a search, she feels, for her "lost father."

Such painful tales became routine over the months, as Charismatics talked to me about their lives; the more so as I started to read scientific studies of conversion and its causes.

In 1899, for instance, one Edwin D. Starbuck of Stanford University in the United States published his seminal *The Psychology of Religion*. In this magnificently left-hemispherical piece of Americana, replete with charts, percentages and more numbers generally than you have had hot dinners, Starbuck writes that for his study sample, in the run-up to conversion, "Fears are a large factor. Hope of heaven is nearly absent. Fears appear to be present nearly fifteen times as often as hope." He sums up: "The sense of sin and depression of feeling are fundamental factors in conversion, if not in religious experience in general."

Shortly after Starbuck there came the yet more influential work of the distinguished psychologist William James, brother of novelist Henry. His 1902 *The Varieties of Religious Experience* went further. Declared James: "The securest way to the rapturous sorts of happiness of which the twice-born make report has as an historic matter-of-fact been through a more radical pessimism than anything that we have yet considered." (Like his brother, William did breathless sentences.) Indeed, he isolates the "neurotic constitution" as crucial to the born-again phenomenon, and asserts that "these experiences of melancholy . . . lie right in the middle of our path." Describing the depression of the "sick soul" in its run-up to conversion, James decides: "Here is the real core of the religious problem: Help! Help!"

There has been a steady flow of studies making similar connections, the volume of which has risen markedly over the years. There was the 1929 Clark study, already mentioned. Heirich's 1977 study found that 83 percent of those converted to a Pentecostal group had experienced personal stress before their conversion. Brown et al. (1982) studied 192 Christians reporting mystical experiences, and found a strong correlation between those enjoying visions of "unity" and "enlightenment," and those expressing self-dissatisfaction in their everyday lives. Hay (1982) found that 50 percent of his subjects had been "distressed or ill-at-ease" before conversion.

In 1990, Lee Kirkpatrick of the University of South Carolina and Philip Shaver of the State University of New York analyzed a sample of 213 respondents to a newspaper survey on love, who then completed a follow-up mail survey concerning their religious beliefs and family backgrounds. "Perhaps the most intriguing results," wrote Kirkpatrick and Shaver, "concerned reports of sudden religious conversions." They explained that:

> Following the religious change items in the survey, respond-ents were encouraged to write freely about their perceptions concerning the factors that might have led to their change in religious commitment at the time it occurred. . . . The vast majority of respondents classified as having experienced a sudden religious conversion described a period of intense emotional turmoil or crisis as a precipitating factor.
>
> The most commonly mentioned precipitating event, especially among those who reported sudden religious conversions after age 30, was divorce or severe marital problems. Six of the nine respondents who converted at age 30 or later had recently experienced divorces; for one of these this was the third divorce, and for another the fourth.

Several of the divorcees also mentioned additional emotional stresses: three miscarriages in one case, alcoholism in another, while a third described a recent "period of intense emotional upheaval and pain." Yet another declared: "I had become so desperately out of control in/of my life that I finally gave up and truly let go of control enough that I could allow the Spirit to give me the experience."

Perhaps the most memorable finding in the Kirkpatrick/Shaver paper lay in the relationship it traced between "sudden religious conversions in adolescence and "childhood maternal attachments." Those who were, as they put it, emotionally "avoidant" as children were almost *thirty* times as likely as the "secure" to convert in adolescence.

In short, a picture begins to emerge of the dramatic—and conversion-inducing—effects of both "tactical" and "strategic" stress. The "tactical" crisis—the divorce, the sacking, the illness—may indeed (especially in combination) be a critical trigger of conversion. But behind it—far more crucial, arguably—lurks the "strategic" history of emotional trauma which may stretch way back into childhood and which will make those "tactical" stresses, when they occur, so much harder to bear.

Such insights may help to make sense of the Charismatic obsession with child abuse. For if we widen child abuse—as we surely should, in this context—to include children who have been ill-loved—or even orphaned—one can see how a Charismatic convert might feel particularly Evangelical about this issue: it is one of the factors that may have helped trigger his or her conversion in the first place.

If one accepts some variant of this stress/conversion connection, then it is pertinent to ask what mechanisms—psychic, psychological, or even chemical—cause such triggers to translate into such effects. Curiously, the process of conversion turns out to be virtually inseparable from the process of Charismatic healing. Take those physical symptoms described earlier by Charles Colson when he experienced his conversion: it felt like water, he said, "not only running down my cheeks, but surging through my whole body as well, cleansing and cooling as it went." Here, in turn, is a woman describing being "healed" of arthritic legs during an EST training session: "It was too much, the pain in my legs was so intense. Then I felt waves of heat come over me, and all the pain went away. I wouldn't choose to go through that pain again, but since that day I haven't had a single pain in my legs."

This woman had just been regressed, in therapy, to the psychological roots of her disease—just as Colson had, involuntarily, been brought to a consciousness of his own psychological pain. In both instances, a similar climactic exposure of the source of suffering led on to a similar plateau of calm—with the simultaneous achievement of an appropriate belief system: in Colson's case, God; in the woman's case, new-found "self-worth."

The real difficulty in examining these different kinds of "conversion" is less in finding the things they have in common; rather, it is in identifying ways in which they fundamentally differ. Little wonder that they often happen simultaneously. The pre-war English scientist and author J. B. S. Haldane declared that since the day he had accepted Communism into his life he had never again suffered from gastritis.

From stress the mind converts to serenity; from disease the body converts to ease, or wholeness (holiness); overall, the organism converts from that greatest of all human agonies, turbulence, to that deepest of all human aspirations, peace: the blessing both Judaism and Islam put before wealth, happiness or even love. *Shalom!* (A closely related Hebrew word, incidentally, is *Shalem*, meaning "wholeness.") The quality these various transformations share is the process whereby various forms of disorder "convert" to new forms of order. The key question is not what is being moved away from or toward, but how that movement is achieved.

No one was more struck by these similarities than the British psychiatrist William Sargant, author of the 1957 classic on brainwashing and conversionism, *Battle for the Mind*. Indeed, the very parabola of Sargant's career is revealing: he started out treating shellshock and trauma cases during the war (healing); moved thence to the study of the political U-turns effected on captured Allied prisoners during the Korean War (brainwashing); and finished up studying the processes of religious coming-to-belief (conversion). At each stage of his career he was struck by the similarities of each process to the others.

When dealing with trauma, he noted the impossibility of "converting" a traumatized catatonic from a state of dumbness to a state of speech unless the patient actually relived the original pain—and relived it in the form of the most profound, consciousness-subverting emotional explosion. The parallel here seems to be with the kind of emotional climaxes which are midwife to the conversion process at religious meetings, or in the apparent nervous breakdowns of desperately embattled individuals like Charles Colson or Pauline Rawle. Sargant found that the mere logical, verbal articulation of their experiences gave his patients no therapy. So he developed a technique of luring his patients, aided by drugs, toward rather than away from emotional crisis.

He described, for instance, how he had to treat a soldier from the Normandy beachhead who had been virtually catatonic after horrendous experiences at the front. After unsuccessful treatment with milder drugs, an intravenous barbiturate was given, which relaxed him sufficiently for the doctors to be able at least to get his story out of him. He'd been under mortar fire for eight successive days; then, when several comrades were killed by mortar fire near him, he lost his voice, burst into tears and became partially paralyzed. "But the barbiturates induced very little emotion as he gave this recital," and there was no change in his condition. That afternoon, however, Sargant used ether instead of a barbiturate.

> When taken over the same ground again, he told the story this time with far greater emotion, and at last became confused and exhausted, tried to tear off the ether mask, and over-breathed in a panic stricken way until the treatment was stopped. When he came to and rose from the couch, an obvious change had occurred in him. He smiled for the first time and looked relieved. . . . This improvement was being maintained a fortnight afterwards.

The technical word for this process is "abreaction," defined by the psychiatrist Sadler as "a process of reviving the memory of a repressed unpleasant experience and expressing in speech and action the emotions related to it, thereby relieving the personality of its influence," and it dates as far back as Breuer and Freud's early studies into the treatment of hysteria, when they noticed patients could be helped "just by talking it out"—with the proviso that, as with Sargant and his soldiers, Freud found "affectless memories, memories without any release of emotion" did not do the trick. The original trauma had to be lived, *experienced*.

Sargant was further impressed by the parallels between these kinds of "medical" cures, or conversions of emotional state, and what he began to hear about conversion techniques in religion.

One day, he visited his father's house and picked up one of his books at random. It happened to be John Wesley's journal of 1730–40. He was struck by extraordinary similarities between the effects of Wesley's hellfire sermons and the abreactions of his soldiers. "The fear of burning Hell induced by his graphic preaching could be compared to the suggestion we might force on a returned soldier, during treatment, that he was in danger of being burned alive in his tank and must fight his way out. The two techniques seemed startlingly similar." As were the effects, for both processes led to profound changes of worldview, or "belief."

"The main difference," Sargant dryly observes, "lies in the explanations given for the same impressive results."

The application of all this to experiences like those of Charles Colson, Pauline Rawle and policeman Peter is plain to see. As their crises developed, the strains gradually built up towards the explosion, until finally, when the climacteric came (Charles Colson's tears, Pauline Rawle's supermarket vision), the mind flipped into its new-found state, and a new stability was born.

As the process reaches its climax, the mind becomes suggestible. When Pavlov did his experiments with dogs back in the Twenties, one of his favorite ploys was to scare the poor creatures to death because this, he found, got them into a state he called "transmarginal inhibition"—roughly the equivalent of the withdrawal state of Sargant's soldiers—and it was then that they could be most readily programmed with new Pavlovian behavior patterns, or "beliefs." In the same way, it is the most frightened individuals—whether the fears are relatively recent, like Charles Colson's, or whether they stretch right back to childhood, like Pauline Rawle's—who are most susceptible. Sargant reminds us that such levels of fear can be induced in anyone at all—on a battlefield, say, or in a torture chamber—and then virtually anyone can be converted to believe virtually anything.

Although there are, apparently, two social groups who are impervious: the exceptionally individualistic—artists, eccentrics, geniuses perhaps—and the insane.

Having looked at the contributory factors and the actual psychological mechanics of conversion, one might also ask what the science of neurology reveals about these processes.

Among the neuroscientists studying conversionism, the work of the Canadian, Michael Persinger, stands out, for he sits square on the notion that if the appropriate chemical and electrical impulses are applied to the appropriate bits of the brain you can produce quite predictable visions, hallucinations and other "neurological events."

Or as Persinger puts it in his 1983 paper *Religious and Mystical Experiences as Artifacts of Temporal Lobe Function: A General Hypothesis*: "According to the hypothesis, the actual mystical or religious experience is evoked by a transient (a few seconds) very focal, electrical display within the temporal lobe. Such *temporal lobe transients* (TLTs) would be analogous to electrical microseizures," while their emotional flavor, in turn, would depend on "the relative inclusion of reward (good: heaven) versus aversive (bad: hell) neuronal centers." Remarkably, this could then give an individual access to: "(1) infantile memories of parental images (perhaps even perinatal representations of proprioception), and (2) images from before four to five years of age and memories for which there are no retrieval formats." And the interpretation of such images? "The former would be a universal source of God (parent surrogate) images while the latter would foster conclusions of 'previous lives' or other memories."

What Persinger seems to be saying is that the electrical impulses generated by these neurological activities could actually retrieve lost-to-consciousness "memories," and that such memories, re-experienced, could seem divine. This is reminiscent of the work of the pioneer, midcentury neuroscientist Wilder Penfield, who applied electrical stimulation to the brains of more than five hundred temporal-lobe epileptics and evoked, in their minds, a startling range of "reminiscences," including "voices," "music," "feet walking," even a "dog barking."

The literature records plenty of other examples, many "mystical," all evoked by stimulation comparable to Penfield's. These include out-of-body experiences (OBEs), "vestibular sensations" like the sense of spinning through time-space, even "auditory experiences" like "rushing sounds" (like, for instance, the "swish" Mary's friend Susan heard during her vision), or "the voice of a god or spirit giving instructions."

The neurologist Oliver Sacks, in his remarkable book *The Man Who Mistook His Wife for a Hat,* suggests that such experiences, and the memories underlying them, are evidence that "the brain retained an almost perfect record of every lifetime's experience, that the stream of consciousness was preserved in the brain, and as such, could always be evoked or called forth, whether by the ordinary needs and circumstances of life, or the extraordinary circumstances of an epileptic or electrical stimulation."

The connection between visionary experience and those electrical brain-storms we call epilepsy is long established. Not only is modern neuroscience replete with titles like "St. Paul and Temporal Lobe Epilepsy," but, as far back as Classical times, epilepsy was known as the "divine" disease. The conversion-inducing Sargant was himself struck by the similarity between epilepsy and those abreactive "climaxes"of his patients. When he and others attempted to induce the same results by the extraneous application of electric shock treatment, Sargant defined such processes as "simply the artificial inducement of an epileptic fit."

It is worth noting that Persinger sees a familiar pattern of causation. TLT precipitants, he says, include music, smells, drugs and hypoxia (mountain top reveries). But he also highlights factors which sound more familiar: pain, fatigue, and social isolation. He adds: "Two life crises, the anticipation of self-demise and the loss of a loved one, are notorious biochemical disruptors that particularly influence TLT probability."

The visionary experiences of Pauline Rawle, Lloyd Kuehl and Mary's friend Susan at *their* climacterics of existential stress again come to mind. What is plain is that such pressures can lead to paranormal experience quite as readily as they can precipitate new belief.

Vision-seeing and supernatural experiences are, in fact, even more fundamental to conversion than plain changes of state, however profound, so one can see why Michael Persinger sums up: "Given the profound capacity to evoke pleasurable and meaningful experiences, reduce existential anxiety and generate the security of old parental experiences (the origin of god images), TLTs are potent modifiers of human behavior. A singular episode, in the appropriate context, can be followed by long-term behavioral changes."

Temporal Lobe Transients, epileptic fits, "nervous breakdowns": with subjects like these Persinger et al. are majoring on the electrical impulses discharged during such "events," which can, impacting on the appropriate portions of the brain, mean that people do quite genuinely "experience" extraordinary things. Oliver Sacks devotes a whole chapter of *The Man Who Mistook His Wife for a Hat* to the migrainous basis of the visions of the medieval mystic Hildegard of Bingen (1098–1180). But there is another category of mental triggers—one which one might broadly call the chemical. These can give comparable results, and are also often intimately connected with stress-inducing "life events" such as illness or divorce.

Endorphins are natural opiates released by the brain in times of stress—and they can be thirty times more powerful than morphine. Indeed, all of us have experienced their benign effects to some extent—for endorphins are responsible for the terrific lift we get immediately after exercise, otherwise known as "runner's high" (and also known as one very good reason why people become exercise junkies). Beyond that, some psychologists believe that the intensity of this "benign" chemical explains the rapturous states so often reported by people who suffer so-called near-death experiences. Then there is that perhaps more familiar category of drugs ingested from outside rather than manufactured from within. For they too have the capacity to induce the most profound transcendental experiences—a fine example of drug-induced conversion in its pure form follows in chapter eight. Typical were the experiences of the Sixties author Carlos Castaneda—seminal, indeed, to the whole countercultural experience—and his insights, under the tutelage of a South American Indian, into the remarkable, vision-inducing possibilities of peyote or "mescalito." But to get a real impression of just how profound drug experiences can be you have to go back a bit further, to the era of "beat" rather than "hip," and that remarkable record by Aldous Huxley of his controlled mescaline ingestion, *The Doors of Perception,* first published in 1954.

So vivid a writer is Huxley that it's worth enlisting him to help remind us just what such visions can really mean (it's not all sign-burning at Marks and Spencer). Under mescaline, Huxley goes into the garden:

From the French window I walked out under a kind of pergola covered in part by a climbing rose tree, in part by laths, one inch wide with half an inch of space between them. The sun was shining and the shadows of the laths made a zebra-like pattern on the ground and across the seat and back of a garden chair, which was standing at the end of the pergola. That chair—shall I ever forget it? Where the shadows fell on the canvas upholstery, stripes of a deep but glowing indigo alternated with stripes of an incandescence so intensely bright that it was hard to believe that they could be made of anything but blue fire. For what seemed an immensely long time I gazed without knowing, without wishing to know, what it was that confronted me. At any other time I would have seen a chair barred with alternate light and shade. Today the percept had swallowed up the concept. I was so completely absorbed in looking, so thunderstruck by what I actually saw, that I could not be aware of anything else.

Garden furniture, laths, sunlight, shadow—these were no more than names and notions, mere verbalizations, for utilitarian or scientific purposes, after the event. The event was this succession of azure furnace-doors separated by gulfs of unfathomable gentian. It was inexpressibly wonderful, wonderful to the point, almost, of being terrifying. And suddenly I had an inkling of what it must feel like to be mad.

Out of all this, finally, a mental map begins to emerge. Human stress, in its widest sense, can lead to brain "events," which can, in turn, lead to "conversions," or changes of state. The actual triggers of these processes within the brain—impelled by existential pressures—can be electrical or chemical. Equally, both electrical (electric shock treatment) and chemical (Huxley and his drugs) input from outside the body can induce comparable effects.

There are, in fact, a whole range of potential triggers of such electrical or chemical effects. Stress, shock therapy, mescaline— we are familiar with these. But many other agencies have been employed, throughout history and by all manner of belief systems, to similar ends: fasting—diet has profound and swift effects on the brain; dancing—the real reason for the whirling of the Dervishes is that they whirl themselves into a trance; smell—this too can have similar effects, as Proust famously records (hence the heavy use of incense in Roman Catholic services, and also the origins of aromatherapy).

The list goes on. A knock on the head can do it: studies have shown a correlation between mystical experience and head injury. A tumor on the brain can do it: Oliver Sacks describes examples of the visions, often entirely benign, that cancerous tumors induce. A swift, sudden flash of terror can do it (as opposed to the steady, more insidious build-up of "stress"): Pavlov described the effect on his dogs of the 1924 Leningrad flood, in which several very nearly drowned and many lost, in its entirety, all the lately programmed Pavlovian behaviors—their brains "washed" clean of all recently acquired "beliefs" by the sudden trauma.

Why, even a thunderclap has been known to do it—but the point, hopefully, has been made: the number of agents which can induce a state transition of the brain is almost infinite. What remains constant, however, is what you might call the "morphology" of the experience: the original stability, the wavelike buildup, the explosive climax, the new-found calm.

That is the story, indeed, of virtually all of nature's infinitely varied and, at a fundamental level, interrelated "conversions." Einstein reminded us that mechanical systems, too, move from one "coordinate system," as he puts it, to another—with turbulence in between (for instance, a train in a station and a train travelling at sixty miles per hour are two stable coordinate systems, with gravity and other forces working normally; but when the train is between states, accelerating or decelerating, turbulence occurs, baggage falls out of racks, coffee spills, and so on). The ancient Greek tragedians practiced a kind of theatrical conversion called Catharsis, whereby they brought an audience to a pitch of emotional anguish, then sent them out at the end of the play emotionally "cleansed." Hysterical illnesses display "conversion symptoms" as psychology calls them—"steady state" before the onset of psychological trauma; relative calm come the masking symptoms of the illness; turbulence in the transition. Even the retail "conversion rate" mentioned by Pauline Rawle follows the same pattern, converting the customer's uncertainty into the "steady state" of commitment. Not for nothing is there this Coates/Rawle/Roddick retail/Evangelical connection.

Underneath all these conversions—religious, retail, psychological, political, theatrical, ecological—lies the same fundamental evolutionary shape, a shape of nature, surely: calm, tension, turbulence, climax, new-found calm.

Peace at the last.

Which leaves us with a last, and crucial question. Do such psychological and scientific rationalizations "explain away" such experiences? Do they refute the religious interpretation?

William Sargant thought not. "Must a new concentration on brain physiology and brain mechanics weaken religious faith and beliefs?" he asks, in *Battle for the Mind*. "On the contrary, a better understanding of the means of creating and consolidating faith will enable religious bodies to expand much more rapidly." As someone of strong religious beliefs himself, such expansion was, he felt, highly desirable.

Michael Persinger thinks not. His work does indeed show, he argues, various mechanisms whereby transcendental experiences can be induced. But who is to say what these experiences really mean, or, come to that, where they actually "come from"? Unlike the more confident or arrogant scientific atheists of an earlier age, those of Persinger's generation (Michael, for example, was born in 1945) are more circumspect. Oliver Sacks, in particular, puts it well. True, St. Hildegard was migrainous, as was George Eliot, but does that detract from the beauty of Hildegard's writings, or the truth of a George Eliot novel? Indeed, is it not even possible, as Henri Bergson thought (and as Huxley suspected his mescaline visions confirmed) that all these different state-changing agents might not, in crucial ways, be *widening* our customarily policed and watered-down perceptions rather than narrowing them? Awakening us, in fact, from what Blake called scientism's "Single vision/and Newton's sleep"?

Sacks argues further: the fact that such experiences have "clear organic determinants . . . does not detract in the least from their psychological or spiritual significance. If God, or the eternal order, was revealed to Dostoyevski in seizures, why should not other organic conditions serve as 'portals' to the beyond or the unknown?"

Portals . . . yes. Here is one arena, in particular, where neuroscience has shed crucial light. For wherever, or whatever, the Kingdom of Heaven may finally turn out to be, this much is sure: the Kingdom of Heaven, as Jesus said, is *within* us. Inexpressibly great, but, simultaneously, unfathomably small. Unimaginable.

As also is the Kingdom of Hell.

8

Visions of Heaven and Hell

It was while I was with Ichthus that I came across twenty-three-year-old Jill and twenty-four-year-old Edward, both members of the Wells Way Ichthus congregation down the road from Mike Pears. Their conversion had resulted from experiences with drugs—experiences which had run the full gamut from dream-trippy rhapsody to the awesome terrors of the damned. Not that the fact that drugs were their particular "portal" meant their conversion in any sense lacked meaning. Indeed, it was two years after their conversion "event" that we met, and their Christian involvement was, if anything, steadily escalating, with both spending many hours a week on Ichthus worship, celebrations and projects. But then to Edward and Jill, their conversion experience, far from being less real (because drug-induced) than the rest of their lives, was a thousand times more real than anything they had ever known. So it is quite natural that their commitment, so deeply embedded in their consciousnesses, was so passionate and strong.

Their triggers had been two soft, green tablets they'd taken simultaneously in a club off the Charing Cross Road—not so different, perhaps, from Persinger's minute quantities of electricity, or Huxley's "four-tenths of a gram of mescaline" dissolved in half a glass of water. In their background, too, lay a history of sadness or stress, as became plain during the unfolding of their vision, though it seemed to be less "tactical" (associated with overt, immediate crisis) than "strategic" (long-term, buried deep).

When we first met, they came across with that familiar, militant ordinariness so characteristic of New Christians. She is a languages graduate, unemployed, short, neat, streetwise, with close-cropped hair; he is blond and bronzed, a dentist, fresh-faced—you can guess how his East End father must have looked as a sailor in the Second World War. Both came from that apotheosis of aspiration, materialism and Eighties common sense—Billericay in Essex. Thatcherism incarnate, blue in tooth and claw, the duo seemed.

However, their particular brand of Eighties lifestyle majored heavily on the club scene—several nights a week at Kinky Disco off Shaftesbury Avenue or Pure Sexy at the Milk Bar or Fresh at Legends in New Burlington Street—and among club-goers, from 1987 onwards, there'd been this drug U-turn: the mouthy, sharp-edged culture of cocaine had been ousted by the dreamy, tactile culture of Ecstasy, or "E," complete with neo-Sixties ramifications of peace, love and togetherness—all in weird counterpoint to the Lawson-boom pandemonium going on outside. One evening, said Jill and Edward, they'd been offered this stuff, green, soft in texture—E, they'd thought, and taken it. What *was* it, exactly? "I wish I knew," said Edward with feeling.

At first the effects were benign: "I felt myself slowing down," said Edward, "a bit wobbly, a bit out of touch. Next thing, I saw this bloke's reflection in a mirror: his image seemed to be dancing twice as fast as he was." Then, escalation. . . . Both Jill and Edward's heads began "whirring" and they instinctively hit the dance floor—but there one of the characteristics of the next twenty-four hours quickly emerged. For both of them began seeing, independently, the same visions—a kind of joint hallucination, in fact (a mysterious, yet well-documented phenomenon in such situations). So, for starters, both saw the dance floor as a kind of "cattle market," half human, half grotesque, dancers with horses' heads, dancers with faces for ears, dancers with cloven hooves like cows, all making this weird, terrifying din, braying, barking, neighing.

So they swung off the dance floor and sat at the bar: and now the walls seemed like they were "bleeding"—and then, as they looked down, the floor beneath them seemed like it had vaporized and they were staring down into this vast pit, immeasurably deep. In a word, they were into what is routinely called "a bad trip." But this was more. "At first we thought we'd sweat it out in the club," said Edward, "but around six a.m. we realized we needed money so we went looking for a bank." They emerged, like two rubbernecking Frankensteins, into the early-morning London streets—where, it seems, the bad trip turned horrific.

A roadsweeper walks past them . . . and he's got the head of a pig. Edward turns to Jill . . . and she's a corpse, black eyes, green complexion, months dead. It gets so Edward stops looking into shop windows, so scared is he of what might be reflected. They wander into a crowd of kids, turn-outs from another club, and they too have the purple faces, the leprous skin, the animal heads, these great, green crests on their heads like they are birds. And then it turns out they're Mohicans, for Heaven's sake. These kids are *real*. . . . They drop in on some friends, and they look like corpses too. So they flee back, finally, to Edward's place. And there, on the twenty-fourth floor of a council block in Bow, they finally experience their own, personal, climactic Dante's Inferno.

Everything in the world is now corpse-like, decomposing; their minds are desperately spinning, spiralling out of control; this filthy taste in their mouths, as of the very tang of Evil; and above all, this suffocating sense of wrap-round wickedness, immanent, somehow, in the very walls, the furniture, the ceiling! And then Edward remembered how his Mum had written to him and said she thought this music culture he was involved in was Satanic, there was Satanic power in those lyrics, and how he'd laughed at her, but now. . . . Suddenly he notices this ornament thing in the corner of his flat, he'd had it a while, but now. . . . No! God help them both! It had this head on it, yes, a ram's head, and horns, it was . . . the Devil! Satan! The Devil himself, God help them both, right there in their very own flat!

"I just hope—*pray*—I never feel fear like that again," says Edward, and leaves it there.

The horrors kept on coming (that Devil image, in particular, recurred) till well up to 12 o'clock in the morning; then a change came about. "Eventually we felt like we were coming down," said Edward, "and suddenly I had this really objective vision of myself. I saw myself as someone who'd taken money off my parents and bought drugs with it, how I was vain, selfish, and unthinking, and yet my mother was always writing me these beautiful letters, just full of love. So suddenly I realized just how little I really thought of myself and I felt this terrible rush of remorse and self-hatred and I cried out to God, "O God I'm so sorry, help me please!" And this extraordinary thing happened. I was sitting against the wall and suddenly I was hurled across the room, it was as if I was kicked by this electric shock at the base of my spine: as if something actually went into me, tingling up and down my body from the tips of my toes to the top of my head.

"And then I actually *saw* it, right there in front of my eyes. It was . . . like a strip of water hanging in the air yet made of light and shimmering and it was at that moment I realized what had shot through me: it was the Holy Ghost."

At which moment, in turn, Jill burst into tears and suddenly *her* hands started tingling too, they became really painful, until eventually she found the only way she could hold her hands without them hurting her was to bring them together as if for prayer. So she and Edward started praying together—and at last, finally, blessedly, Jill started hearing the voice of God, calling on her to repent.

It was at this stage, says Edward, that things really took off.

"I saw this vision of the Cross," says Edward. "I say vision, not hallucination, because with a hallucination—I've had plenty, what with the drugs—you see it yet you know it's false; but with this, I saw it and I knew it was *real*. This dark, awesome wooden cross, towering up above me, right there in the flat: and, as I looked, blood started trickling out of it, then flowing, yet in some weird way the blood seemed to be—how can I put it—independent, as if the corpuscles were moving under their own power. What I'm really saying, in fact, was that it felt like the blood was *alive*.

"And as I saw it I suddenly understood and realized: It's the blood of Christ.

"So I put my hands in the air and I cried out, 'Take me God, I'm yours!' And with that I felt my body pushed backwards as though I was bent in two, double, and I was wobbling, my center of gravity behind me—and my arms went out and my body was shaking from my feet to my fingertips and I opened my mouth and out came this *roar*, from deep inside me, past my vocal chords somehow, without touching me, as if something terrible had cried out from deep within."

And at that same moment some impulse made Jill reach out and run her hand from Edward's thigh right down to his ankle, and it was, he says, as if she drew this "slug" out from his leg. Or was it a curse? "Because I'd always been prone to injuries on my left leg, sprains in particular—and, since that moment, I've never had problems again."

Edward had, in fact, abreacted to the core of his pain; and linked in with the spiritual event a "health conversion," or cure, seemed to have taken place. Here was another instance of the similarity between religious conversion and Charismatic cures.

From then on, the experience turned benign. "Put simply," said Edward, "God visited us for three hours."

For now that all-pervasive sense of wickedness was gradually replaced by the most profound joy either Edward or Jill had ever known. More, the voice of God Himself was in the flat there talking to them. Kindly, understanding, wise, telling them they'd be married eventually and have this wonderful life. Assuring them it would be Edward's calling to minister to adults, Jill's to help the young.

Then Edward had this Word telling them that Jill's hands, which still felt most comfortable in the prayer position, would develop the ability to heal. And Jill had this vision of the two of them walking up this shining path toward these gates, with Jesus at the end, welcoming them.

Both Jill and Edward, now, could only see each other as beautiful. Jill, in particular, began to see Edward as more than just beautiful, somehow transcendent—as did Edward himself. As he put it: "For the rest of the day I felt really happy and bubbly and fresh and clean and I went into the bathroom and looked in the mirror—and I was amazed at what I saw. My skin radiant, my lips all red and glowing—it sounds incredible, but I was looking at the face of an Angel!"

The whole episode lasted around twenty-four hours—and the two have never been the same again. Edward does retain some slight, lingering doubts as to whether the Devil was actually in the flat, but he is absolutely certain—more certain, indeed, than of anything in his life—that he and Jill had a genuine visitation from God.

In the immediate aftermath, Jill and Edward's lives entered a strange period of flux, with periods of profound rapture followed by sudden intrusions of panic and fear—times which Edward and Jill interpreted as the Devil doing his damnedest to win them back. There were dreams: Jill, for instance, dreamed she was being put through a sausage machine; Edward dreamed he was going through a meat mixer; Jill started having terrible nightmares in which she was murdering Edward, all this dreadful screaming and blood.

Then there were voices: some benign, like the voice of God

telling Jill she should confess to Edward about the times she had been unfaithful to him—which she did, and he forgave her, utterly, and it was a profound and beautiful moment; others, however, were diabolic—still more last-ditch attempts by the Devil to win them back. Still others were more equivocal. They *seemed* Godlike—one divine injunction Edward obeyed was to destroy his "demonic" music collection, six hundred tapes and records, all smashed apart—but would sometimes tell the couple to do unaccountable things.

"One night," said Edward, "there was this voice telling us that God wanted to test our faith and, if we truly believed, we would take the car out without lights, drive down the wrong side of the road and God would preserve us. So we did just that, and took the car out onto the main road, no lights, wrong side of the street, just as we were told. And suddenly this car was coming straight at us—but it swerved and missed us, so we were spared.

"Another time we were told to lie down in the road, at night again, and risk being run over. Once again, God would preserve us. So again we did it. But this time we saved ourselves—when a car came we made a dash for it." This, they eventually decided, was not God's word at all, but the Enemy, working in disguise. The voices, the nightmares, and the panic attacks went on for weeks, strangely mixed in with all this joy. For some reason, Jill was especially singled out for Satanic attack—so that finally they decided to put Jill in the hands of a "deliverance" team—to exorcise her, in fact. In the event, it was Edward's sister Chris and her husband, both Evangelicals, who did it: they came up from Billericay with a couple of friends and carried out the exorcism in the council flat in Bow, in Edward's bedroom.

"They started off by praying over me," said Jill, "and very quickly I began to feel awful—physically sick. It was these spirits rising up inside me, I realized later. And yet I never knew which spirit would rise up next; but Chris would recognize them, and call them out, bang, bang, bang, one right after another.

"So I'd suddenly feel this spirit of hatred, say, and she'd call it out, and it would come bursting out with a howl, I'd find myself going 'Grrrrrrr!' and it'd be out. And then she'd go on to the next one, lust, say, and she'd call that out—I'd go splutter, cough, and out it would come, then onto the next, self-pity, say, and another cough and that would be out, and so on.

"Until finally Chris identified this spirit of rejection welling up inside me, and I felt this terrible, deepest misery of all. And as she called *that* out I found myself yelling out, from somewhere deep inside me, 'I was an accident, an accident!' And THAT, I realized later, was all about this deep, deep feeling I'd had all my life that I wasn't a planned child: that I'd been, in fact . . . unwanted.

"And yet until that moment I'd never known it consciously; and yet unconsciously, it ruled my life.

"Because in a way that spirit of rejection was the deepest feeling of all, as it lay behind all the other things before I converted—the spirit of lust for instance, the way I'd betrayed Edward with all these other men. Because the real reason I did it was this sense that I lacked self-worth: I slept with men to prove to myself that I could be . . . yes, wanted.

"Well, you can imagine how I felt after I'd discovered that. I'd unearthed, and expressed, my deepest pain. I'd writhed and screamed and threshed about in torment. But I'd come through it all, and now, although I was exhausted, shattered, I was cleansed. Incredible!"

And, indeed, Jill's abreaction—just like Edward's—was duly followed by the deepest, most sublime experience of peace.

Both Jill and Edward became steadily more confident in their faith. A few weeks after her deliverance, Jill talked in tongues; Edward developed a passion for Bible reading and traditional hymns; both felt, as Edward put it, that they'd somehow "come over the brow of the hill."

Peace, self-affirmation and sobriety became the keynotes of their lives. They plunged into a typically busy and highly structured Christian schedule. Out went the clubs, the drugs, the music, the sleeping around. In came a life of order, meetings and self-improvement: two days a week voluntary work for Jill at Ichthus primary school; two days at Welldiggers, another Ichthus group; prayer meetings on Monday for Edward, Welldiggers for him, too, on Wednesday; youth meetings for both of them on Friday (Jill is now an Ichthus youth leader). On Sunday they both might go to two services in one day. And so it goes on, week after sober week. Now and then they might pop out and eat, La Bella Italia in Camberwell's very nice; and now and then they'll take in a movie, something jolly, preferably: *The Jungle Book*—now there was a movie they both enjoyed.

If you happened upon Jill and Edward tomorrow, they would come across as the most ordered, ordinary citizens you might ever meet.

9

Magician Heal Thyself

Do Jill and Edward's experiences merit a specifically transcendental interpretation? Could they not be better described, for all their extraordinariness, in the language Michael Persinger, for one, prefers: that such experiences are, in shorthand, "dreams"? Waking dreams, of course, but it is worth bearing in mind how infinitely more "real" any dream will always feel, compared with that emotional cocoon we call wakefulness.

Or to use the language of psychiatry, was this not an example of that specific form of "abreaction" known as "drug abreaction"? Was Jill and Edward's experience a do-it-yourself drug-induced abreaction (albeit involuntary) to childhood pains and pleasures rather than to any "genuine" God or the Devil—the religious imagery a kind of metaphor, culturally induced?

As modern psychology grows ever more sophisticated in its understanding of the workings of the brain, it's becoming ever warier of taking our conscious mind's interpretations of such "visions" at face value. As psychiatrist Ray Wyre (himself, interestingly, an ex-Charismatic who has experienced at least one vision) of Birmingham's Gracewell Foundation puts it: "It's wrong-headed, and dangerous, when people move too readily to stick supernatural labels on such experiences—for the simple reason that you don't need the supernatural to bring such experiences on. You just need the abreaction!" This can be particularly insidious, reckons Ray, when people put the supernatural tag on the dramatic (though often strictly temporary) "cures" that can occur in the "group abreactive" circumstances of, for instance, an Evangelical healing meeting.

"The problem is that your average participant—and this can include the healers themselves—tends to be unaware of just how powerful such psychological forces can be. So that when a meeting uses music, or dance, or the kind of intense emotionalism that speeds up breathing and affects the brain, lots of people will be genuinely amazed when someone who hasn't walked for months suddenly gets up and proceeds—quite genuinely!—across the stage. 'It's a miracle!' they cry. And indeed it is, in one sense— because it is, unquestionably, quite extraordinary what the mind and body are capable of. But that doesn't make it the work of God. And it's here that people can get tragically misled." To remind ourselves of such powers, it's worth looking at two examples of avowedly "secular" abreactions. In the introduction to his 1970 expressionist-psychological classic *The Primal Scream*, Dr. Arthur Janov describes how he first happened on what must be the abreaction theory *par excellence* of the last quarter century.

> Some years ago, I heard something that was to change the course of my professional life and the lives of my patients . . . an eerie scream welling up from the depths of a young man lying on the floor during a therapy session. I can only liken it to what one might hear from a person about to be murdered . . .

In therapy Janov had already noticed the man's enthusiasm for a stage act involving childhood regression.

> Danny's fascination with the act impelled me to try something elementary, but which had previously escaped my notice. I asked him to call out, "Mommy! Daddy!"

. . . As he began, he became noticeably upset. Suddenly he was writhing on the floor in agony. His breathing was rapid, spasmodic: "Mommy! Daddy!" came out of his mouth almost involuntarily in loud screeches. He appeared to be in a coma or hypnotic state. The writhing gave way to small convulsions, and finally, he released a piercing, deathlike scream that rattled the walls of my office. The entire episode lasted only a few minutes, and neither Danny nor I had any idea what had happened. All he could say afterwards was: "I made it! I don't know what, but I can feel!"

"What happened to Danny baffled me for months—" Janov wrote. Nevertheless, come another therapy session:

A thirty-year-old man, whom I shall call Gary Hillard, was relating with great feeling how his parents had always criticized him, had never loved him, and had generally messed up his life. I urged him to call out for them . . . halfheartedly, he started calling for Mommy and Daddy. Soon I noticed he was breathing faster and deeper. His calling turned into an involuntary act that led to writhing, near-convulsions, and finally to a scream.

Both of us were shocked. What I had believed was an accident, an idiosyncratic reaction of one patient, had just been repeated in almost identical fashion.

Afterwards, when he quieted down, Gary was flooded with insights. . . . He became alert; his sensorium opened up; he seemed to understand himself.

Over the following months Janov repeated the process with a string of patients. "Each time there occurred the same dramatic results."

I have come to regard that scream as the product of central and universal pains which reside in all neurotics. I call them

Primal Pains because they are the original, early hurts upon which all later neurosis is built.

The parallels with Edward and Jill's experience speak for themselves, although one might underscore the specifically regressive nature of Jill's cry, "I was an accident, an accident!"; and, most striking of all, that climactic moment of Edward's vision, when: "I opened my mouth and out came this *roar.*"

A primal scream? Yet again, perceived boundaries dissolve. The parallels between Jill and Edward's religious "visions" and post-Sixties healing therapy—both part of the same counter-cultural evolution, after all—are striking indeed.

But then all these manifestations—primal scream, EST, drug abreactions, Charismatic conversions, the entire transcendental language of the New Age movement—are, despite their differences, crucially alike, above all in their dependence on the twentieth-century rediscovery of the "unconscious" (in Nineties-speak, the "right hemisphere") and the parallel collapse of mind-body dualism. It is thus to be expected that a Western culture which has become ever more obsessed with the possibility of sudden mental transformation (whether religious or secular) should also become ever more susceptible to the associated notion of sudden physical transformation, or healing.

It is easy to forget that Freud's starting point was that of "healer" in the conventional Western sense: when he qualified in 1881, aged twenty-six, it was in medicine, and the theories which first caught his interest (those of Charcot and, later, Breuer) concerned hysteria—specifically, patients who would return again and again to their doctor with a different symptom every week. Such people were incurable so far as the conventional medical wisdom of the West was concerned, but incurable victims of overtly *physical* ills. The great breakthrough of the late nineteenth century, of which Freud was just one part, was the linking back of physical symptoms (matter) to the emotional traumas imprinted in the deepest vaults

of memory (mind). The collapse of Cartesian mind/matter separation, or Western "dualism," was built into Freud's revolution
from the very start—and thus also was the symbiotic relationship
between emotional recovery, twentieth-century style, and physical
"healing." Even conventional Freudian analysis was, in effect, a
kind of slow burn "abreaction." It might take fifteen years rather
than fifteen minutes, and it might use the mighty Western *logos*
rather than electricity or drugs, but nevertheless, it was based on
the same essential—and to Western medicine revelatory—premise:
the profoundest possible exploration of a quite newly conceived,
because mentally and physically indivisible, memory.

From the start, this was memory of emotional state, of "affect"
—and as psychiatry advanced in tandem with the century's broader
cultural emancipation, "affect" was granted ever-greater therapeutic
clout. The "experiential" therapies of the Sixties and Seventies,
complete with touchy-feely hold-me-love-me physicality, were a
natural progression.

This approach coalesced into what U.S. psychologist Abraham
Maslow christened psychology's "third force," although it was
always more a state of mind than a movement. What brought its
spiritual content ever closer to an overtly religious sense of mind's
power over matter was not just its penchant for overt religiosity
(although a new respect for religion was very much part of it—one
of Maslow's best known works is *Peak Experiences,* an exploration
of the paranormal and of visions) but, even more significantly, the
way its ideas spilled over into medical realms previously regarded
as exclusively material.

The result was a whole new secular notion of the power of
the mind, or spirit, to heal. Whether it was Wilhelm Reich (a
major influence on Janov) enlarging Freud's theory of sexuality
as a spiritual, psychic force to redefine it as a physical force, with
concrete energy flowing through the biological organism giving
profoundly beneficial—or destructive—effects; or Carl Simonton,
in the early Seventies, arguing that the way to cure cancer is

to address the emotional problems of which cancer is merely one manifestation; or R. D. Laing highlighting the connection between "nervous" breathing and the symbolic holding back of breath we call asthma; or the Johns Hopkins pediatric research investigator Robert Blizzard arguing the connection, in children, between emotional sustenance and physical growth (a deprived child, he said, put into a nurturing environment, can produce the normal flow of growth hormones within five days, and grow ten inches in a year)—whichever way you looked, come the Seventies, it was the same story: an ever-broadening sense of the capacity of the mind to effect physical cures on the body.

Perhaps the real discovery was that whereas the part of the brain we call "Mind" or "intellect" does seem able to dissociate itself from the body, this late-nineteenth-century arriviste, the unconscious, cannot. One of the crucial themes of that 1928 antidualistic blockbuster, Lawrence's *Lady Chatterley's Lover*—and Lawrence, as a sensibility, was surely one perambulating "unconscious"—was Lawrence's notion that the body had its very own autonomous, self-regulating world and being, quite separate from the intellect. In expressing this, he almost seems to equate the words body and soul—for not only does he argue that the body, if ignored, will bring all manner of visitations on the mind (the sexually deprived Lady Chatterley's terrible dreams, her irrational surges of anger and so on) but, in a kind of Janov-in-reverse, that it may induce spiritual neurosis in later years. Lawrence certainly knew plenty of Victorian-matron models for that.

Rediscover the unconscious and you rediscover a mental universe in which body and soul are inextricably one: each capable of acting "causally" on the other. Or as Jung himself put it, writing, like Lawrence, as far back as the Twenties:

Psyche cannot be totally different from matter, for how otherwise could it move matter? And matter cannot be alien to psyche, for how else could matter produce psyche?

As this post-Cartesian *Zeitgeist* gathered momentum through the Eighties and gained popular appeal in the form of New Age in the Nineties, its noisiest fans seemed sold not merely on mind over matter, but also on what amounted, in effect, to "magic."

Not that neo-Cartesians, deeply shaken by all this, distinguished much between such shamanism and—for instance—holistic healing traditions which, while new to Europe, had centuries of civilization behind them. The crystallization of English medical conservatism around groups such as Healthwatch, and their views on the new tangled holistic treatments for cancer, has already been mentioned—as has the U.S.-based CSICOP and its war against paranormal "irrationalism." Nevertheless, while scientists were disturbed by any number of the flood of alternative cures on tap by the early Nineties, it was, above all, the religious manifestations of all this—those claims of actual "miracles"— which really riled them.

The claims the Charismatics were making, worldwide, were so extreme: cripples walking, sight restored, the dead (for heaven's sake!) raised back to life. Such cases offered a clearer target for Cartesian demo squads than the more opaque claims of, say, acupuncture. And unquestionably their attack—in the areas in which they have chosen to concentrate—has been quite devastating.

In the U.K., for instance, medicine's best-known miracle investigator has long been Dr. Peter May, a Southampton-based GP. Dr. May is himself a committed Christian, a member of the General Synod. He has been investigating claims of supernatural healing for twenty years, and indeed has an interesting history himself. When he was sixteen, he was diagnosed as having a life-threatening tumor and scheduled for an operation. "Relatives and friends knew about it, of course, and were praying for me," he says. "But the operation proved that what I had wasn't cancer and was curable with surgery. Wrong diagnosis." Nevertheless,

Dr. May says some may have thought there'd been a "miracle"; and, reckons Dr. May, when "miracles" are based on that kind of error, something basic has gone wrong. Today he investigates such claims with the help of some five thousand colleagues worldwide, members of the Christian Medical Fellowship—and a profoundly rigorous, left-hemispherical affair it all is. In twenty years, in fact, Dr. May believes he has not yet encountered one single medically proven claim.

Perhaps the best known "miraculous" healing is that of Jean Neil, star of the internationally sold video *Something to Shout About—The Documentation of a Miracle*. The film shows Jean being "healed" by the German Evangelist Reinhard Bonnke, after which she leaps from her wheelchair and runs around. Her "multiple condition," we are told, includes spinal injury, a hip out of joint, one leg two inches shorter than the other, and angina pectoris. More, the video says that over twenty-five years she has had fourteen operations, spent four years in hospital, suffered three heart attacks, been confined to a wheelchair, and swallowed twenty-four tablets a day. Dr. May looked into all this. His conclusions, as described by the investigative reporter Peter Martin in London's *Evening Standard Magazine*, were these:

Contacted by Dr May, Mrs Nell sent him crucial orthopedic reports from her medical records.

These revealed:

SPINAL INJURY: the removal of the coccyx [the little bones at the very base of the spine] after a fracture in the 60s, and three other operations on her spine to relieve pain. In 1988, six months after Mrs Neil's healing, the orthopedic surgeon's report stated: "X-rays have been repeated today and these confirm that there is absolutely no change from the X-rays taken prior to this evangelical healing."

HIP OUT OF JOINT: the orthopedic surgeon reported that an

X-ray taken three months before the healing showed her hips to be "quite normal."

ONE LEG TWO INCHES SHORTER THAN THE OTHER: there was no record of a short leg.

HEART DISEASE: the papers made no mention of heart attacks. Writing six months before the healing, however, her GP stated that her chest pains, "after vigorous investigations, were felt not to be cardiac in origin."

FOURTEEN OPERATIONS: four on her spine, plus two Caesareans, an operation for a hammer toe, some small surgical attentions to her elbows, and having her appendix out. Mrs Neil could not recall the other operations.

CONFINED TO A WHEELCHAIR FOR 25 YEARS: in the 15 months prior to the healing, Mrs Neil was getting about with both walking sticks and a wheelchair. But at no stage was she "confined to a wheelchair."

FOUR YEARS IN HOSPITAL: this was the estimate of all her hospital visits over 25 years.

In brief, in the unforgiving searchlight of Cartesian analysis, Jean's claims dissolve, leaving Dr. May so victorious, indeed, as to be magnanimous: there is, he allows, no doubt of the "amazing improvement" in Jean's "sense of well-being and enjoyment of life." But this is an utterly different matter, clearly, from the dramatic, overtly paranormal events originally on offer—and which continue to be flogged around Europe and Africa by Mrs. Neil and the indefatigable Bonnke.

Before leaving Jean Neil, one other aspect of her case should be highlighted—because it recurs time and again in such situations —and that is the extent to which the whole episode rests on misdiagnosis. This appears to be one of the key preconditions of such "miracles": the plain fact that the patient never had the condition in the first place. Indeed, argues Dr. May, still generous, such mistakes are often perfectly genuine:

> It can so easily happen. Someone is rushed to hospital, and the junior casualty doctor, erring on the side of caution, puts what he suspects is a broken leg in plaster. Fracture X-rays can be very difficult to read. The patient goes home and prays. Come Monday morning, the specialist looks at the X-ray, deduces that there was no break after all, and orders the plaster taken off. But the patient is left believing his broken leg was healed by prayer. A miracle!

Peter Martin further describes Dr. May's investigation of the case of Jennifer Rees Larcombe, who claimed divine healing of four attacks of viral encephalitis—and wrote a book about it, *Unexpected Healing,* selling well. This, too, was based on false diagnosis—with the difference that the diagnosis in this case was made by Jenny herself. No doctor ever diagnosed her encephalitis —*the interpretation of her symptoms was her own.*

These, remember, are some of the movement's star case histories —and yet they are typical of the way such stories turn out. America's answer to Dr. May, James Randi, actually offers a $10,000 reward in his book *The Faith-Healers* to anyone who can produce a properly authenticated instance of paranormal powers —his version, plainly, of May's "no medically proven claim in twenty years."

James Randi, it must be said, is a rationalist of some style. Not only has he the highest clout among a bevy of bright people, those anti-irrationalist CSICOP scientists; not only did he secure a MacArthur Foundation (so-called genius) Prize Fellowship to fund his research; not only did Carl Sagan, no less, write the preface to his book; but Randi has a surprising yet deeply relevant qualification for his miracle-busting role: he is, himself, a professional conjuror—a stage magician. "I possess a narrow, but rather strong expertise," he says. "I know what fakery looks like."

Add to this a splendidly dry, pellucid Enlightenment mind, some truly hilarious, charlatan-busting stunts, and one of America's finer Father Christmas white-beard-and-whisker sets, and you have a veritable Last American Hero, a true back-to-the-future eighteenth-century Yank.

Randi and his team (assorted scientists, academics, conjurors) sure had some fun with all this. For a start there was a whole mass of straight miracle bustings in the Dr. May/Jean Neil mold. Then there were those conjuror's perspectives on how a faith healer gets his results—the memorable variant on that never-had-the-illness-in-the-first-place theme perpetrated by the U.S. faith healer W. V. Grant, for instance. Grant's big number, at healing services, was raising people out of wheelchairs who would then walk out of the hall. Scam? They'd arrived on foot—Grant supplied the wheelchairs and persuaded them to sit in them till "healed." End of story.

Another favorite at healing services is the phenomenon of "calling out." In this scenario, the faith healer identifies people in the audience with specific problems and illnesses, people he has never met before, and magically tells them where they come from and what they're suffering from. Randi reckons this is a very old chestnut, a conjuring cliché. What you do is get helpers to talk to people as they come in, then smuggle the info backstage in time for the main event. A hi-tech rendering of this, exposed by Randi on the Johnny Carson show, was the Evangelist Peter Popoff's use of a miniature radio receiver in his left ear.

The list goes on. There's the leg-lengthening scam, for instance, (also a golden oldie), achieved by moving loose-fitting shoes an inch or two up or down the foot. Grant once inadvertently "healed" the same woman in two separate, successive healing services. As skeptics observed, if both hearings were real she must once have walked with one foot in the ditch. . . . But the mother of all Randi's exploits, the ultimate deflation, concerned a well meaning but less than rigorous research investigation into parapsychology— a caper Randi and team code-named, possibly with an eye to the film rights, the "Project Alpha Experiment." It involved the surreptitious introduction, like some dread plague bacillus, of two conjurors into the McDonnell Laboratory for Psychical Research, a pristine new $500,000 parapsychology research institute funded via Washington University, St. Louis, Missouri.

The background was that Randi and other CSICOP folks were increasingly concerned about the lack of rigor in parapsychology —especially the possible introduction, as with the faith healers, of plain conjuring tricks. To give the project director, physics professor Peter R. Phillips, every chance Randi sent him a long list of relevant difficulties concerning the kind of tests they intended to carry out, and included an offer of Randi-the-conjuror's own presence at the experiments, for free, as an observer. The offer was not taken up.

Bizarrely, out of three hundred-odd applicants for the tests, just two were picked—and they were the Randi conjurors, both teenagers, both part-time magicians. Presumably they did great letters of application.

These kids soon had the researchers believing they'd found *serious* psychics. The boys "saw" inside sealed envelopes. They transmitted pictures by mental powers. They blew fuses, magically. They bent bars, paranormally. They even mind-boggled the workings of a video camera, so the resulting images swelled and shrank very spookily indeed. . . . And yet each stroke they pulled, it turned out, was pure (and often extremely elementary) conjuring—if not straight duplicity—none of which was detected by the lab. For instance, in the words of Randi's report:

One device, developed at the laboratory for testing the Alpha subjects, consisted of an overturned aquarium bolted and padlocked to a stout table. Objects would be put inside and left overnight. Since the locks on the doors were of excellent quality, and Phillips wore the padlock and door keys around his neck, security was thought to be absolute. It was not. Edwards and Shaw simply left a window unlocked, and returned to the premises at night. There were several ways to open the sealed aquarium, and they were free to do anything they pleased with the contents, which were discovered in the morning by lab personnel to have been bent, twisted, broken, and moved about by mysterious paranormal forces.

A part of the aquarium test used a shallow box in which dry coffee-grounds were spread in a thin layer. Small cubes and other objects were placed therein, and were found to have spelled out strange cabalistic symbols when examined in the morning. This evoked much wonder among the investigators.

Indeed, herein lay one of the real curiosities of the investigator-psychic relationship: the profundity of the investigators' commitment to their subjects' powers. They called them "gifted psychic subjects," and dreamed up their own special label for them: "psychokinete." In fact, when the first rumors worked their way back from the magician community that there were conjurors in the lab, the researchers, in turn, passed this on to their tame "psychics" as an excellent joke.

One hardly dares imagine the moment when finally, after three years' research, Phillips and co. were finally confronted with the truth. Randi feels the McDonnell team finally learned from the experience and subsequent experiments were appropriately adjusted. But before we feel too much sympathy for the researchers, we should remind ourselves that Randi offered that free anticonjuror consultancy from the start. And, more significantly, we should note that the tendency towards self-serving credulity the scam revealed—habits common to all of us but supposedly transcended in a scientific setting—is more powerful than one might imagine. Almost anyone will believe almost anything, it seems, especially in a group.

Dud healers and flawed experiments don't discredit the whole argument about the interconnection between body and soul. The cancer therapy pioneered by Carl Simonton, for instance, gives an average survival time twice that of the best U.S. institutions for cancer therapy and comparable therapies have produced similar results. Beyond which there is a whole series of paradigm-busting experiments which are neither the scams of con-men nor the fruits of credulity. (And one should never forget just how mixed up straight chicanery and genuine healing used to be in the early days of what we now regard as establishment medicine.)

There's the so-called Ganzfeld procedure, for example: this pride of modern parapsychology tests for telepathic communication between human "receivers" and "senders." An analysis of twenty-eight such studies (835 Ganzfeld sessions) revealed a hit rate of 38 percent, against an assumed 25 percent if chance alone were operating—statistically highly significant, as the probability that this variation could have arisen by chance has been estimated at less than one in a billion.

Even more remarkable are the experiences of those working at that headquarters of supertechnology, Denver, Colorado, at the University of Colorado Health Sciences Center, where they devised an experiment to monitor "therapeutic touch." They have been both practicing and teaching it here for twenty years—ever since the onset of our oral/tactile counterculture. Moreover, the professor of Nursing there, Janet Quinn, has noticed over the years that her own health has improved during therapies, as well as her patients'. (She has heard similar tales from therapeutic-touch nurses operating elsewhere.) At Colorado, they decided to test the effect of therapeutic touch on the immune system. For that purpose, they found four subjects who were grieving or had recently suffered bereavement (in an interesting parallel with the stress-conversion relationship we saw earlier, the capacity of stress to lower our immune capacity is long established). They then chose two therapeutic-touch healers, added one subject who would not receive healing, as a control, and set to work.

Blood samples were taken before and after the experiment from all participants, and they found just one—remarkable—change: in immune lymphocyte cells known as OKTeights. These, it turned out, had dropped an average of 18 percent in all patients, and in both healers—but not in the control. As cellular immunologist Dr. Tony Strelkauskus put it: "What we have shown in this study is that therapeutic touching has a direct effect on a population of immune lymphocytes. So some specific immune cells, which might be in excess, and suppressing the immune functions in grieving patients, have been reduced."

There are reasons why a patient who sincerely believed in the efficacy of this process might show such an improvement. But what about the claim, which so many healers stress, both lay and spiritual, that there is a kind of omnipresent healing energy in the universe which can be invoked by a healer regardless of a patient's suggestibility or otherwise?

Californian psychologist Dr. Daniel Wirth developed an experiment to try to answer that question. Using forty-four volunteers, he had identical, surgically induced, eight-millimeter-wide wounds put into his subjects arms. He then had a healer "heal" half of them. The subjects' arms were stuck through a kind of masked "porthole" into the healing room so that none even knew they were supposed to be being healed (they thought they were testing out a new kind of medical photography). On completion of the study, thirteen of the treated group were "completely healed," while ten were well on their way. In the untreated group there was no significant wound healing at all. No Sargantian suggestibility, seemingly, here. . . .

But then even the "energy fields" apparently invoked only

activate, argue the healers, a curing process which is, in the end, self-activated. They finish up sounding strangely reminiscent of Albert Schweitzer when he tried to reconcile his Western "healing" techniques with what he saw succeeding, all around him, in the African bush: "The witch doctor succeeds for the same reason all the rest of us [doctors] succeed. Each patient carries his own doctor inside him. We [doctors] are at our best when we give the doctor within each patient a chance to go to work."

Whether one is talking about the abreactive techniques of a Sargant, a Janov, or a Charismatic; or the "enabling" therapy of a Simonton cancer cure; or Western antibiotics, slowing down the reproduction of the invading bacteria sufficiently for the body's own immune system to fight back; or those Colorado healers also influencing the immune system—in all cases we find we are looking *inward* for the cure. Like the Kingdom of Heaven, it seems that God's healing power, wherever else it may or may not be, lies within.

Rationalism is, unquestionably, impeccable as far as it goes: but it only goes so far. The problems arise when rationalism—down-to-earth and square as it must always be—moves from its tried and tested stamping ground, the particular, towards the general. William Sargant, no romantic, put it nicely in *The Battle for the Mind*: "My concern here is not with the immortal soul, which is the province of the theologian, nor even with the mind in the broadest sense of the word, which is the province of the philosopher, but with the brain and nervous system, which man shares with the dog and other animals." Sargant's whole project is shot through with a wise and modest self-limitation —a self-limitation, above all, *that knows itself*. Or as quantum physicist Werner Heisenberg summarized it:

1. Modern science, in its beginnings, was characterized by a conscious modesty; it made statements about strictly limited

relations that are only valid within the framework of these limitations.

2. This modesty was largely lost during the Nineteenth Century. Physical knowledge was considered to make assertions about nature as a whole. Physics wished to turn philosopher, and the demand was voiced from many quarters that all true philosophers must be scientific.

3. Today physics is undergoing a basic change, the most characteristic trait of which is a return to its original self-limitation.

If science cannot "make assertions" about "nature as a whole," what can? Newton himself stressed his work was concerned not with the ultimate question of *why* something happens, but the immediate question of *how*.

Re-enter mysticism. . . . For as U.S. scientist Ken Wilber points out in his recent anthology of modern physicists' philosophical writings, in which he extracts the work of Heisenberg, Schroedinger, Einstein, De Broglie, Jeans, Planck, Pauli and Eddington: "They were *all* mystics of one sort or another."

Positivism is fine just so long as it stays in its box—and knows it is in a box in the first place. For it is indeed, a fine, well-ordered box: a touch square around the edges, but full of clean, well lit, well ordered corridors, of numbers and grids and right angles as logically eloquent as any U.S. city, and utterly, and very healthily, antipathetic to all the sillier forms of cant and self-delusion. The problem arises when it pulls down the lid and announces: "That's it! There's just the box! If it moves, measure it! If you can't, forget it!"

Or as Wilber puts it in the introduction to his book, addressing, in effect, all of Boxville's assembled squares:

I would simply ask, you of orthodox belief, you who pursue disinterested truth, you who—whether you know it or not—

are moulding the very face of the future with your scientific knowledge, you who—may I say so?—bow to physics as if it were a religion in itself, to you I ask: what does it mean that the founders of your modern science, the theorists and researchers who pioneered the very concepts you now worship implicitly, the very scientists presented in this volume, what does it mean that they were *every one of them, mystics?*

Does that not stir something in you, curiosity at least?

10

A Crisis of Self-Worth

In the summer of 1992 the American evangelist Morris Cerullo's healing show hit London. It turned out that he'd been coming over from the U.S. for thirty-five years, but this was the first time the British public had really registered him: partly because he'd taken over the vast Earl's Court 2 auditorium, and partly because of his startling £150,000 come-see-the-healings poster campaign, featuring discarded wheelchairs, smashed white sticks and thrown-away dark glasses. Furthermore, supernatural spirituality was finally getting into the air. Turn on the TV and there'd be yet another Charismatic saying how he'd lost his job in the recession but it no longer mattered because, thanks to Jesus, he was "beyond materialism." Parents discussing what they feared most for their children came up not with pregnancy, or drugs, or unemployment, but Charismatic Christianity.

The result was a tremendous focus on Cerullo's circus: the tabloids covered it and the qualities covered it and Joan Bakewell did a CSICOP-style exposé of it on TV. The whole caravanserai unfolded, in fact, in true Evangelical form—genuine old-time, top-down U.S. fundamentalism, heavy on the manipulation, bouncers, corporate image-making, suits.

The audiences were huge: black Pentecostalists, folks in wheelchairs, men in T-shirts with their hands in the air. There were lengthy "sermons," biblical quotations, "callings out." Then,

151

as in any skillfully orchestrated narrative, came the promised healings/conversions in a grand, climacteric pay-off.

After the tour there were claims that the final miracle score was 476, no less; Peter May (who was there, and did one of his investigations) said that there had not been a single one; Joan Bakewell's miracle count was also zilch; there were, more insidiously, allegations of miracles that backfired—in particular, an epileptic woman stopped taking her medicine after a Cerullo "cure" and died six days later; there was talk of all the money Cerullo was making—an annual turnover of £6.5 million was mentioned; and there were expressions of distaste from the straight church at such shenanigans.

Odd details were surprising. One was Cerullo's appearance: short, squat and glad-handedly Italian, he and his chums did look very much like a Mafia convention, very little like, say, Jesus. (But then Cerullo's own publicity machine said he originally wanted to be a state governor.) Another surprise, given the feel and flavor of all this, was just how ready the cooler, more level-headed New Christians were to accept it. Gerald Coates, in particular, who'd met Cerullo previously, said he'd been struck by Cerullo's "poise," his "self-effacingness," his "modesty." The conundrum is familiar: on the one hand, the high seriousness, the profoundly suggestive arguments of the Sargants, Janovs and Heisenbergs, with their implication that something remarkable, albeit highly mysterious, *is* going on; on the other, the seeming absurdity of so much Evangelical practice—of so many "conversions," "vision experiences" and mass "healings." If Heisenberg's or Einstein's God was really about to reveal Himself to a surprised late twentieth century, would a Marks and Spencer sign or a Cerullo healing meeting really be His chosen venue?

Yet such a vocabulary, for good or ill, is unquestionably, so often, the actual language of Charisma, and of believers who are, whatever else, genuinely moved. Even in such an improbable venue as Earl's Court, and even under the full blast of secular skepticism, not all of Cerullo's healings were "disproved." Forty-five-year-old Sheila Lambshead, a long-term sufferer from back pain, was "cured," she said, by Cerullo way back in 1990. Since then, she affirmed, her pain had gone and her whole life had been dramatically enhanced—so much so that, at the suggestion of the Bakewell program, her specialist took new X-rays . . . and found her organic condition quite unchanged. Nevertheless, her *experience* seemed to be of a life utterly transformed. How could a man like Cerullo have done it? Could there be some connection between, say, his emotional history and his capacity, if not to give legs to the limbless, at least to radically transform mood?

The British psychiatrist Anthony Storr postulated a link between the much-documented clinical depressions suffered by that secular Charismatic Winston Churchill and, paradoxically, his capacity to raise the spirits of the "depressed" British in 1940. Is depression (or "stress," to use our earlier language) something we are *more,* rather than less, likely to find in a Charismatic leader—as we have already seen with Charismatic followers? Could the degree of depression be related, via some unexpected emotional confection, to that leader's very capacity to transform mood? Could he lift his own depression at the moment he exalts his audience? And could such emotional chemistry be rooted, in turn, in the kind of childhood trauma which seems to lie at the roots of conversionism, that very pain Janov tried to exorcise with his primal scream?

For Cerullo (according to Philip Greven's 1990 book *Spare the Child—The Religious Roots of Punishment and the Psychological Impact of Physical Abuse*) turns out to have experienced as much childhood tragedy as any convert he might "exploit" today. As did Billy Graham—as Greven also shows. As did John Wesley, too. As did the eighteenth-century American Evangelist Jonathan Edwards. As did Churchill, by the testimony of his own letters, and his Charismatic contemporaries Stalin and Hitler. As did Gerald Coates. As did Lloyd Kuehl (his father's death, his step-father problems).

Leaders, followers, "victims," "exploiters"—all (depending on the moment at which you catch them) seem to be revolving in the same sequence of intense emotionalism, intense Evangelization and/or intensely cherished belief; all, though emotionally in different gears, bound, finally, on the same wheel of fire.

All roads lead to childhood, to those most innocent years.

Morris Cerullo lost his mother when he was just two years old. He ended up in an orphanage, where he was regularly beaten "with a paddle." In the words of his own publicity material, "life began to look fearfully bleak as the cold truth in the meaning of the words orphan, orphanage and foster home gradually dawned on him." Indeed, he was "tortured by bitterness, resentment, rejection, rebellion and loneliness."

At the age of fifteen, these experiences seem to have been expressed in a vision. In *Spare the Child*, Greven quotes Cerullo looking through a "hole in the sky" one evening and seeing:

> The very flames of Hell. I saw them rising and rising until they were literally burning right underneath the hole which had been made by the presence of God. In the midst of those flames were multitudes of lost souls. No mortal tongue can describe the anguish. If a messenger was sent straight from Hell to warn the sinner, man still would not comprehend the awful anguish and torment that awaits the unsaved in that dreadful place. Oh the screams and the cries of these anxious souls! . . . Throughout the endless ages of eternity these souls would be constantly reminded through the torment of their souls of the awful sin of rejecting God's love and mercy.

And yet, as Greven shows, such torments are not unusual in the childhood of Charismatic leaders; if anything, they are the norm. Take Billy Graham, in the words of his biographer Marshall Frady:

His father would sometimes withdraw a wide leather belt to apply to him, once when he was discovered with a plug of chewing tobacco bulging in his cheek, another time snatching him up from a church pew where Billy had been fretfully squirming, shoving him on out into the vestibule and there strapping him thoroughly. Over all the years since then, Billy maintains, what he still remembers most about his father is the feel of his hands against him: "They were like rawhide, bony, rough. He had such hard hands." In one instance, after Billy had gained some size, his father stood over him flailing away with the belt as Billy was lying on his back, and "I broke two of his ribs, kicking away with my legs."

Said Graham's mother: "Mr. Graham was right stern. . . . We thought that little disobediences, you know, were terrible things." As Marshall Frady puts it, Billy Graham's parenting represented the "inflation of menial errancies to proportions of the cosmic and dreadful."

Or take the early childhood of the eighteenth-century founders of Methodism, John and Charles Wesley, as described by their mother Susanna:

When turned a year old (and some before) they were taught to fear the rod and cry softly, by which means they escaped abundance of correction which they might otherwise have had: and that most odious noise of the crying of children was rarely heard in the house, but the family usually lived in as much quietness as if there had not been a child among them . . . No sinful action as lying, pilfering at church or on the Lord's Day, disobedience, quarreling etc. should ever pass unpunished.

In the case of Gerald Coates, his autobiography, *An Intelligent*

Fire, describes how any torments he suffered seemed largely self-inflicted. He describes his "confusion and sadness" in adolescence, his mother's "massive migraine attacks" and, more generally, her "recurring negativism—which had a debilitating effect on all that surrounded her." But most remarkably, he describes his own, quite staggering series of accidents and disasters—virtually all, in some way, self-orchestrated, even if he is not always the only victim.

There was the time, for instance, in boyhood, when he and his father stuffed themselves with plums—and Gerald spent three months suffering from gastroenteritis. He nearly died—at one stage he was so ill he couldn't be moved to hospital. Then there was the time he nearly drowned in a flooded stream: the footbridge was submerged, Gerald stepped off where he thought it should be, missed and was swept away. He was rescued just as he was about to disappear into a deep drain. Another time he set fire (intentionally) to the kitchen of a café where he was working, nearly burning the place down. At another job, he knocked a fire extinguisher down and covered a work-mate with acid powder. Gerald also nearly drowned himself in a swimming pool.

When he was seventeen, Gerald crashed a friend's motorbike, fractured "almost every single bone" in his body, suffered head injuries, and took seven days to regain consciousness. At one stage his parents were told: "Your son has about four hours to live." He did live, but only to repeat the performance a few years later when working as a postman: this time he was knocked off his bicycle by a car, broke his leg, and reopened the head wounds he'd suffered earlier.

There were other, more conscious, ways in which Gerald set up his own vulnerability: notably in giving up his job as a retail display manager shortly after he got married, to "live by faith." He duly describes the shortages suffered by his wife and two sons, the lack of clothes, food, holidays, not to mention the day the electricity man appeared at the front door to cut the Coates family off.

Gerald does not venture to speculate on how all this might be interpreted. Indeed, he hardly seems to notice what he is telling us. But then the whole book is written, somehow, at one remove (the first draft, incidentally, was written in the third person) as if Gerald were dissociated from his own story. In the following darkly enigmatic passage, he describes life around the age of seventeen:

> Despite a stable family life and fulfilling career, I was strangely unsettled. It wasn't that I needed to leave home, nor could I see myself leading an Oxford-Regent Street display team, or forming my own freelance company. I was yet to learn that self-disillusionment is necessary for spiritual maturity. But instead of seeing disillusionment as a friend, I viewed it as an enemy. It was on these rare and infrequent occasions that depression turned to darkness and I took excursions into the pleasures of sex with friends. It certainly relieved the tension, but afterwards I felt even deeper guilt and shame. To me they were excursions into a betrayal of important moral values. I knew I was spoiling other lives as well as my own.
>
> It was playwright Jonathan Miller who, on a national television broadcast, stated categorically that the "orifice into which one puts one's private parts" was unimportant —and yet has nothing to do with morality. AIDS was not yet discovered, but I knew he was wrong.

What is Gerald telling us?

Examples of the connection between childhood misery, depression and Charisma are everywhere. Ignatius Loyola's mother died shortly after birth, Ignatius was sent for suckling with the village wet nurse, and his father was absent on military campaigns. Martin Luther wrote: "My mother whipped me for stealing a nut until the blood came. Such strict discipline drove me to a monastery." Comments biographer Erik Erikson: "Luther all his life felt like some sort of criminal." Kathryn Kuhlman, twentieth-century American Evangelist, had a childhood "punctuated by encounters with punishment and pain," with a mother "never once able to acknowledge any love for her daughter." Winston Churchill called his depression "black dog," and once said: "I don't like standing near the edge of a platform when an express train is passing through . . . a second's action would end everything." Of the Puritan mystic Florence Nightingale biographer Cecil Woodham Smith wrote, "As a very young child she had an obsession that she was not like other people. She was a monster. . . ." Or, more succinctly (Lytton Strachey) "a Demon possessed her." Hitler's father, in the words of his psyche-biographer Walter C. Langer, was "brutal, unjust and inconsiderate," and "played the part of the bully and whipped his wife and children who were unable to defend themselves."

As for Joan of Arc, psychologist Michael Argyle, writing in a section of his *The Social Psychology of Religion* entitled "Mental disorder in religious leaders and clergy," says, "She has been diagnosed as lesbian, transvestite, schizophrenic, paranoid, creative psychopath, hysteric and epileptic."

Given all of which it becomes a little less mysterious when William James, summing up, writes:

> You will in point of fact hardly find a religious leader of any kind in whose life there is no record of automatisms. . . . The whole array of Christian saints and heresiarchs, including the greatest, the Bernards, the Loyolas, the Luthers, the Foxes, the Wesleys, had their visions, rapt conditions, guiding impressions and "openings."

The parallels with Charismatic "followers" are clear: that desperate sense of "unwantedness" in young Jill; those childhood sadnesses described by Lloyd, Susan and Mary; more broadly, the importance assigned by academic studies to childhood trauma; that overweening concern of Charismatics with the specific trauma of sexual child abuse (which Freud notably linked with adult hysteria) and its appearance in Charismatics' own histories—or, come to that, of a "celebrity" convert like Michael Reagan, the ex-president's adopted son: "Born Again" in 1985, sexually abused (by a youth worker) in 1952, when he was eight.

How is it that depressives are able to lift their followers' spirits so decisively? Depression is just one sidestep from obsessiveness: the tremendous hours Evangelicals put in may be the workaholic's escape from human reality, but they get results—and results thrill followers. And then depression is also one further step from insecurity, and any inflexibility that insecurity brings about, may, from the point of view of followers, look more like strength. Nor, indeed, does obsessiveness or escapist ducking away from real relationships hurt anybody's capacity to use others politically; nor, further, does it inhibit associating with all manner of other yet more powerful figures, and basking in reflected glory. Billy Graham moved effortlessly from associations with first President Johnson (Democrat), then Nixon (Republican), then Carter (Democrat), then Reagan (Republican) and now Messrs. Clinton and Gore (Countercultural).

But the real significance of the tragic childhood lies in its internal emotional dynamic, otherwise its "process," and above all in that particular process known to psychology as "dissociation." Greven defines it thus:

> Dissociation is one of the most basic means of survival for many children who learn early in life to distance themselves, or parts of themselves, from experiences too painful or frightening to bear . . . , children often discover ways to survive their pain through disconnecting and splitting, in the most extreme cases creating alternate selves and personalities, which bear and express feelings which otherwise would be overwhelming in a small child.

Indeed, there can be as many as sixteen personalities, as with the daughter of one apocalyptic fundamentalist—but that's exceptional. More typically, dissociation can, for instance, involve an attempt to deny a loathed parent's paternity (perhaps replacing that parent with splendiferous if imaginary "substitutes"—one theory behind Adolf Hitler's "discovery" that he was "divine"). Or it can lead to a history of hallucinations, including "shadowy figures, persecutory voices, and inner helper voices"—as the American psychiatric worker Ellenson reported after studying forty female incest survivors aged sixteen to fifty years and finding that *all* suffered problems with perception, including certain types of illusions and visual and auditory hallucination. Various Charismatic "events" may come under the same category, as Greven explains:

> The ability to speak in tongues, characteristic of Pente-costalism, is rooted in dissociative states of mind. The extraordinary scenes described in Helen Koolman Hosier's *Kathryn Kuhlman: The Life She Led, The Legacy She Left* . . . fit the depictions of dissociative states by others. Given the childhood encounters with her mother's whipping, Kuhlman's ability to disconnect and disembody herself when preaching ought not to be overly surprising. Other biographies and autobiographies of Pentecostals reflect similar dissociative experiences and states in the context of their religious worship and lives.
>
> Robert Anderson's cogent description of Charismatic and Pentecostal worship notes that "belief in spirit possession often leads to altered states of consciousness that produce unusual psychological and physical effects. Since these effects are dissociated from full consciousness, they are perceived as coming from some external, supernatural force." He also observes that "many experienced tongue speakers are able to enter a state of dissociation with such little effort that neither

they nor others are aware of the change. Yet the underlying alteration of consciousness is normally there, as it is in the case of all automatic behavior."

As is also, one might add, that most critical dissociative process of all, the collapse of any integrated sense of self. Because while it is scarcely necessary to develop quite sixteen personalities for the full effect, nevertheless, the fundamental, primal split—between, as one might put it, "good" self and "bad" self, or, more precisely, "felt" self and "compensatory" self—lies at the heart of Charisma.

The American psychiatrist, Walter C. Langer, in his analysis of the charisma of Adolf Hitler, shows the power that such duality may bestow:

> As one surveys Hitler's behavior patterns, as his close associates observe them, one gets the impression that this is not a single personality, but two that inhabit the same body and alternate back and forth. The one is a very soft, sentimental, and indecisive individual who has very little drive and wants nothing so much as to be amused, liked, and looked after. The other is just the opposite—a hard, cruel, and decisive person with considerable energy —who seems to know what he wants and is ready to go after it and get it regardless of cost. It is the first Hitler who weeps profusely at the death of his canary and the second Hitler who cries in open court: "Heads will roll." It is the first Hitler who cannot bring himself to discharge an assistant, and it is the second Hitler who can order the murder of hundreds, including his best friends, and can say with great conviction: "There will be no peace in the land until a body hangs from every lamp-post." It is the first Hitler who spends his evenings watching movies or going to cabarets, and it is the second Hitler who works for days

on end with little or no sleep, making plans that will affect
the destiny of nations.

Two people, in fact, in one body: "Hitler," as Heiden put it, and
"The Führer"; vacillating, depressive Hitler, and the euphoric
Führer. Now, apply such a psychology to that most critical
Charismatic moment, the mood-transforming oration. Langer:

> At the beginning as previously mentioned [Hitler] is nervous
> and insecure on the platform. At times he has considerable
> difficulty in finding anything to say. This is "Hitler." But
> under these circumstances the "Hitler" personality does not
> usually predominate for any length of time. As soon as he gets
> the feel of the audience the tempo of the speech increases,
> and the "Führer" personality begins to assert itself. Heiden
> says: "The stream of speech stiffens him like a stream of
> water stiffens a hose." As he speaks he hypnotizes himself
> into believing he is actually and fundamentally the "Führer"
> or, as Rauschning says: "He doses himself with the morphine
> of his own verbiage." It is this transformation of the little
> Hitler into the great Führer, taking place before the eyes of
> his audience, that probably fascinates them. By complicated
> psychological processes they are able to identify themselves
> with him, and as the speech progresses they themselves are
> temporarily transformed and inspired.

At such a moment the feedback for the speaker can be overwhelming: as the ex-Evangelical preacher and one-time Billy Graham
associate Charles Templeton puts it:

> You begin really preaching to yourself, and then this interplay
> starts with the audience, they begin responding to your every
> tone, your every movement, your every breath. It becomes like
> all these people—thirty thousand people—they are amplifying

everything you're feeling, everything you're saying, they are amplifying you. You become magnified to the size of all that huge crowd—thirty thousand people, and *they have become an extension, an enlargement of you.*

This is terrific from the speaker's point of view, because that superman sensation, so needed by the weak end of the character continuum, gets overwhelming affirmation from the crowd. And it's terrific, simultaneously, from the crowd's point of view, because, identifying totally with the speaker's emotional transformation up there on the stage, they go spiralling upwards on that very same depression-exhilaration continuum which is so giddily transmogrifying their leader.

So it is clear why no ordinary psychology will do for the full Charismatic range—most obviously, perhaps, among the followers, but just as emphatically among the leadership, too. Because to take the audience on this journey the leader must travel a journey also—and no such journey is possible unless the polarity is there, the sheer drama-filled distance between the depressive-euphoric extremes.

I stumbled across a curious secular instance of this process while reading a newspaper letters page in the early Eighties. A middle-aged housewife had written in to say how much she had enjoyed the recent final of the World Snooker Championships. The finalist had been Alex Higgins, rogue and maverick Northern Irishman. Suffice it to say that Higgins has won international fame for his wild, depressive, even suicidal behavior, and that his lifestyle is reflected in the dualism of his play: constantly getting himself into desperate scrapes; constantly coming back, brilliantly, from impossible situations. The final had been no exception. Indeed it had been THE example, in Higgins' career, of desperate crisis, followed by breathtakingly exciting recovery.

Most interesting, in this context, was the woman's comment.

She had identified so closely with the graph of Higgins' recovery, had found it so thrilling, so exhilarating, so magnetic, indeed, that it had cured her, she said, of her own, long-standing clinical depression.

11

The Left and Right of It

Given the multiplicity of connections between the psychology and practice of Christian revivalism and broader social, cultural and scientific trends, it is hard not to wonder whether some evolution in our most basic forms of thought is also taking place.

Consider that swarm of new scientific strands which were gathered together during the Eighties under the catch-all title of "chaos theory." The notion "that a butterfly stirring the air today in Peking can transform storm systems next month in New York" is, for instance, redolent of the kind of interdependence that both McLuhan and Bucke characterized as religious. Or consider the self-similarity of nature revealed, in mathematical form, in those extraordinary New Age graphs, the "Mandelbrot sets": here, the micro and the macro are indistinguishable, and Blake's "To see the world in a grain of sand" is made manifest.

This is quantum territory again, but with a moral dimension. For if, as philosopher of science Danah Zohar puts it, the boundaries between you and me, like all quantum boundaries, are indistinguishable and it is no longer clear where you or I or the world stops or starts, then it becomes very much easier to love one's neighbor as oneself. A neighbor who, in the new world view, effectively *is* oneself, and everything else, come to that.

Yet even this idea, suffused with post-Newtonian spirit as it is, seems less radical than the new thinking about the functioning of the brain itself: the discoveries in "hemisphericity" which have been gathering pace, year on year, ever since the mold-breaking Sperry experiments of the Sixties. Not only is every aspect of post-industrial culture shot through with the mental atmosphere of this grand new hero of neuroscience—the gestalt, interconnecting "right hemisphere"; and not only is Western culture's fabled left-hemisphere dominance in ever-steepening decline; but it is beginning to look as if this reconnection with pre-industrial mental processes and our rediscovery of the supernatural might be one and the same thing.

Given that, according to neuroscience, uncertainty stimulates the right hemisphere of the brain, the relevance of this particular field of research seems clear. So, what part has the West's new relationship with what Huxley called the "Mind at Large" played in the religious revival?

Neuroscience has made unprecedented strides in the last thirty years, just precisely the period, in fact, in which both the "counter-culture" and "Charisma" have also boomed. Little surprise, then, that Dr. Peter Fenwick, neuropsychiatrist at London's Maudsley Hospital, and Britain's leading authority on the neurology of religious experience, now finds himself in ever-escalating media demand. Yet when you meet him, Dr. Fenwick seems to have stepped straight out of the nineteenth century: he would have made a very acceptable Oxford don around 1860, say, somewhat in the Lewis Carroll mode; or, alternatively, a highly plausible bishop. The good doctor's voice has a distinctly ecclesiastical twang, especially when speaking in public. And he has a donnish difficulty with things like door keys: when I visited him at the Maudsley there was a moment's crisis before we finally made it into his office. Nevertheless, when it comes to the relationship between religious experience and hemisphericity, his authority is plain.

Hemisphericity became a hot issue in the late Sixties, when

Joseph Bogen, Roger Sperry and Robert Ornstein published the work which showed that the human brain not only consists of two quite distinct (right and left) hemispheres, but that each can, as demonstrated by experiment, operate quite independently of each other: that each of us has, in effect, two brains. Subject to various caveats, each hemisphere has specializations, the most notable, perhaps, being speech in the "left hemisphere" and visuo-spatial calculation in the right. This discovery was followed by a veritable Niagara of further studies into the specialization process and, by the Eighties, it all looked very interesting indeed.

It emerged that the two hemispheres had quite distinct mental cultures: two emotional and intellectual worlds. Logic? Left brain. Intuition? Right brain. Step-by-step solutions? Left brain. At-a-flash inspiration? Right brain. Knowledge (or, as the Americans have it, "cognition")? Left brain. Wisdom (or, as the Americans have it, "experience")? Right brain. Masculinity (a bit dodgy this one, but very popular with the public)? Left brain. Femininity? Right brain.

Most fundamentally of all, these discoveries seemed to offer a neuroscientific basis for all those broader dualisms which every age, one way or another, has identified: science (left), art (right); Classical (left), Romantic (right); yang (left), yin (right); "square" (left), "hip" (right); Apollonian (left), Dionysian (right); Confucian (left), Taoist (right); a thinker like Comte (left), a thinker like Heraclitus (right). You could go on forever, but let us just add one particularly relevant dualism here: just as plausible as science (left), art (right) is science (left), mysticism (right). "The essential point," says Fenwick, with the cadence one feels he might have employed at Evensong in Salisbury Cathedral in 1861, "is that there is a very specific focus within the brain, from which this experience arises. Let me put it this way: God has no hiding place in the brain!" Fenwick is well versed in summarizing all this for lay audiences, since he lectures quite regularly to the neuroscientifically unwashed—a good example of his style was an open lecture to the Oxford Alister Hardy Research Centre religious studies group in 1992.

What, he asked, are the qualities of mystical experience, and how can we locate them in the brain? For a start, he made reference to the constantly reported "ineffable" quality of such experiences (ineffable means "beyond words," and language, of course, locates in the left hemisphere). "Now," declared Fenwick, "you can argue that if you don't have words for it, it's not within—or does not have easy access to—your lexicon. So you've got to argue then that it's probably within another part of the brain, and it's probably going to be right hemisphere rather than left." Next, there is the subjects' oft-reported sense that in a mystical experience they "break down boundaries," become part of everything, while everything becomes part of them. What does that imply?

"Loss of boundaries, or loss of categories of things, me, you, tree, bird, that sort of thing . . . underpinning feelings of special unity and oneness . . . this is an emphasizing of spatial maps . . . We're breaking down categorical boundaries, and we're looking at the thing as a whole spatially, and that's much more a right hemisphere function than it is a left hemisphere function. For example, if I was to destroy your right parietal area, you would not be able to find your way out of this building. You'd lose your spatial maps completely. Obviously then—" in the causation of such experiences—"there is a distortion and a change in those very structures.

"Now, let's look at time—that's very important. You know the prophet's drop of water as it falls from the jar to the desert floor, he sees the 'whole of creation' during that time —it's an enormous expansion, and these experiences usually have a distortion or a change in time." That is, they are not in the "ordinary, everyday time" that we live in now. "Now, disorientations of time, and misordering of events in time is all right-sided, mainly right-temporal . . . so your integration of time, your time sense, is in the right hemisphere. And if you have a lesion there you won't be able to tell me what has gone before and what has come after. . . . Both speeding up and slowing down of subjective time—how we feel time flows, obviously—is found in patients with right temporal lobe epilepsy . . . [epilepsy being a] . . . cerebral discharge, which flows through a particular area of brain. Now this is terribly important, because it's nature's natural experiment. . . . [If] you get these discharges flowing through the brain, it disorganizes it. So we know *precisely* where that area is. If we can see where the discharge flows we *know* what those structures —what the function of those structures—is.

"Now, if it flows through the right temporal lobe, then you get changes in subjective time—it can speed up, or it can stop. The prophet who saw the whole of creation as the drop flowed to the ground would have had his time sense in some way altered. Okay, so that is pointing us to right temporal. . . . You see I'm getting a very heavy right bias."

Indeed he was—and continued to do so, because the number of right brain-mysticism correlations turns out to be legion. There's color for instance. Remember Huxley's vision of "stripes of a deep but glowing indigo alternated with stripes of an incandescence so intensely bright that it was hard to believe that they could be made of anything but blue fire"? Fenwick points out that studies show the right hemisphere not only sees far more variety of color than the left but, above all, sees it with intensity—sees it, you could say, with meaning.

Then there's music. A glorious, heightened sense of music, replete with singing angels, is typical of mystical experiences— and musicality (as opposed to mere ordering of notes, of which the left hemisphere is well capable) is situated in the right hemisphere. Inflict appropriate damage on the right hemisphere, in fact, and you may still be able to hear—even order—the notes, but they won't be music because the notes will have lost (to use typically right-hemispherical language) their value and meaning.

Meaning itself is a further example. People who have had mystic experiences, explains Fenwick, above all stress how such moments radiate this sense of significance, of "meaning": "And where is meaning generated? The application of certainty and familiarity to what is going on around us takes place in one part of the brain —guess where, the right temporal lobe. And how do we know this? Because in patients who have epilepsy they will tell you that suddenly a particular set of experiences has absolute meaning for them—not only that, but they will tell you the whole thing's happened before and they know what's going to happen. . . . And that's in the right temporal lobe. Meaning—the attribution of meaning—is in exactly that same area of the brain."

There is one other quality which Fenwick isolates as typical of the mystical experience: what he calls "paradoxicality." For while one of the deepest feelings in mysticism is a sense of oneness with the universe, nevertheless, at that very moment when "you are at one with the universe . . . you'll hear a bird sing . . . [and suddenly] you will *be* the bird." Or, putting it another way, such visions are characterized by the conjunction of opposites.

We are back in the quantum universe again—a set of perspectives which looks increasingly right-hemispherical. But there is another and most paradoxical belief system hovering around in the background—namely that of Jesus.

It was John Stuart Mill who pointed out that if it's straight answers you want, you must go to the Old Testament, you will never get them in the New. Because it was Jesus who told us that it is those most materially blessed who are furthest from Heaven; and those most reviled who'll be most eternally blessed; and, most paradoxically and Romantically of all, "he that findeth his life shall lose it; and he that loseth his life for my sake shall find it."

Indeed, you could do another of those hemispherical dualisms, quite plausibly, opposing Old Testament (left) and New Testament (right): think of the Ten Commandments, rock-logical, adamantine, numbered and orderly; or the marvellous opacity of the Parable of the Talents, or the over-the-boundaries thinking of the Good Samaritan.

Small wonder indeed, that such right-brain-rooted phenomena as quantum philosophy, "postindustrialism," and the current religious revival (with its focus, above all, on Jesus) should find a natural historical symbiosis together. And small wonder, either, that it isn't just Peter Fenwick who's been getting in on the academic act. For while Fenwick concentrates on the right-hemispherical culture of mysticism, others have noticed a "left brain" religiosity also.

The Catholic theologian Pierre Babin (a man much influenced, incidentally, by his friend Marshall McLuhan) argues in his 1991 *The New Era in Religious Communication*:

> The symbolic and catechetical ways . . . are dialectical ways of entering the one truth. They are two complementary languages, expressing the one and same Jesus. They correspond to the two hemispheres of the brain . . .
>
> Until the sixteenth century, catechesis functioned essentially in "mono 1," with the right-brain hemisphere predominating. Since Gutenberg and the Council of Trent, it has functioned essentially in "mono 2," with the left-brain hemisphere predominating . . .
>
> It would not be wrong to say that printing [which McLuhan regarded, of course, as the "trigger" of our Western, left-hemispherical dominance] gradually led to the emphasis being placed, initially by church leaders and official teachers, on precise concepts and strict definitions, formulas of great uniformity, and logical systems and ideologies of vast dimensions, all of which were seen from a single vantage point.
>
> Slowly but surely, rational analysis, the practice of making logical distinctions and connections, and the cult of obedience to formulas and to canon law became more

important than feeling oneself at one with the church or taking an active part in the liturgy.

Meanwhile others have looked for a left-hemispherical basis for what began as Puritanism ("rational" religion), evolved into science ("rational" study of nature), and developed thence into industrialism ("rational" production). As Matthew Fox puts it in *Original Blessing*:

> The Enlightenment—the en-light-en-ment—has rendered all of us who live in Western Civilization citizens of the light. And of lights. Questers after left-brain—which is light orientated—satisfaction. The invention of the light bulb and electricity and neon lights and handy light switches was a marvellous outgrowth of the Enlightenment's technological achievements. . . . Religion too has become very light oriented in the West. The Religion of Positivism is almost all light.

In brief, just as there is a right-hemispherical religious culture (connection, paradox, tactility, color, belief in "instant" [miraculous] solutions rather than step-by-step strategies, and so on), so there is, evidently, a whole left-hemispherical religious world view too: and it can most economically be summed up by reference to those heroic pioneers of rationalist religiosity, the Anglo-Saxon Puritans.

The prime quality in *this* mental culture has to do with division, fragmentation, schism. Whereas the keyword with Charismatics is that right-hemispherical sense of dissolving boundaries, of "connection," the Puritan keynote is evoked by the word "separate." Indeed, as early as 1572 Whitgift (quoted by cultural historian Patrick Cruttwell) characterized Puritans thus: "They think themselves to be mundiores ceteris, more pure than others . . . and *separate* [my italics] themselves from all other churches and congregations, as spotted and defiled." Cruttwell further observes:

> The Puritan mind, for example, was not only not averse from the multiplication of sects; it welcomed it, as Milton does in *Areopagitica,* for evidence of spiritual liveliness, proof of the enlightenment to come. . . . This particular habit was but a symptom of the general Puritan bent for dividing: religious from secular, church from state, Sundays from weekdays, levity from seriousness.

The more one considers such notions, the less they sound like moral positions, the more like neurological states. Certainly such perceptual styles transcend religiosity, as evidenced by the love of secular sects (or career "specializations') evinced two hundred years after Whitgift by that prime advocate of that other, secular Enlightenment, the left-hemispherical hero Adam Smith, in his *Wealth of Nations.* Smith even advocated that thought itself should be a specialization—best left to intellectuals.

Step-by-step rather than all-at-once, sectarian rather than "One Church," specialist rather than generalist: here is the authentic mental atmosphere of Puritanism—and the authentic flavor, too, of the left hemisphere. Levy-Agresti summed up a wealth of neuroscientific experiment thus: "The data indicate that the mute, minor [right] hemisphere is specialized for gestalt perception, being primarily a synthesist in dealing with information input. The speaking, major [left] hemisphere, in contrast, seems to operate in a more logical, analytic, computerlike fashion."

Method (Methodism), numeracy (those Ten Commandments —Sperry found the right hemisphere had little aptitude for such skills, being unable, for instance, to calculate "even to the extent of doubling the numbers 1–4"), "under-standing" (standing separate from rather than entering into a belief system): these are the words associated with Puritanism. To use Schoenfeld and Mestrovic's phraseology, this is "instrumental-masculine" rather than "expressive-feminine": for while the simple left-right hemispherical divide based on gender doesn't work, neuroscience has found readier interplay between the hemispheres—or "reduced laterality"—among women.

(A classic indicator, incidentally, of modern neo-Puritan America's left-hemispherical dominance is the constant use, in conversation, of the word "understand"—most strikingly where Europeans would use "feel." But then, as Robert J. Trotter indicated, linguistic studies show that the holistic-intuitive Inuit language of Northern Canada and the abstract-deductive American argot occupy opposite poles of the emotional continuum. For a crash course in North American usage of "understand," try "The Oprah Winfrey Show.")

The Puritan aversion to color—black clothes, whitewashed interiors of seventeenth-century churches—is also significant, and indicative of a visual sense which is insensitive to shades, to go with the intolerance of moral or religious ambiguity. Above all, the eternal love affair with text, as opposed to images—the sermon elevated over the wall painting or icon—is classically left hemispherical, and the very opposite of the distaste for "labels" of, for instance, the mescaline-drugged Huxley or the denomination-wary Marchers for Jesus.

The descendants of Puritanism—the modern Evangelicals— are beginning to sound distinctly left hemispherical, as opposed to the Aquarian, right-brain outpourings of Charisma.

Another, broader emotional quality has been attached to the hemispheres—a quality which is highly suggestive in this context. The distinguished American neurologist Marcel Kinsbourne argued, in a 1981 article "Sad Hemisphere, Happy Hemisphere" that the hemispheres differ, also, in their mood. He suggests that:

If the left hemisphere is damaged, leaving the right half in charge, a patient is likely to show a generally gloomy outlook on life, with seemingly unjustified feelings of anger, guilt and despair. . . . When the right half is excluded from control of behavior—by injury, surgery or an epileptic attack—a patient is likely to be cheerful, even elated, and surprisingly indifferent to this abnormal state. . . .

Neuropsychologists in several countries have found evidence that the right hemisphere is involved in negative feelings and their expression, while the left is associated with positive feelings and their expression . . .

The fundamental decision any motile organism must make with respect to a point of reference is to approach it or withdraw. (Fight or fly.) Approach—a left-hemisphere speciality—is positive and direct, indifferent to what is around it. Withdrawal—a function of the right hemisphere —is concerned with the overall picture, how situations and conditions relate to one another.

As Californian professor of psychiatry James P. Henry sums up: "One hemisphere evaluates the pros and the other the cons." Positivism, the grand number-cruncher, is clearly *the* left-hemispherical philosophy. And with the Power of Positive Thinking behind them, it is no wonder those busy, methodical left-hemispherical Puritans and their secular Anglo-American descendants have been so can-do, constructive-minded! Predictably, Cruttwell identified "optimism" as a key Puritan trait, while "melancholy" was characteristic of the holistic, poetic early-seventeenth-century Anglo-Catholics. One thinks, too, of melancholy, Romantic art: Keatsian sadness, Byronic despair.

So that the description of the right-hemispherical religious process of contemplation as "going into retreat" also makes sense (the *Via Negativa,* as theology phrases it—as opposed to the *Via Positiva*). The image is of letting go rather than getting on: as Taoism, that most right-hemispherical of all philosophies, puts it:

He who pursues learning will increase every day;
He who pursues Tao will decrease every day.

The application of all this to the current revival—above all to the movement's Charismatic wing—is plain. Charisma's instinctive, antispecialist need to cross over boundaries and its sense of the union of opposites are both right-hemispherical in flavor. But then in this respect, as in so many others, the social language of the revival is at one with society's broader trends.

Take that right-brain, pattern-recognition capacity: the business "logo" most surely is a pattern before it's a word, while the grand debate in Western schools over reading methods, for instance, is an argument over whether you learn to read step by step, left hemispherically, or by pattern-recognition (word shape). Studies in Japan have compared subjects' strategies using the *Kana* writing system—which is sound-based, step by step, a kind of alphabet—with those used to decode the *Kanji* writing system—which is meaning based, "all-at-once." Results showed that subjects showed a significant right field = left-hemispherical superiority using *Kana*. Then there's that new-found enthusiasm for creativity in business, which, in effect, is enthusiasm for a right-hemispherical approach.

Fenwick described a patient who lost her ability to paint creatively when she suffered migrainous spasms in the arteries that supplied her right hemisphere. Then there's the right-hemispherical feel for color as opposed to the black and white asceticism of the left: it has been thirty years since the so-called color revolution transformed Western cities in the countercultural Sixties; that process went into marked reverse in the black-loving Eighties, but now it's come bursting through again—one of the "Baby-Busters" ' most notable characteristics, declare the marketing men, is their love of "color." Yuppies themselves, for all their number-crunching, have been described, suggestively, as "the triumph of form over content." Well, form is right-brain, content left (more Braun than brain, these yuppies). And as for a high-Eighties TV series like "Miami Vice," all sound and images, no storyline at all—here was wrap-round, wall-to-wall, right-hemispherical TV.

If it is true that Western "laterality" is fundamentally changing, and if we are, as a society, becoming just a bit less dominated by our left hemispheres, then would it not at least seem possible that this might facilitate just those mystical experiences (let alone any other forms of religious perception) that are so critical to Evangelical/Charismatic conversion?

The notion of some genuine change in our communal laterality —change happening right here, today, in the West, not in some learnedly pored-over seventeenth century—does seem hard to take. A Christian might accommodate it all by saying God had changed consciousness to facilitate religious revival. Or a Green might argue that it represented plain self-preservation on the part of poor old Gaia: program in some gestalt, species-preservative thinking quick, before final environmental catastrophe! Nevertheless, any objective enquirer must ask for evidence.

There are obvious problems with mass measurement—charming though the notion of EEG equipment situated on every citizen's head undoubtedly is. However, it has long been possible to measure individual, if not mass, hemispherical change.

There are, for instance, the experiments Robert Ornstein describes in which subjects first arranged separate blocks to match a pattern (spatial calculation), and then wrote a letter (step-by-step linearity), both under EEG. The results showed right-hemisphere dominance while manipulating the squares; the opposite while writing. So the dominance changed. Gott et al. (in 1984) described a businesswoman whose left-hemisphere was dominant when she carried on her business life, holding meetings and making decisions, but whose right hemisphere held sway when she indulged her passion for gardening, or "got turned on by an intimate friend."

But perhaps the most remarkable examples of such tests—and the one most specific to religious experience—were those carried out by Peter Fenwick on a Zen master in London. Peter Fenwick takes up the story:

"I found somebody who has got the authentic stamp of being a Zen master—so he's got a permanent change in awareness; and so the question was, was there a change in brain function?

"His IQ showed that he was not brain damaged in any way. His left memory was normal and his right memory was normal and his EEG was normal. The next thing we tried was to give him a strategy, see how he related to the world."

Fenwick indicates a set of charts: "You can show whether the right hemisphere is working predominantly or the left hemisphere is working predominantly. And if the left hemisphere is working predominantly the electrical change in the brain moves this graph above the line and if the right hemisphere is working predominantly it moves it below the line.

". . . Let's look at somebody whose left temporal lobe we've taken out . . . the whole graph collapses below the line. And that —one exactly like that—was the Zen master! There's nothing wrong with his brain, but when he brings a cognitive set to anything" (for instance, when he does any of Fenwick's tests) "his brain functions as if he had got no left temporal lobe. Fascinating. So he looks as if he's just using right-hemisphere strategies all the time. So," Fenwick sums up, "is that what this permanent change is, a changeover in the way, the cognitive way, that we see the world?"

There are many ways, not just the Way of Zen, in which we can move ourselves over to our mind-at-large. There's dancing. There's sound: baroque-musical concordances, studies have shown, reverberate in the right hemisphere, Schoenbergian dissonances in the left. There's the aromatherapy of incense, there's "tongues," there's prayer, there's drugs. And above all—

in the "strategy" rather than the "tactics" of personal psychology —there is the habitual dissociation which can be the result of a tragic childhood, with a loving God providing the instinctive "continuum" memory of the love any human being is programmed to expect—however abusive their actual experience.

In this context it is interesting that those hunter-gatherer Indians the anthropologist Jean Liedloff studied have familiar patterns of religious belief, despite childcare traditions of which Janov himself would have been proud. As Liedloff puts it:

> That we are so universally subject to a conviction that serenity has been lost by us, cannot be accounted for solely by the loss at an early age of our place in a continuum of appropriate treatment and surroundings. Even people like the relaxed and joyful Yequana, who have not been deprived of their expected experiences, have a mythology that includes a fall from grace and the notion that humanity lives outside that lost state. . . . From the continuum point of view, it would seem that in that enormously long period, running to hundreds of millions of years, before our ancestors developed an intellect able to reflect on these troublesome matters of morality and purpose, we did indeed live in the only blissful way: entirely in the present. . . .
>
> It is not hard to imagine that the eons of innocence have so impressed themselves upon our most longstanding expectations that there remains a feeling that the serenity that comes with innocence can somehow be had . . . it seems so near, yet so far; one can almost recall it.

It almost sounds, for Liedloff, as if that unworrying, unthinking, pre-left-hemispherical psychology is indeed our Kingdom of Heaven, once lived out in fleshly reality right here on Earth. And there are others, too, who see the right hemisphere as the royal road back to our long-lost spontaneity—not to mention those milliards-old aggregations of species-wisdom we call "instincts."

Just a year after the publication of Jean Liedloff's book, in 1976, the Princeton psychologist Julian Jaynes published his *The Origin of Consciousness in the Breakdown of the Bicameral Mind,* in which he argues that as recently as three thousand years ago human beings did not "think" at all: rather, they acted purely on the basis of "voices" from what today we call the unconscious, and that these voices represented the instinctive, deep-memory wisdom of the species—developed later, as our consciousness evolved, into our notions of "gods."

In particular, Jaynes suggests that these divine "voices" would announce courses of action when our ancestors were pondering tough decisions—or, as Jaynes suggestively puts it, when they were suffering "stress." When we finally evolved out of our capacity to make this direct, instinctive relationship with the wisdom of the dead, the relationship survived, in etiolated form, in our capacity to hear inward, admonitory "voices" at critical moments, to receive oracular commands or, alternatively, to regain such contacts via priestly intermediaries—who originally consisted of that portion of humanity still retaining capacities others had lost.

The seat of these voices, of these gods, is naturally in the right hemisphere, which is so rapidly moving from status of "minor" hemisphere to its new position as "mind at large." Jaynes's theories are, not unpredictably, widely challenged. Nevertheless, the real surprise is less the objections to such ideas, rather that they're now being taken seriously by quite mainstream commentators. As Sally Springer and Georg Deutsch put it in their sober and well received round-up of the latest hemisphericity research, *Left Brain, Right Brain*: "Although there is considerable controversy surrounding Jaynes's theory, the idea of connecting the voices of Gods in ancient times to a stage in the cultural development of language is fascinating."

You can see how both Jaynes and Liedloff are themselves part of the same late-twentieth-century "continuum" (Liedloff's title, indeed, is *The Continuum Concept*)—part of an evolution of ideas which has left the Lockian *tabula rasa,* clean-slate-at-birth mind behind in favor of connection, in this case, way back across the generations to the consciousness of human beings thousands of years dead. This is within a whisper of an overtly religious idea, and it is no wonder these books have made a stir in today's ever more supernaturally conscious climate.

Julian Jaynes, incidentally, like so many today, has had his own paranormal experience. When in his late twenties, there was a time when he was living alone and was under stress. He writes in *The Origin of Consciousness*:

> I had for about a week been studying and autistically pondering some of the problems in this book, particularly the question of what knowledge is and how we can know anything at all. My convictions and misgivings had been circling about through the sometimes precious fogs of epistemologies, finding nowhere to land. One afternoon I lay down in intellectual despair on a couch. Suddenly, out of an absolute quiet, there came a firm, distinct loud voice from my upper right which said, "Include the knower in the known!" It lugged me to my feet absurdly exclaiming "Hello?" looking for whoever was in the room. The voice had an exact location. No one was there! Not even behind the wall where I sheepishly looked.

While acknowledging that this could have been his own experience of the very phenomenon he writes about, Jaynes is nevertheless dismissive of the content of his vision, describing it as a "nebulous profundity."

Nebulous profundity? Isn't Jaynes being a bit self-critical here? "Include the knower in the known!" What succincter expression of modern thinking could be asked for? Interconnection, the measured and the measurer entwined . . . it says it all, really, in just six words.

Why, the man's had the world's first quantum vision!

One day in January 1993 I was leafing through a back number of *Numinus*, the journal put out by the Alister Hardy Centre in Oxford (which collects and analyzes case histories of religious experience). In a footnote to a report on a lecture about religion and neuroscience given by none other than the "neurophysiologist" Peter Fenwick, I read this:

> Members who heard Dr. Peter Fenwick's lecture to the London group last June will be interested in a report from Canada that scientist Michael Persinger of Laurentian University has invented a helmet that he claims induces mystical experiences by stimulating the temporal lobe with magnetic forces. After a few sessions under the helmet many of Persinger's subjects found that the presence of a cross or background music could send them into a mystical state. Persinger states that all human brains can be found on a scale going from the most sensitive temporal lobes to the least, and people who are "temporal lobe sensitives" are most likely to have mystical experiences as well as epileptic seizures. He claims that his theory still holds good if the supernatural exists, since there must be a physical mechanism for the transmission of supernatural experiences.

It emerged that Michael Persinger was indeed performing such experiments. They involved entering a sound-proofed chamber and putting on something like a motorcycle helmet with electrodes, and having electric charges targeted to specific areas of the brain, with the results described. One subject, indeed, reckoned he'd seen God; another ran out of the chamber declaring it should be exorcised because the Devil was in there.

So anyone ought to be able to have a mystical experience, courtesy of Dr. Persinger, at the flip of a switch. And as mystical experience was the starting point of so many of my conversionary case histories, I felt duty bound to try the equipment myself. So I called Persinger and asked him whether he would like to tell me about his work, and even give me a ride on his machine. Sure, he said, but had I considered how this might go down with my Evangelicals? He had himself, apparently, had a bunch demonstrating outside his office at Laurentian University—they'd claimed that both he and his equipment were demonic.

Nevertheless, we fixed a date.

12

God in the Brain

So, to the frozen north. It's been observed, of medieval pilgrimages to shrines, that the journey itself was quite as crucial to the experience as anything discovered at the end of it. So it occurred to me—en route to my very own mystic experience in Sudbury, site of Laurentian University—that maybe I should see my own pilgrimage like that. The reflection was most especially insistent around the eighteenth hour of the journey north through Canada—I'd cleverly fixed to do the last leg by train, the object being to view a little of the country-side en route, not realizing, however, how I might feel around hour seven of the ride, on top of the earlier flight to Toronto.

So, onward through the glacial darkness, onward goes the pilgrim band . . . lake, forest, lake, forest, hill, forest, forest, lake, all sliding, slithering, clanking past at a tantalizing, better-safe-than-sorry, wintery twenty miles per hour, the entire doomscape hushed and silent under the ice. The smart money is flying up these days, it must be said, in under the hour.

As for Sudbury, the (unlikely) Mecca in this instance—well, suffice it to say it's one of those places even the locals are wry about. The architecture of Sudbury is quite devastatingly common-sensical; and the other striking things about the place are the all-pervasive slag heaps, legacies of the city's copper-mining industry, which give the landscape its distinctively gaunt, view-from-a-spacecraft appearance.

Indeed, the word is out locally, in that wry Sudbury way, that they trained the NASA moonshot pilots up here, the better to give them the feel of their destination.

So that's Sudbury, of which this much could be said that gruesome March evening as I cabbed in to the Pied Piper Inn —almost anything looks better under three feet of snow.

As indeed it does under a brilliant blue morning sky, the sun leaping off the snowdrifts. I took a taxi out to Laurentian University and, there in the bowels of Laurentian's Sixties brutalist campus, met Dr. Persinger himself: surprisingly suburban, striped-suited, formal, with a superbly hawk-like scientist's profile.

Without more ado, we kicked off with a quick tour of what Persinger and his staff, a touch discouragingly, call "the Dungeon": the acoustic chamber, plus surrounding school-of-Star-Trek equipment, in which his "subjects" are duly worked on and where, in the course of time, I would be too.

An approach along labyrinthine corridors, neo-Maginot-Line; a room about the size of a squash court with, at the center, a room within the room, like a workmen's hut—the acoustic chamber: serried ranks of dials, wires and computers against the chamber walls; and, inside, an armchair for the "subject," a red light on the wall, and two motorcycle helmets with yellow and black stripes, duly wired up.

"Yeah, this is where it all happens," said Michael, speaking in a regular, no-problems voice, such as might introduce the production line of, say, Nissan Sunderland. "What you have to understand—" he gestured—"is that first the computer gets the wave frequency right, then the pre-amps amplify the computer signal, then the commutator, via the interface, shifts it into the acoustic chamber and then the solenoids on the Koren helmet project the magnetic field into the subject's brain."

"I see."

"And as for the visions," continued Michael, "well, they're

context dependent, of course—I mean a Catholic, for instance, is more likely to see Mary, a Protestant will see Christ, an Islamic, of course, Allah. Although more typically it's less a 'vision' exactly, more a sense of 'presence'—a presence, nevertheless, usually understood by subjects as supernatural."

"Okay. And there are also, I gather, er, negative experiences?"

"Okay. A small percentage see demons, ghosts, and yes, there was one who said the chamber should be exorcised, we'd got the Devil in there. And, yes, we've had subjects, too, who've clamored to be let out."

"But this is rare."

"It's rare. Most subjects find the experience highly positive. Indeed they want to try it again. They want more!"

Which was encouraging indeed, given my intention to give the helmet a go myself. After all, "presences," "visions," the odd "ghost" even, I can cope with, but I draw the line at the Devil.

As we wandered back to the main lab, Persinger filled in some background.

Born in 1945—the counterculture generation premium year—his education was in the best over-the-boundaries, inter-disciplinary style. Along with neuroscience, he is interested in sociology and history, and he pursued graduate degrees in psychology, physiology and geophysics. After which, in appropriately think-locally, small-is-beautiful mode, he took a job in the provincial university of Sudbury specifically because, he says, he hoped to be able to get on quietly here with the kind of research some might find a little strange; also—an interesting coda, culturally—it might, in a relatively small university, be easier for him to "cross the disciplines."

His first research interests might seem even more surprising than what he is up to now. He wrote papers relating UFO sightings to stresses and strains in the earth (including so-called "earthquake lights"—those ghostly luminosities which can precede earthquakes, and which are emissions of electricity and other forces from the

Earth's crust as a result of tectonic strain). There was more: for given the capacity of electric charges to impact experientially on a subject's brain, was it not possible, reasoned Persinger, that these tectonic emissions could be responsible for events *inside* as well as outside the brain? Could experiences generally referred to, historically, as visions, be caused by Mother Nature, obliging with an appropriate electrical charge? More papers followed, and more statistical correlations. So it was via this neuro-environmentalist route (it gets less esoteric as you think about it) that Persinger arrived, eventually, at his current experimental position: could not he do Mother Nature's work for her, employing machinery, rather than earthquakes, to induce visions right here in the lab?

By the early Eighties, the experiments with the helmet had begun. As Persinger put it, with rather breathtaking academic restraint, "By stimulating lobes with our helmet, we achieved a widening and deepening effect. After several sessions it took little to trigger the mystical state of mind."

We swung into Laurentian's main neuroscience laboratory— little bigger than a railway station waiting room—the place that Persinger and his twenty-odd graduate students call home. There is a blackboard with recent hieroglyphics; also cupboards; also labels, marked suggestively: "Rat Brain Slides," "Surgical Instruments," "Sliced Human Brain."

"Of course, you understand that the helmet is just the technology," said Persinger. "The real thing, of course, is the theory and that took *years* to put together."

Persinger duly took me on a Cook's tour of his neuroscientific theories; and, predictably, our starting place was hemisphericity.

"You could sum up my position like this," he said: "Put an individual, or a group—or a culture—in a situation in which the structure in their environment is being decayed away—in conditions, above all, of *uncertainty*—and their right-hemispherical activity, the seat of enhanced vigilance, or anxiety, goes up.

"So that a subject, say, suffers intolerable stress, pain, or, indeed, child abuse. Now, the left hemisphere, as well as being the seat of language, is also the seat of self; and one brain strategy, under intolerable pressure, is for the sense of self, in a kind of psychic failsafe, to close down. Otherwise known as dissociation. When this happens, the right hemisphere effectively takes over; and right-hemispherical experience—visions, dreams, hallucinations—come rushing through."

Persinger's theory further postulates a right-hemispherical equivalent of the left-hemispherical sense of self—and it is this right-hemispherical sense of presence, intruding into left-hemispherical consciousness as described, which is perceived by the subject as a "visitor." "Because our left-hemispherical, daylight consciousness never entirely closes down," said Persinger. "Maybe diminished is a better word than closed. Of course, what you may also notice," he added, "we certainly did, is that this is just what Julian Jaynes was saying, in his *The Origin of Consciousness in the Breakdown of the Bicameral Mind* all those years ago."

So far, Persinger would seem to have quite a lot in common with the English neuroscientist Peter Fenwick; but at this stage, they part company. "Because the result of repeated right-hemispherical invasions of this kind is, paradoxically, to kick-start new activity in the left. And as the left hemisphere has this culture of optimism," (as opposed to that right-hemispherical culture of negativity, or "retreat") "the next thing the subject understands is this great surge of optimism, joy. All fearful, right-hemispherical affect falls away, confidence comes flooding in and, if the conversionary process goes far enough, other left-hemispherical processes cut in too —an *enhanced*, rather than fragmented, sense of self, including self-esteem, a pressing need to structure all these brave new feelings into a system, otherwise moral code, a determination to make sure everyone else feels just exactly the same way too. In a word, if the process goes far enough—" Persinger smiled,—"We have what is generally called religious bigotry."

Added to which, there is the neuroscientific angle on depression. "What we also found," said Persinger, "was that people, typically, in mild to moderate depression end up in religious conversions. More, these periods of repeated depression were in many respects similar to what neuroscience calls "kindling" episodes, so there would be a depression and then a recovery, a depression and a recovery, and after a few of these, bang, you get the left-hemispheric stimulation and the religious conversion. It's not an accident that religious conversion often follows a period of serious depression."

Persinger stressed that it doesn't have to be disaster, or pain, or abuse that activates the right hemisphere. It can, of course, quite simply be a direct electrical charge—hence his helmet. Moreover, the subject doesn't have to be psychotic or in any other way especially susceptible. "Because what research has also shown is that we are all on a continuum of susceptibility; and high emotionality —something quite different from, say, psychosis, so long associated with vision-seeing—is related to just the kind of temporal lobe sensitivity that makes people liable to mystical experiences."

High emotionality? "Yes, people like the more sensitive among my students, for instance, five hundred of whom we tested for just this, and who are, also, just the kind of ordinary people we like to test on the equipment."

Ordinary people? Ordinary people are susceptible to visions?

"Oh yes," said Michael. "People just like you and me."

It must be said that it's hard to imagine a human being on this planet less likely to go cosmic than Michael Persinger. For all that gestalt quality that informs his research, his thought processes, his very manner indeed, seem utterly left-hemispherical. Not only does he work all hours God sends (including Sundays, complains his wife), not only does he use the word "understand" nicely, in all those inappropriate-to-a-European contexts, but his time management is segmented in the extreme, even by the high standards of North America. One of the more heroic moments came when he offered me one twenty-minute slot just after one lecture, just before another: "We could talk from two-ten to two-thirty," he said, and meant it. And did it.

So in a way, with Michael too, you saw the familiar leitmotif —twin poles of logic and instinctiveness jammed together in yet another late-twentieth-century union of opposites: the manner pure Classicism, the subject matter rollercoaster Romance.

Once we got to the actual workings of his machinery, we were plumb square in the left hemisphere again.

"Okay. So why the helmet? Well, what we do is target very low doses of electricity—the field our equipment throws is less than a hairdryer or a word processor—to highly specific parts of the brain. And for that to work out we must ensure the field is absolutely accurately targeted and, therefore, that the equipment sits absolutely steadily on the head. That's the sole reason for the helmet. Indeed, we could have built something more overtly scientific ourselves, but our budget's small, and it does the job, so we use it."

Which is also why Persinger's team uses strips of iron attached to the helmet, pointing in at the head—as the actual sources from which the current is transmitted: they too offer a means of precisely targeting the field. "Because we wanted to keep the field highly focussed rather than diffuse, because a focal field produces focal current and that's what produces effects."

So, iron strips, a motorbike helmet, that "commutator" he mentioned earlier, the solenoids, all maximizing the effect . . . And into the acoustic chamber we go, where all those confusing, extraneous sounds get screened out by the chamber walls. Confusing, extraneous sights are dealt with by yet another piece of North American pragmatism: ping-pong balls, one on each eye indeed, like some kind of monstrous eyeball. There's little a subject will see that could look much scarier than the subject . . .

So now, finally, neither sight nor sound will intrude on the neuroscientifc quietude inside the head. Switch on, and the electrical field goes into the brain's amygdala and hippocampus, which turns out to be Persinger's preferred target because "these are the most electrically labile parts of the brain, that's why seizures are often associated with them."

(All of which, Persinger stresses, perhaps a little surprisingly, is entirely safe. There's the smallness of the dose for a start, and a range of other precautions, including prior tests on animals.) Then, during a couple of sessions of twenty minutes or a half-hour each, the subject awaits the effects. Which are?

"Oh, I don't know, visions . . ." says Persinger, abstractedly. "Look, I know I sound blasé, but after the first couple of hundred experiences it gets a bit mundane. Okay, typically, as we have seen, people report a presence in the chamber—that's very frequent. Also 'bright' images. . . . One crucial quality is the expectancy created by the setting. In one study we had, in the background, the theme song from *Close Encounters of the Third Kind,* in another we had a cross hanging, slightly elevated, fifteen degrees to the left. Not surprisingly, the content reflected the setting. With the cross in particular, there were these death themes, religious experiences."

But perhaps the most remarkable phenomenon was the direct correlation Persinger's team found between visions and quite measurable brain "events."

"One time we were using a strobe and this individual saw Christ actually *in* the strobe—at the same time generating good old-fashioned temporal lobe spikes. Then there was the subject who, after a sharp spike in the right temporal region, saw this gnarled hand thrust into her left visual field. Now we know from monkey studies, and indirectly from human studies, that there are neurons that actually code for complex shapes like hands. The result? If some stimulus—in this case, our equipment—makes them fire spontaneously you're going to see, right there before you, the material the neurons are coded for—in her case, hands.

"Then there was this transcendental meditation teacher. In the last two minutes of a twenty-minute session, she experienced God in the laboratory, visiting her. And afterwards we looked at her

EEG, and there was this classic spike and slow-wave seizure over the temporal lobe at the time of the experience—the other parts of the brain were normal. We never told her, actually."

Because, of course, not everyone can cope with that kind of knowledge. "So before one goes blundering in there saying, "Okay guys, you've just had a routine electrical seizure", there's a certain clinical consideration to be accommodated. Even though you may suspect, as a scientist, that this is an electrical phenomenon similar to thousands of others, it doesn't change the fact that for the individual such an experience has been been awesome, tremendous, utterly without precedent. I mean, your God coming and sitting down next to you, that's a pretty freaky thing."

Persinger's work forms part of a series of experiments being done in neuroscience labs around the world, although few have taken them to quite such lengths.

Ronald Siegel, for instance, at UCLA's Neuropsychiatric Institute, has induced client hallucinations in his lab—he managed to evoke a Black Hole for one subject. Like Persinger, he uses a dark, soundproof laboratory chamber: extras include a photo-stimulator that flashes bright, pulsating lights.

Then there's the Munroe Institute, where they've developed a tape that induces coherent sounds in both ears, thus facilitating "hemispherical coherence": result, sensed presences and out-of-body experiences.

Or consider the work of neurophysicist Barry Beyerstein: his favorite hallucination, he says, was that of the patient who saw "a troupe of squirrels marching along wearing army helmets singing in unison." Or the new biofeedback techniques: when first developed, sessions lasted perhaps one hour, but now they can extend to eight, causing multiple hallucinations, usually mystical—golden rams running through the acoustic chamber, and so on. Much of this owes a great deal to the pioneering work of Wilder Penfield at Montreal, way back in the Thirties. Applying electrical stimulation to patients' brains, he found he could evoke forgotten childhood memories, hallucinations, out-of-body experiences and, most relevant to present purposes, "homunculi"— monstrous presences threatening attack.

Then there's the more wildside research of someone like neurophysicist Dr. John Lilly, better known for his dolphin studies: Lilly's particular interest is a flotation tank he uses to meet extraterrestrials. Get floating, courtesy of Lilly, and—a boost from the hallucinogen ketamine does no harm—you too can be the recipient of messages from deep space, pumped direct into the brain. (One notes, in passing, the Roper survey which found that 20 million Americans reckon they've had out-of-body experiences, including abduction by aliens; also, the therapy groups currently running at Harvard for deep-space abductees.)

The tool which these techniques have in common is the sensory-deprivation chamber: and this device is central also to the work of Raymond Moody, M.D., who is much fêted around TV (both Joan Rivers and Oprah Winfrey have "done" Moody). Moody's speciality is that he puts clients in touch with the dead.

"I use this psychomantium," says Moody. "It's a kind of booth, built in my home, modeled on structures employed by the ancient Greeks."

Moody's set-up, to the casual eye, resembles Persinger's: there is the darkened chamber, there is the easy chair; but in his case, on the wall opposite the client, there is also a large, gilt-framed mirror, on which will appear (hopefully) the face of the deceased.

But where Moody differs markedly from Persinger is that apart from the room, the darkness, the mirror and the couch—and maybe a bit of music—there's no intervention by Moody himself: no electricity, no lights, no drugs. All "events" are generated spontaneously by the client. Nevertheless Moody's results are impressive—typical is the reported advent, *à la* Persinger and Munroe, of undefined "presences." Moody's New Age clientèle, he says, includes luminaries like Carl Simonton (the systems cancer

man) as well as Oprah Winfrey and Joan Rivers—indeed, Joan
Rivers managed an out-of-body experience on air, wherein she
"flew," while in the booth, to her daughter's flat in California.
Moody even runs seminars for psychotherapists, so would-be
communicants can build their own psychomantium in the privacy
of their own homes—do-it-yourself, apple pie supernaturalism. As
one of his suburban clients explained, she had this empty bedroom
anyway, so the psychomantium "kinda solved that problem."

One feels such a fool, these days, without a psychomantium
. . . but this is one of many areas where Persinger parts company
with certain colleagues. Not unpredictably, he's had zillions of
entrepreneurs who want to market his equipment—"I've got tired
of keeping their names"—but such exploitation would, he feels,
be "inappropriate."

Oh, and the other thing one should get quite clear, stresses
Persinger, is just how little his work has in common with virtual
reality, despite the seeming similarity of the helmets. Virtual reality
is essentially pre-programmed stuff dreamed up by scriptwriters,
going in from the outside. "Ordinary percepts through the
ordinary pathways," as Persinger puts it, however wild. Whereas
the Sudbury techniques, conversely, "tease the brain into releasing
images which are individual-dependent." Whatever the subject
sees is dreamed up by the subject—birthed in the brain.

All of which, memorable though it may be, was not the point of
my trip—which was, I had to admit, the moment when I finally got
myself down there in the chamber, got psyched up, plugged in and
then. . . . The truth is, I was scared. Okay, hundreds had been there
before me, but what happened if this hundred and oneth time Doc
Persinger's hand slipped. Or, more probably, what if I were one of
the favored few who *really* saw something . . . Beelzebub, God,
you name it. I accepted there was nothing in the chamber that
wasn't in my own mind. But that was the problem. God knows
what might be down at the bottom of *my* mind.

I found myself counting off the days, and then the hours, much as I used to before visits to the dentist as a child. And then the day before the off, I rang the lab to check final details and got Yves, one of Michael's postgraduate assistants.

"You'll have final tests in the morning," said Yves brightly, "then Dr. Persinger will see you in the afternoon."

"Sounds a bit like an operation," I said.

"It's just like an operation!" quipped Yves.

So at ten o'clock the next morning I duly showed at a little room just near the chamber itself, where Michael's assistant Pauline was setting up tests.

Pauline was reassuring. Bright and homey with her long hair, trousers and red sweater, she felt for all the world like a primary schoolteacher.

"Sooooh," said Pauline cheerily, "Heeear we go!" And off we went into a battery of brain and brain-body co-ordination tests, many of which were predictable, some a touch bizarre. For each test she gave a short spiel of instruction, finishing up with a high little squeak of encouragement, "Off you go!" just right, indeed, for this most leery of subjects.

"Soooaaah!" said Pauline. "Here's a test devised by Michael Persinger personally!" she squeaked. "I draw on your fingers and toes, and you have to work out which one I'm touching, it's ever so easy! Off we go!"

Well this one, I did fine—"You've got excellent toe-mind co-ordination," glowed Pauline. Emboldened, I connected numbers on a piece of paper (pattern recognition) and numbers linked up with the alphabet (left-hemisphere dominance) and I ticked or crossed psychological questions like:

"I like reading mechanics magazines."

"I have had a vision."

"I have been taken aboard a spaceship."

Until, that is, we got to the lights question, and there, alas, I met my nemesis. Different lights flashed on and off, and I had to figure out what the pattern was, and could I do it? Could I never. Indeed it seemed to me that we established that very early on, but Pauline would keep getting me to do it again, and again and again and again and again. . . .

At last, however we stopped. "All done!" said Pauline.

"Just a couple of other little tests this afternoon before you actually go in there, and then," she finished brightly, "you'll be on the helmet!"

Around 3:30 that same afternoon I was duly installed: eyes covered with ping-pong balls, head wired in under the helmet, ears plugged up, nails targeted in, intercom on, dials a-whirr, door shut, total darkness. The observer was about to become the observed: to have his own very personal visionary experience, duly monitored, right there in the chamber. Pauline switched on.

It began with . . . silence . . . followed by little prickling noises, which I took to be the electric charges going in . . . and more silence . . . and more little prickling noises. . . . Until slowly my consciousness seemed to turn into a kind of video camera, much like a dream, and I drifted back to the great white Edwardian house I had grown up in, and those sultry sunny days so long ago. . . . The bright blue sky through my childhood bedroom window, the radiant clouds parading slowly, luxuriantly, heads thrown back, across the sky. . . . And then the video camera moves down from the window, and into the passageway, and there's the oil burner my parents put there when I had pneumonia when I was eleven. And then back in the bedroom, and up the bedroom wall, and alighting on this paper frieze with all those nursery rhyme pictures on it, a duck, move three inches to the right, a monkey in a tree, move three inches more, a windmill, now, that was always, for some reason, my favorite. . . . And now something I had forgotten for thirty years until this moment . . . . the plastic cover on the top of the round table by my bed, the one with the intricate little pattern of red roses, all set into this geometric framework of black squares.

. . . Outside, still, those regal clouds, parading slowly, splendidly across the sky. . . .

The whole of that first session continued (very typically, I gathered, later) in that dreamy childhood-recollecting mode, the most striking quality of which, apart from its idyllic, elegiac quality, was the utter absence of any family or other human beings; only this video-camera consciousness making its tour of a 1947 interior, with this endless, extraordinary recall of long-lost detail.

And then Pauline's voice was calling me over the intercom, as, after around twenty minutes, the first session was over.

But during the second session, about ten minutes later, things really began to move. This time a little background sound was added, some vaguely New Age, Eastern temple bell sounds. Appropriately suggestible, my mind began a whole new mental tour, this time with a distinctly Eastern, Tibetan feel. It gradually increased in intensity and conviction, until suddenly, with a kind of booster rocket of realism, I was actually *in* a temple, *in* a line of solemn, Tibetan monks, grave-eyed, brown cowls around their heads, the bells tolling loudly now, re-echoing in my head, in fact I too was a Tibetan monk. . . . But then I always had been, I now realized—what had happened was that I'd finally understood this obvious truth for the first time. We were processing off to make our observances as we had, day after day, from time immemorial: bells, high seriousness, magisterial pacing, those solemn, monkish eyes. . . .

At which stage Pauline's pert voice came bursting in over the intercom again, and that session was over too.

The session had felt exactly like a dream, but a waking dream. I had described my experiences over the intercom throughout, knowing with one part of myself that I was in the chamber: it was almost like being in a film of the *Who Killed Roger Rabbit* school, with cartoon characters intermingling with conventionally filmed reality, two universes merged seamlessly into one.

There was a funny thing about that second session, as Persinger pointed out after he had looked at the print-out of my EEG. The moment of that "booster rocket" of seeming reality, the time when I started describing, over the intercom, the sudden intensity of the Tibetan vision, coincided with the moment when I very briefly (as recorded by the instruments) fell asleep. Dream consciousness had taken over from waking consciousness but, extraordinarily, although I promptly "woke up" again, dream and waking consciousness somehow carried on in tandem, entwined inextricably together. "Reality" and the transnormal had co-existed side by side, much as it had with Jill, Edward, Lloyd, Pauline and all the other visionaries I had talked to for this research.

No wonder my visions—and theirs—felt so real. And no wonder Persinger's subjects feel as convinced as they do by the things they "see" in the chamber, the presences, demons, saviors, visions of God. Indeed, as I took one last look back into the chamber, it struck me that I was, arguably, gazing into the twenty-first-century equivalent of a church. For here was what centuries of experiential techniques had been refined down to, all those bells, smells, fasting, dancing, drugs, terror-preaching and music making, all the innumerable ways and modalities we have encountered whereby transcendental experiences can be induced in the brain. From here on out, it seems, all could be induced at the flick of a switch: brave new other-world.

Yet when Persinger and I met the next day to discuss it all, he was at pains to re-emphasize that his processes did not, in his view, discount religious experience.

"It all goes back to your philosophy of reality. Johannes Muller once stated that you are only aware of the states of your nerves. So if a psychotropic drug, or a maintained electrical series of seizures, or even a tumor, effectively induces new connections in the brain, then you may indeed perceive things hidden from others.

"Even the fact that we can actually insert a God experience doesn't change the fact that the process is there for some functional or evolutionarily significant reason. If one accepts that God created the universe, then why not have a brain mechanism whereby these experiences take place?"

After all, declared Persinger, there are interesting parallels in the realm of art. Few would declare, presumably, that artistic perception is unreal *per se,* and yet, "We know that poetic capacity is a manic feature; we know from studies that at least 70 percent of contemporary writers and musicians who are considered *avant garde* or at the edge of our culture are manic depressives. The manic phase activates the brain to such a degree that parts of the brain functionally interact that normally would not.

"And thus they can see things in the universe and even make predictions that are beyond the ordinary person. And that is what we call talent—or intuition."

Until very recently in the common-sensical West, visionaries, whether aesthetic or transcendental, have been marginalized. And yet it is precisely that marginalization which is being so dramatically altered in our time: back in the early twentieth century, virtually no Christian Charismatics at all; by the Nineties, no less than 25 percent, or 400 million in the Christian communion worldwide; by the end of the century, an estimated 30 percent, almost one in three.

Said Persinger: "It's quite remarkable, how few people have grasped the implications of all this." For underneath it all, he argues, lie two profoundly important developments: the first is that recurrent leitmotif of this tale—uncertainty.

"Some physicians argue that anxiety attacks have increased so much that they amount to an epidemic. And, as we have already seen, from the neuroscientific point of view anything that interferes with the sense of self can produce disruptions. The left hemisphere becomes subdued, the right gets stimulated, you get intrusions, "kindling," and then the new, reconstituted left-hemispherical assertiveness we call "conversion": uncertainty, in fact, has been reconstituted into a new sense of self, otherwise "identity"—the great psychological yearning of our time.

Now, if you have enough people doing that, it's called a social movement.

For this is what links the disparate crises of yuppydom (that label culture reacting against contemporary loss of identity), the Iranian revolution (Islamic identity crisis, reacting against Westernization), and the left-hemispherical certainties of Evangelicalism (reacting against information-society uncertainty, relativity): the psychological sequence uncertainty-depression-crisis, followed by resolution into new certainty, and new "self."

"And it's usually something simple-minded. It has to be, that's the nature of anxiety. That's why, more than often, it's a religious or neo-religious movement—because they're simple. Historically, it's happened time and again. Social disruption, confusion, disorientation: and then, in tandem, these great surges of paranormalism. Typical was the situation at the very start of the century, another period of extreme social flux, when you had the Welsh Revival—the first great twentieth-century surge of Charisma—*and* people seeing, simultaneously, balls of fire in the sky, spaceships, flying saucers.

"Because, just as it's no accident that, in the individual, religious conversion so often follows a period of uncertainty and/or serious depression, so it is with society at large.

"The Great Depression of the Thirties, for instance, was a fine source of Charismatic belief."

As is what the Indian-American economist Ravi Batra has called "the Great Depression of 1990"; not to mention that deeper process of which the "Depression" is but a symptom—the cultural time-bomb called the "Information Revolution."

What of the other of the two "developments" Persinger mentioned?

"The really crucial question is whether there is actually some fundamental cultural shift taking place, something beyond the mere strains and stresses of uncertainty. Some kind of refashioning, if you will, of consciousness itself, something that will make

Charismatic experience that much more readily available to everyone."

Interestingly, Persinger virtually lines up here with McLuhan—unthinkable for a neuroscientist even twenty years ago.

"McLuhan's been underestimated. His essential thinking, intuitive though it was when it first appeared, seems to me to be scientifically sound: yes, we are moving from a culture of literacy, with all its associated forms of thought, to what one might, indeed, call an aural/tactile culture; and yes, that does involve profound changes of awareness."

Persinger paused for a moment; weighed his words.

"True, such changes won't be genetic, that's far too slow. But other things can happen: we know from rat studies, for instance —and we study rats just precisely because the neuro-electrical and neuro-metabolic qualities of their brains are so similar to ours —that environmental enrichment changes the cortical thickness of their brains; and if you change cortical thickness, which is a crude gross measure, you must be altering the subtlety of micro-structure.

"Now, it's perfectly possible that we, too, have changes taking place in our environment or culture that would allow susceptibility to previously unsuspected stimulus patterns—that comparable processes, in fact, are taking place in human brains.

"Ever since Hubel and Wiesel won their Nobel prize with their work on learning patterns, neuroscience has been profoundly aware of the extent to which individual brains create their own, quite individual synaptic patterns based on experience. And as with individuals, so, perfectly plausibly, with whole cultures."

So it is, to put it at its mildest, entirely possible that contemporary stimuli—McLuhan's TV—and radio-based "audiotactile" environment, just for a start—could be evolving brains that perceive quite differently from even thirty years ago?

"Oh yes. It really is very difficult to overestimate the impact of all this, sociologically, on the twenty-first century."

To all this was added, from my personal point of view, the following suggestive coda, when Persinger and I had our final meeting the next day. Michael had got my EEG data out, plus the results of those psychological tests. His first comments were routine enough. "Most of your data's normal," he said, "excepting that we did find these spikes on the EEG of your right front temporal lobe. This ties up, actually, with the problem you had with that test involving lights. Visual-spatial calculation, pattern-recognition, these kind of problems. Don't tell me, you drive your wife crazy leaving things around the house?"

Spot on indeed; but there was more.

"Now this bit. . . ." A look of concern came over Persinger's face, such as when one drops the bombshell about the cancer. "Let me re-emphasize," he said kindly, "that we're all on a continuum in this, it's not that you're *fundamentally* different from anyone else."

Well?

"It's these psychological tests," said Michael. "Quite simply, you're much higher than average on depression. I wouldn't worry too much about that, though. As we've seen, that can be quite handy for a writer.

"But there's something else, too. . . . We have this research data that enables us to look up your category and make certain predictions. Now let me see." Michael fingered his way down a printed page. "You're an A-thirty-nine." Michael looked intrigued. "Hmmm, that's an uncommon profile. . . . Can involve attacks of acute anxiety. . . . Hello, there's something else: not only are subjects in this category depressed, but they are liable to deal with their depression by developing these . . . conversion symptoms."

Persinger gave me what Dostoevsky calls "a subtle look."

"You know, you could be *just* the person to write this book," he said.

13

In Our End Is Their Beginning

In which Michael Persinger was, of course, quite right. For being both outside and inside the world one is writing about, however uncomfortable, is, undeniably, the most creative posture of them all. Include the knower in the known! And he was right, too, both about the depression (well, my mother had died six months earlier) and the conversion symptoms (since when I had been suffering rheumatism in all limbs, a typical reaction on my part, to stress). What I'd never experienced, however, were *religious* "conversion symptoms"; but then perhaps a state's first cousin is as good for understanding it, if not better, than the state itself.

With the Clinton-Gore "It's time for a change" election of November 1992 as its watershed, the Nineties began to evolve its own quite distinctive change-conscious, rather than change-avoidant, sensibility. And soon a whole new range of uncertainties had come rattling in to add to the cultural confusion, trailing, as ever, conversions in their wake. There were, for instance, the knock-on effects of the collapse of the Cold War and its monolithic, black-and-white politics of confrontation. As the ultimate nuclear Armageddon receded from public consciousness, the likelihood of a limited exchange, paradoxically, increased. And how many nuclear explosions do you need to feel insecure? Just three or four, surely, will do nicely. This development further challenged both Eastern and Western senses of self. As Jim Garrison put it in *The Russian Threat*—"The threat of the 'other' has been so deeply internalized within both American and Soviet cultures that the very *self-identity* of many people today is bound up with the ideological assumptions of the Cold War." The relationship of loss of identity to conversionism has already been described.

Then there was the ever-escalating sense of worldwide environmental catastrophe, both man-made and "natural." Storms of unprecedented ferocity had been pounding the U.S. and Europe since the mid-Eighties. Graphs of solar radiation and atmospheric pollution steepled upwards. Welsh hill farmers continued to complain about the knock-on effects of Chernobyl.

Above all there was the ongoing, if rarely admitted, structural crisis of the world economy. By 1992, the first green shoots of conventional recovery were peeking through, but in America, especially, that desperate sense of job insecurity (nearly 50 percent of those in work expected to be fired or temporarily laid off) continued to grow.

As for Black Africa, South America and, most perilously of all, the ex-Soviet Union. . . . Suffice it to say that what was happening there, economically, really didn't bear thinking about. By the early Nineties, Russia, in the words of one economist, "was almost on the brink of turning into a Third World country." Small wonder it soon produced its own, home-grown, secular Charismatic: Vladimir Zhirinovsky.

To all of this was added a further factor: a magic number. The year 2000. The millennium. For as the decade crept on, this most symbolic of dates hovered ever closer to consciousness. It should not be forgotten that this is a Christian date—in Islam 1995 is 1415—and even in a world as apparently secularized as the West this lowering number cast its spell.

To the overt crises, then, of economic, environmental, and cultural transformation was added the subliminal sense of religious "end times." Or as John Naisbitt and Patricia Aburdene put it in *Megatrends 2000*:

> Religious belief is intensifying worldwide under some gravitational pull from the year 2000, the millennium.
>
> One thousand years ago, in the 990s before the last millennium, the Christians of Europe's dark ages believed the end of the World was at hand. . . . As we approach the year 2000, it is happening again.

But then we have, surprisingly, been there before—or somewhere very close—in almost living memory. It turns out that the rather less dramatic date of 1900 had similar effects. As Cambridge critic Frank Kermode put it in his *The Sense of an Ending*: "Our sense of epoch is gratified above all by the ends of centuries." He goes on to describe the "fin-de-siècle phenomena" at the end of the nineteenth century. "There was a deal of apocalyptic feeling at that time, not least in the revival of imperial mythologies both in England and Germany, in the "decadence" which became a literary category . . . in the utopian renovationism of some political sects and the anarchism of others." Kermode sums up: "There is a real correlation between the ends of centuries and the peculiarity of our imagination."

Millennialism, much of it secular and subliminal but all of it intensely felt, has been the defining psychological characteristic of the last quarter of the twentieth century. Its impact is clear in the apocalyptic vision offered by the Greens: for however you interpret the figures (and the argument has rumbled endlessly on from the first Green stirrings in the countercultural Sixties) what is undeniable is the "endist" flavor of it all. A Great Reckoning is upon us, a *Fate worse than Debt*—to quote another famous Green apocalyptic, Susan George, whose analysis of the Third World in 1988 drew together financial and ecological strands into one desperate debacle: dodgy Western loans lead to still dodgier attempts at restructuring, which in turn results in the assassination of the forests and the decimation of the poor.

There have been similarly apocalyptic diagnoses of the world of business and finance—a theme which, as noted at the start of this book, spawned a whole publishing category of books about The End—in 1988 I got a whole article out of it, "The Good Gloom Guide," for the London *Evening Standard*, listing, with no trouble at all, a good half-dozen of the hottest financial-Armageddon titles in town. When, in October 1987, the first, much-predicted mini-apocalypse actually came to pass, the entire financial world (and press) went Apocalypse crazy. In the U.K. by the early Nineties, money melt-down stories were appearing on average once a fortnight in the Sundays (typical was *The Sunday Times'* business section lead of 3 April 1994: "Markets Fear Selling Frenzy," plus sub-heading, "Global markets in turmoil"—it never happened). The psychology shaped up like that of the hypochondriac who knows his last dozen health alarms were false, but can't get it out of his head that this, the thirteenth, might just be true.

Nor should one forget how one vocabulary of Apocalypse can shade, even evolve, into another. For while by the early Nineties the language of yuppy short-termism was that of money and business, ten years earlier, when the essential world view of such thirty-somethings was being formed, short-termism was rooted in *nuclear*, rather than financial, fears (this was the height of Evil Empire confrontation, after all). A poll taken by the American Psychiatric Association of Boston teenagers in the early Eighties showed that almost all believed their lives would be cut short by nuclear war, while in West Germany over 50 percent of those aged between 18 and 24 believed nuclear weapons would destroy the world. It is hardly surprising that they later became short-termists in business.

The various Apocalypses are indeed hard to separate. Take the Green concern with pollution. As McLuhan commented:

"Pollution is merely the revelation of a changing [cultural] situation at very high speeds. We now regard all our institutions as polluted, because we can see that they have many patterns that have nothing to do with the function they are supposed to perform." It's plain enough that the Green pollution apocalyptic is at least in part metaphorical—and from McLuhan's perspective one can see why Westerners would simultaneously be becoming obsessed with moral pollution, or "corruption"—an obsession comparable to that which overwhelmed the Puritans at that other period of social transformation, the start of our current 300-year-old Newtonian adventure.

By the Nineties, the corruption story, hardiest of all media perennials at the best of times, was rarely off the front page: Clinton's financial peccadillos, his sexual mishaps, the dire shenanigans of Eighties money mobsters in both the U.K. and U.S., the 1994 Westminster homes-for-votes scandal, the government corruption scandals in Spain (Spanish youth unemployment rate in 1994: 25 percent), Watergate, Whitewatergate, Irangate, Iraqgate, Camillagate, Squidgygate, Troopergate—the very language strained to shape these rows into a pattern. And yet underneath it all, as McLuhan suggested, the subliminal feeling was this sense of inappropriateness: the outmoded and decaying failing, utterly, to accommodate the fresh; new wine in very old bottles.

So that for those looking out for the ultimate Apocalypse, the clincher to prove the end-times were finally here, what was really needed was something which fed on all these diverse elements, encompassing them in one psychic catch-all. And, starting in the Eighties, gathering pace as the Nineties wore on, such an apocalyptic duly presented itself—child abuse.

It was the 1991 child-abuse allegations in the Orkneys that were the watershed in the U.K.; soon, the Evangelicals were piling in there too; later variants included the eighty-four cases of Satanic child abuse investigated by Professor Jean La Fontaine of the London

School of Economics on behalf of the Department of Health, all but three of which turned out to be unsubstantiated. But the climax came during the depths of the U.K. recession in February 1993, when a child of two, James Bulger, was murdered by two ten-year-old boys, to the outrage of the nation. Here was corruption to end all, for what devilment could compare to innocence abused? This theme hooked straight into individual apocalyptic psychology, too: for, as Philip Greven pointed out in *Spare the Child,* "The painful punishment of children creates the nuclear core of rage, resentment, and aggression that fuels fantasies of the apocalyptic end of the world. This has been true at least from the early seventeenth century to the present. The most consistent thread connecting apocalyptics generation after generation has been the experience of pain, assault and physical coercion resulting from harsh corporal punishments in childhood." No wonder the Evangelicals were into it.

Child abuse stories seem to fit into just that same "endist" consciousness Frank Kermode described, and thus might reasonably have been expected to have surfaced in the 1890s, as well as in the run-up to the year 2000. For are they not, after all, the ultimate evidence of the arrival of the "latter days," the worst thing imaginable, earthly manifestation of the end?

The American historian Larry Wolff, in his remarkable 1988 book *Postcards from the End of the World,* an "investigation into the mind of fin de siècle Vienna," shows how that same Vienna which was, for Hermann Broch, the city of "the gay Apocalypse," and for Karl Kraus, "an experimental laboratory for the end of the world," debauched, uncertain capital of an imploding empire with just nineteen years to run—this same Vienna was also, for the last three months of the millennial year of 1899, a city obsessed with child abuse.

Four sensational cases of child battering and murder virtually took over the newspapers in the last weeks of 1899 (then promptly vanished as Vienna clear forgot about "child abuse" with the new century). To add to the deadly Viennese cocktail, another of Vienna's millennial obsessions, anti-Semitism, got mixed up in the child abuse stories. The result, writes Wolff, was that:

> For the Viennese who created and patronized the extra-ordinary culture of the fin-de-siècle, there seemed to exist, however briefly, some profound inner relation, perhaps neither fully conscious nor explicitly articulated, between the horrors of child abuse and those of anti-Semitic blood libel. In November 1899 they were two specters, darkly presiding over the apocalyptic death of one century and the birth of the next.

Wolff is not arguing that Vienna invented its child abuse cases, or that apocalyptic psychology created a fantasy that was unreal. What he is saying is that there are certain millennial times and circumstances when such apocalyptic notions are more readily brought to consciousness than others. And those times are periods of huge unease and cultural change (child abuse next surfaced during the Sixties); and, most especially, periods in which such unease is further boosted by transcendental symbolism like magic dates. As in 1899 Vienna, so in the run-up to the year 2000.

When secular apocalyptics have been so active, it is small wonder that religious apocalyptics have been yet more so, especially in the era of the counterculture, post-1970.

In all the high drama of the Evangelical/Charismatic belief system it is end-times theology, as we saw with Pauline Rawle, that is wildest of all. Most Evangelicals today are so-called "premillennialists." This means they believe Christ will appear on Earth before the 1,000-year preparatory period which will precede the end of the world, as opposed to "postmillennialists" who believe He will return thereafter. And while, for premillennialists, Christ's reign will indeed be characterized by unearthly justice and joy, there is a catch: the utter horror of the trauma, or "tribulation," attendant on His coming.

As with most such notions, versions vary, but current contenders include: (a) the idea that the European Community comes together under the rule of the "Beast" of Revelation, who then initiates a kind of reconstituted Roman Empire, tyrannous beyond belief; (b) the Beast's big number becomes a financial New World Order, centralized, computer-coordinated, with diabolically conceived credit cards used to keep tabs on us all; (c) that after a terrific end-time war in the Middle East, the Battle of Armageddon climaxes in a nuclear exchange between Russia and China, fought out in remotest Asia; and (d) there meanwhile occurs a remarkable event known as the "Rapture"—essentially a jump-jet job whereby the Elect are plucked instamatically skyward to get them away from all this (hence such bumper stickers as "Beam me up Jesus" and "In case of Rapture, this car will be driverless"). In short, while earlier millennial thinking involved at least some sweetness and light, today's big emphasis is on comeuppance.

And instant comeuppance at that, for the stress is on the sudden transformation, the miraculous change. It is hereabouts that premillennialism reveals its roots in the early-nineteenth-century Romantic movement, with its feel for suddenness, spontaneity, the "all-at-once." For it was then, roughly contemporaneous with the first modern appearance of that other piece of religious Romanticism, speaking in tongues (first recorded in 1830, in two parishes in the West of Scotland), that the present premillennialist bandwagon really began to roll.

Typical of this connection was the friendship struck up between the Romantic poet Samuel Taylor Coleridge and Edward Irving, one of the pioneer British Charismatics. Of commanding presence, 6¢ 2 tall, Irving wore his hair parted "left and right" so it hung down on his shoulders "in affected disorder": Coleridge considered him "the greatest orator I ever heard." When the

Evangelical leader Thomas Chalmers, obviously a less inspired personality, met them together, he said, "There was a secret and to me as yet unintelligible communion of spirit betwixt them, on the ground of a certain German mysticism and transcendental lake-poetry which I am not yet up to." Irving's congregation was one of the very first in which tongues were spoken, for which scandal Irving was kicked out of his own church by the trustees.

Even in millennialism, curiously enough, there is hip and square. Earlier postmillennial theology was full of optimistic, eighteenth-century left-hemispherical thinking—a key signal, believers reckoned, would be a palpable bettering of the human condition, which is why the American and French revolutions were taken as hopeful signs—but the premillennial notion, by contrast, was shaped by typically Romantic melancholy: Christ would come before the millennium precisely because the outlook come the conservative 1830s seemed dire indeed. In Classical post-millennialism, in fact, the end-times indicator would be that things were getting better; in Romantic premillennialism, that they were getting worse. In premillennialism, there is thus the need for that further Romantic event, Christ's sudden, dramatic intervention. In this pessimistic world, all that eighteenth-century, step-by step, "cause, effect, order and gradualness," as David Bebbington puts it, was passé. The at-a-stroke syndrome, great-grandsire to "The Oprah Winfrey Show," was born.

And if the growth of this attitude was encouraged by the negativity of the 1830s, how much more was it enhanced by the cultural character of the twentieth century. Neo-Romantic movements like Expressionism helped to feed twentieth-century Charisma; then, to this broad, right-hemispherical tide, add on the two world wars, the Great Depression, the death camps, nuclear overkill—then, finally, two landmark political events: first, the creation of the state of Israel in 1948; second, the Israeli capture of the old city of Jerusalem in 1967.

These Jewish events were special. Had not the Jews' return to the Middle East been predicted in the Bible, as *the* sign of the latter days? Small wonder that by the Seventies, end-times theology was on such a roll.

The grand watershed was 1970, when Hal Lindsey's seminal *The Late Great Planet Earth* was published. This book, by an ex-Mississippi tug-boat captain, sold 18 million copies, surfing in on just that shift from hippy religiosity to overt Christianity that so many counterculturati were then making.

Essentially what Lindsey did was update the rather creaking millennialism of the past by changing the language. The Antichrist became "that weirdo beast"; the Rapture was "the ultimate trip." Zechariah's description of the decay of human flesh becomes, "Exactly what happens to those who are in a thermonuclear blast." The nuclear concern is very big in Lindsey, whose key notion is the recycling of the Apocalypse as the Third World War, the ultimate nuclear exchange. Such imagery was by no means unattractive to twenty-something ex-hippies whose late, great demonology had been the nuclear state.

Lindsey, for all his hip appeal, became one of the key protagonists of the nuclear Apocalypse so popular among Eighties conservative fundamentalists—one of his better known readers was President Reagan himself, a prophecies freak from way back. Indeed, Reagan was on record as declaring, at a 1971 political dinner in Sacramento after a leftist coup in Libya: "That's a sign that the day of Armageddon isn't far off. . . . Everything is falling into place. . . . Ezekiel says that fire and brimstone will be rained upon the enemies of God's people. That must mean they'll be destroyed by nuclear weapons."

Where nuclear Armageddon got problematical, however, was with the collapse of the Cold War. Where was the enemy now, with The Enemy belly up? Yet anyone who thinks this presents theology with more than a hiccup doesn't know the genre. By the early Nineties, key adjustments had been made, with the result that the new enemy swiftly became, as in the good old days, Satan himself. And the cosmic conspiracy theory, essence of so much apocalyptic thinking, moved out of the Kremlin and back into the ether where it belonged—still manifesting on Earth, of course, but changed.

Grassroots, do-it-yourself theology now seized on Bush's New World Order, insisting that it was inspired by Satan, and all part of the preparation for the Rule of the Beast, vilest tyranny of them all. Computerization and use of credit cards was all part of the plot, for this way the rich (the demonology abruptly switching, recession-led, from poor-bashing to rich-bashing) could increase their stranglehold on the unwary, could impose their dream of a single world currency. It was all part of the run-up to Antichrist's rule, Revelation 13 and 17!

This kind of interpretation became particularly weird wherever esoteric numerology turned up. The point about "666"—the Beast's number as recorded in Revelation 13—is that it manifests pretty much anywhere you care to find it. 666-spotting was once mainly concerned with names (as, for instance, the Protestant who in 1612 found that the numerical values of the Pope's name added up to 666), but today's 666-freak finds it more in credit card numbers, computer bar codes, and all the complex numbering systems of modern finance. Entire books have been devoted to 666-spotting, Mary Stewart Relfe's 1982 *The New Money System 666* for instance; one advanced school suggests that today's hi-tech Antichrist will actually *be* a computer. You can prove it. If the letter A is taken as 6, B as 12, C as 18 and so on, the numerical values of the word "computer" add up to . . . 666.

Such reflections are evidently at the fruity end of the millennial theme and would rate little more than a chuckle were it not for the number of people who believe them. (Adherents include Pat Robertson, fundamentalist candidate for the presidency of the United States, also Lloyd Kuehl and Pauline Rawle; while in 1988 Ronald Reagan changed the number of his California mansion from 666 to 668.) The real danger of such beliefs is the conspiracy psychology they represent, for conspiracy psychology, when it takes millennial forms, can lead us down some very dark and dangerous paths indeed.

Not all apocalyptic thinking is old-style fire and brimstone. Just as the Greens show every sign of having their own Apocalypse psychology, religious apocalyptics have been going green. The book of Revelation, it is explained, can be read as the ultimate environmental catastrophe. Or, as the end-times publication *The Omega Letter* put it in 1991, "Revelation 16 actually describes effects now being attributed to the hole in the ozone layer."

Nevertheless, while millennial thinking does shade into more familiar, and thus less threatening, countercultural concerns, the perils of that conspiratorial world view remain. True, today the conspirators are perceived to be the rich, which goes together quite nicely with all that post-Eighties, new-hatched populism. But has not the twentieth century already seen where millennialist populism can most tragically lead? And are not the objects of such hatred, demonstrably variable, less important than the fact of it?

Norman Cohn, student of medieval millennialism, also wrote *Warrant for Genocide* about the Nazis' millennial, 1,000-year-Reich attack on the Jews. And he identifies the roots of Nazi thinking in centuries-old Christian anti-Semitism. More, he shows the ways in which Germany's Jews—artists and intellectuals as well as rich businessmen—came also to symbolize, in the culturally traumatized German consciousness of 1933, everything amoral, threatening, *new*.

Should the New Christianity, with its heady populism, ever go on a real hate trip, it's not impossible that it would take off in a similar direction. After all, there's not exactly a shortage of candidates: as well as the rich, the child abusers, the occultists, and the channellers, how about, say, the gays? Amoral, irreverent, artistic . . . and above all, *different*. If Christian populism ever were to evolve into Christian fascism it is apocalyptic psychology, with its obsessions, fears and demonization, which would supply the fuel.

None of this, of course, has anything to do with what Matthew Arnold called "the Spirit of Jesus." But that could be the point. It was D. H. Lawrence, in *Apocalypse,* who argued that the key point about Revelation—which appears in the New Testament, after all—was that the human psyche needed something else to balance out all that altruism. Your average citizen just wasn't up to so much sweetness, peace and love. He really shouldn't attempt it. Otherwise, sooner or later, something in him would snap. And then—watch out!

However the real mystery of the apocalyptic canon is how such extremely bad news can have such wide appeal. After all, 666 and all that is only the start of it; just wait till the sun falls down, the moon spouts blood, the nuclear missiles go their deadly way . . . The American sociologist William Martin wrote in 1982:

> Pre-millennial teaching is probably most attractive to those who feel that the world, or at least their segment of it, is out of control, and can only be brought to a good end by supernatural intervention. Such feelings of marginality are likely to be especially acute when established ways of life are being threatened.

As with the poor old monkeys described in chapter 1, it's better to know that there's a pattern to the flux of contemporary life—even if that pattern is horrific—than to remain unsure. People will believe anything, endure anything—kill anybody, if it goes that far—just so long as they can convince themselves that they know (a) who they are, and (b) what will unfold.

14

The Priesthood of All Believers

By the winter of 1992, the Western economies were bumping along the bottom of the deepest recession for sixty years. And prominent among the ever-broadening flood of casualties was, of course, poor Pauline Rawle.

I tried calling her at her country house—and got a security man, who put me onto the auctioneers selling her estate, who put me on to her solicitor, where I left a message. A week later the phone rang and it was Pauline—we duly met.

Pauline had, it turned out, ended up just a couple of miles from my wife and me in suburban Maidenhead: as a guest in a polite, trim-lawned villa owned by the mother of a friend from the Cobham Christian Fellowship.

"Not that I heard much from them, when I needed them," said Pauline. "I was in hospital at one stage with a blood disorder and they visited twice and that was it."

Nevertheless, the lady she was staying with, Sylvia, herself a Christian, had come up trumps. "She phoned me every day when I was in hospital, when I wasn't even sure I wanted to live." And now Sylvia had taken her into her home. So Pauline sat there, more poignant than ever, in this hushed suburban sitting room with its pastel shades, seascape on the wall, pile carpet underfoot —still dressed to slay, even now, in cream top and trousers, brown shoes and chunky gold.

"I've lost everything," she said matter of factly. "I went into hospital on the eighth of September and was made bankrupt on the ninth: I've lost my house, my furniture, my crockery, my family photographs, every last thing, in fact, except my clothes. Even my Bible has been taken from me to be sold."

Pauline gave her blow-by-blow version of the events leading to the debacle; how Body Shop pursued her remorselessly till she went down; how her credit lines were cut off; how, yes, she *had* suggested staff might attend child abuse classes, but no way, absolutely not, had she forced anyone to attend against their will; how she'd offered, come the crisis, to form a co-operative with her staff; how only a handful took up the offer, so she'd got teams of Christians in, from the local church, to keep her shops open; how Body Shop had got an injunction, finally, to close her down. . . .

"You know," she said, "it sounds strange, but if anything my faith has been strengthened by all this. I mean, where would I have been if Sylvia hadn't helped me? Fifty-one years old, unemployable, and nowhere to go?

"I've found this great little church in Reading, scripturally based, supportive congregation, and I'm beginning to make plans. Why, even though, as an undischarged bankrupt, I can't start a business, I can help form a co-operative, and I've met this local group of unemployed executives, including two Lloyds names, and we're starting this group to go in and help companies in just the kind of dire straits we've been in ourselves." For all such rather brittle optimism, there were moments, that afternoon, when there was a simplicity about Pauline that seemed new.

"Through all this," she said, "just one thing has remained constant, and that's Jesus' love. So that now, strange though it sounds, I feel something I've never felt in all my life before, not even when times were good. Weird to say, I know, and yet, I feel secure. Because wherever I go, whoever I am with, whatever my life may bring—I'm not alone."

This poignant, gentle Jesus quality had rarely been visible in my earlier talks with Pauline. Nor did it last, it must be said, so very long now—because within moments, like knocking a wound, the talk veered around again to Body Shop. Ah, Body Shop! Once again I saw that old, apocalyptic fire in Pauline's eyes:

"Just look at their share price!" she cried, brandishing a print-out of their chart which she happened to have handy beside her chair. "Down by half! And still dropping! It's perfectly obvious what's happening isn't it?" A death-ray look. "God's punishing them for their wickedness. It's obvious! And it's quite plain what the upshot's going to be, too, isn't it?" Another Look. "God's going to take their company away from them," declared Pauline, "just as they took my company away from me, and it will be a just retribution for them, God be praised, and it will be their punishment, richly deserved, for the unspeakable wickedness of their ways!"

To which I had, I must admit, no ready reply.

The only contacts I had with Pauline after that were in similarly apocalyptic vein, and it was quite a question whether her conversion had left her better or worse off than when she started. It was revealing, by contrast, to catch up with "my" other convert, Peter the policeman, because his new-found Christian lifestyle had taken him off in quite another direction.

He had moved, too, since I met him last—out of the flat where we'd first met into a brand new four-bedroom house, which he'd rented initially but had finally taken the opportunity to buy. Sitting there with his wife Julie (they had married in October 1992) on their plush new sofa, with new carpets and freshly decorated cream walls, both Peter and Julie looked almost unrecognizable as the couple who'd been under so much pressure so very few months before.

Although the last six months of 1992, said Peter, had been a nightmare. Pauline Rawle had been right—he had been before the courts—a data protection offense, said Peter, no criminal conviction, but a fine. And yes, he had been dismissed from the police, so there'd been all that, plus the desperate uncertainty of wondering what on earth he was going to do for work. As for Julie, well, there'd been all the rumbling, endless trauma of her divorce—not to mention the ongoing problems of her illness, or the property sales both Peter and she had to carry though, or the move into their new place. Purgatory.

Yet suddenly, they told me, there was a transformation! "This whole series of things went right just as if they'd been planned," said Peter. "First, this old friend finds me a job in security. Next I land this even better job in a bank."

"Then my divorce comes through," said Julie. "Next, my MS sees this dramatic improvement, the result of healing services and of prayer."

"And then," said Peter, "we sold our houses within two weeks of each other, started renting, and this house comes up for sale so we buy it and avoid the trauma of another move."

Career rescued, health saved, home sorted out. Then, of course, there had been that October wedding; and that had been an amazing blessing too—not least because it had been, it turned out, as fine a piece of quantum, do-it-yourself religiosity as could be imagined.

"We did the legal bit down at the Register Office first," said Peter, "and then we booked this venue called the the Old Barn Hall —*the* local venue—for our service, which we designed ourselves.

"We were amazed at the way all these church people helped out: one lady did the flowers, Pete the Greek, a chef, did the moussaka for the reception. Then, for the service itself, we had this pastor, Paul, from Pioneer and a four-piece band and a ribbon dancer and all our favorite modern hymns: we even wrote our own vows. I suppose there were about a hundred and twenty people there, Christians and non-Christians, and at the end, instead of the usual prayers, we invited anyone who felt like it to come out and pray over us or proph-esy.

"Then we shifted the chairs around and held the reception in the same building.

"But I guess the best moment was when Paul pronounced us man and wife and the whole crowd erupted into this spontaneous cheering."

Not quite Aunty Beryl's wedding down at the local C of E—and the local group's offerings amounted to rather more than 50p in the collection box.

"There's this big Pioneer project cooking up," said Peter, "whereby we hope to buy this empty aircraft hangar, prime local position, to convert into a center—and from a congregation of five hundred, last March, we had two hundred and fifty thousand pounds collected in one go. In this recession! Then last November we had a pledge night, and people committed themselves to yet another two hundred and seventy thousand, deliverable within weeks—over five hundred thousand pounds in total. People were going without family holidays, selling their cars. . . ."

So far as community and commitment go, Peter and Julie are in there with the best. For as well as Sunday worship and their fortnightly network group, and one-offs like that trip Paul did to fit the plumbing in the orphanage in Romania, they'd run an Only Looking Group, for people considering joining up with the church. All this is on top of Peter's job, and looking after Julie's two teenage boys; as well as all the hours Julie puts in with her fancy-dress hire business, run from their home. Indeed, the stability, even exuberance that Peter and Julie's conversion has brought them stands in marked contrast to the very different experience of Pauline.

As Peter puts it: "Who would ever have thought, even a year ago, that in just these few months Julie would have been healed, that I would have lost one career, found another, and that we would have moved, married and even bought ourselves a brand new four-bedroom home?

"It was as if God took our lives, threw them up in the air—and remade them, utterly anew."

Many lives were being broken, and rather few remade like Peter and Julie's, by that spring of 1993. In Britain, the jobless figures continued their remorseless upwards grind; a watershed was "Black Wednesday"—16 September 1992—when the government, overwhelmed by events, raised interest rates 5 percent in one day to defend the pound. They were down again the next day, but the trauma remained. In the U.S. the first signs of recovery were finally there, but the psychology was still of the most profound economic insecurity, even despair.

Most significant was loss of faith, not just in the economy, but in those very institutions whereby such problems as the economy were traditionally supposed to be fixed. By 1993, this same all-pervading loss of faith, economic and moral, spreading northward into Canada, would lead to the slaughter of Canada's Eighties-dominant Progressive Conservatives at the general election: 154 parliamentary seats reduced to two! Jobs, politics, institutions, communal morale: it was no longer just the radicals who were blaming the "system" for their ills: hard-hats, blue-collars, the mainstream middle class itself—everyone was at it.

So that the growth of self-organizing groups like the New Churches—systems that dreamed up their own brand-new organizational forms, mutual support systems, even morality, outside the old power blocs—was less surprising than might at first seem. And how they grew! Take Pioneer, for instance, the church of Peter's family and, formerly, Pauline Rawle: Pioneer had around ten thousand members nationwide in 1992, if you included linked churches, compared with under five thousand when I first encountered them back in 1990. Or take a New Church organization like Bryn Jones's up North: it showed a 17 percent rise in 1992. Or good old inner-city Ichthus, batting steadily along at 6 percent. Or London's Kensington Temple: a mere five hundred strong ten years ago, they had five thousand plus now, and were reportedly buying a warehouse. Consider the endless spawning of those amoebalike cross-denominational initiatives.

A charity like ACET (AIDS Care, Education and Training), launched by a house church back in 1988, was, by the early Nineties, the largest independent provider of AIDS home care and information in the U.K., in touch with over 250,000 students in schools alone, and with education and home care programs as far afield as Romania, Uganda and Thailand.

Dawn 2000, the church-planting organization, is a further example. Amoebically entwined, in the best New Church traditions, with such like-mindedly global organizations as March For Jesus (both are rooted in globalism and interdenominationalism, Dawn having started out in the Philippines, in the early Seventies, with the express aim of getting cooperation across local denominations for evangelism), Dawn U.K. was, by 1993, in touch with several hundred interdenominational leaders, and had already spawned at least thirty subgroups nationwide. Just one of these, the Shine group at St. Helens, Liverpool, comprised forty of St. Helens' sixty-two churches, and was planning no less than thirty New Church plants by the year 2000. The Salvation Army, as its Dawn contribution, had a target of a cool five hundred new centers by the same date.

Dawn 2000, in particular, is one of the finer instances of that strange, diaphanous, hi-tech New Church mode. Not only is their hierarchy amoebic in the extreme, not only are their conferences full of authentic, postindustrialist language ("network," "facilitate," "bottom-up," "Dawn is a process, not a club") but my abiding memory is of Chris Forster, Roger Forster's son and Challenge (Dawn) 2000's U.K. coordinator, standing there in his new offices, one day in 1992, at the Forest Hill Ichthus HQ.

Twenty-five-year-old Chris, who has a computer science degree from London University, was in true New Age mode—tracksuit, trainers, ring in his ear—and his room, which was quite small, contained at least five computers, gleaming white. Like his Dad, Chris has this way of chuckling as he talks.

"Hee-hee!" went Chris. "Know what this can do?" He whistled

some computer graphics onto the screen. "It's got so much info that it can home in on any street corner in the land, unpack the local data, and give you a breakdown on every household in that street, its size, family make-up, sex, numbers of kids, you name it. Not bad for Evangelism targeting, eh? Hee-hee!

"And do you know who were its chief designers and programmers?" said Chris, with dancing eyes. "A couple of Christians from California, would you believe, and now it's being used by marketing organizations and secular businesses throughout the world!

"And yet despite the use being made of it now, commercially, it was developed for just the Christian purposes we're using it for right here! Evangelization! Yes! Would you believe it! Hee-hee!"

Not everything on the New Church front was spiralling quite so unreservedly up. The half a million pounds collected for Pioneer's new center was still sitting there, accruing interest, some months later because Trafalgar House, who own the site, are being most unwelcoming to Gerald's advances. ("Unwise of them," Gerald told me, momentarily Rawlesque. "Their shares have fallen from one-ninety to forty-five pence, they're trying to sell the Ritz and no one wants it, and the QE2, which they own, goes and runs itself aground. So I say to them: 'Do you believe in God? Well, Why do YOU think all this is happening?' ")

Still, maybe's that's just a blip. Because with one thing and another you can see why Gerald Coates got an invitation from George Carey, the new archbishop of Canterbury, to pop round to Lambeth Palace for drinks. But then Carey, before his promotion, had not only been one of the established church's few Evangelicals but, to boot, the sole Charismatic.

When Gerald duly showed up at the Palace, there were about forty other high-flyers there, including a sprinkling of bishops. But the real shock came when Gerald and Carey were introduced: The Archbishop said to him, "I feel I know you so well already!" with many smiles, and then reached forwards and gave Gerald, "this big hug—I mean a real *bear hug,* mark you!" The imagination strains to express the enormity of such a moment. Not only do we have an Anglican Archbishop of Canterbury whose reputation is already sufficiently Charismatic that the word is out he has himself "talked in tongues" (although Lambeth Palace, understandably, have played this down); not only is he now embracing, in every sense, one of England's most noted religious mavericks; but he is doing it right on the C of E's home ground, in its very heart and central nervous system, Lambeth Palace! And right in front of these other, straight, properly appointed bishops, looking amiably on, grinning!

Maybe the Charismatic Carey just has a feel for the future. For by the mid-Nineties it has become apparent that the New Christian movement has muddled, hunched and intuited its way into some very Big Ideas indeed. There is its postrationalism, its do-it-yourself instincts, its quantum, boundary-crossing culture, its feel for unions of opposites or, in the vogue phrase, "paradoxicality," its "tight-loose" organizational structures, its group psychology at once Romantic and Square; not to mention its embracing of the Green balancing act expressed by "think globally/act locally," of which the classic New Christian application is International March For Jesus, taking local community organizations and instincts —typically those of London's Ichthus—and welding them into a multinational, global force.

Nowhere is this happening more dramatically than in the U.S. With the dazzling success of March For Jesus has come an increasing U.S. interest in the English groups' wider philosophy: that Ichthus Christian socialism, for instance. So that America, which throughout living memory had been the Charismatic inspiration for the U.K.—most notably via Billy Graham—is now experiencing the reverse process. The U.K. is calling the shots in the U.S. to such an extent that, even though the MFJ leadership in Britain want the Americans to run their own show, the Americans keep coming back to them for "quality control."

Now, Forster, Coates and co. periodically commute to the U.S., at the Americans' invitation, to give advice. Nor is there any lack of traffic the other way. Tom Pelton, in particular, U.S. MFJ's national coordinator, is a regular visitor to the U.K.

As for Ichthus's Graham Kendrick, MFJ leader and author of all those New Christian praise songs, he is rapidly turning into a North American superstar. It is getting to the point where he turns up at Christian festivals and is virtually mobbed. "Beatlemania" is how one MFJ leader put it.

15

Seizing the Power

At some point in the future, early in the 1990s at best
... must come an ideological re-orientation. Such a re-
orientation will most likely include a new sense of the
mystical unity of all mankind and of the vital power of
harmony between man and nature ... some form of Judeo-
Christian socialism will be the new political ideology.

William G. McGoughlin,
Revivals, Awakenings and Reform, 1978

One spring evening I was sitting in yet another mass meeting of
Evangelicals, but this time in the Harvey Addison Hotel in Dallas,
U.S.A. It was the grand, 400-plus leadership meeting of American
March For Jesus. The organization Tom Pelton had nursed from
1991 until now, 1994, when it encompassed the entire American
continent—Canada, the U.S., and South America too—was making
plans for the future.

Here, moreover, was the New Christianity, English and American, rubbing shoulders in the same room. The star speakers at
Dallas were none other than Gerald Coates and Graham Kendrick.
And what a welcome Graham got, when he walked into the hall!
The congregation erupted. But then Kendrick is not only a leader
of English MFJ, but one of the leading figures also of Ichthus—*the*
role model of the New Christianity in North America. Of course,

Kendrick's other quality is that he is the revival's troubadour, its musician *par excellence,* and music is crucial to Charismatics.

Never did I hear "Shine Jesus Shine" sung more shatteringly than that night; for here was the maker of these marvellous sounds, their very spinner and weaver, right here with the believers in the hall!

I had been following American MFJ since 1992, when I first met Tom Pelton, at that same meeting where I met Lloyd Kuehl, the would-be healer of John Ellen in Yorkshire. I'd heard about this embryo American MFJ offshoot, and had a hunch, somehow, it would take off. The meeting place, back then, was a little room in Tom's local Quality Inn motel in Austin, Texas, and there were just forty-seven U.S. marches signed up. Yet right from the start, Tom's enthusiasm for his English model was remarkable.

Six feet, four inches tall, cowboy-shirted, with Latin looks and lush, curly black hair, he couldn't have been much further from English notions of religiosity. Nevertheless, he felt quite different, too, from American right-wing fundamentalism of the Robertson and Bakker variety. For one thing, you never saw him in a suit. For another, his manner towards those around him was strikingly easy, self-effacing and friendly.

Soon after the introduction, I met him in his office just off an Austin freeway, which he shared with the Austin house church where he was an assistant pastor. So why England, in particular, I asked?

He'd first heard about English MFJ back in 1990, got intrigued, and was sent over by a group of Austin churches to check it out. From the start, he said, he'd been blown away by the English instinct for "reconciliation."

Reconciliation?

"Reconciliation between the denominations for a start," said Tom, looking moved. "Because the marches aren't just for Charismatics, they're for everyone. Reconciliation *within* the denominations, even: we've got Baptists over here who aren't talking to other Baptists. Reconciliation, come to that, with Britain herself—" Tom shot me a slow-burn, bounteous smile —"reconciliation with the motherland after two hundred years!"

One can see the appeal of this to Americans—the blood-feuds of U.S. denominations are notorious, and the power of postmodern "interconnection" is attractive. But there was more. It was not so much the March itself, Tom went on, as what it symbolized: a quite new spirit of Christian expression, which he saw coming particularly from England, especially Ichthus; the rediscovery, in fact, of the "communal" spirit of the early church, "The way they used to sell everything, hold everything in common."

Was this really an American talking? From the land of "prosperity" theology?

"Yes, indeed," said Tom, glowing, genial. "A Christianity that is relationship rather than property based. So if a guy next door's my neighbor, and his house gets burned, or he loses his job, and I've got money and he hasn't, why yes, I do believe I should give him what I have. As neighbors. Yes."

This was about as far from "right-wing fundamentalism" as you could get, yet soon Tom was finding a flood-tide of support from Christians nationwide, many of whom were even keener on MFJ than Tom. As veteran Austin pastor Dan Davis put it: "This movement completes the revolution started by Luther." When you ask Dan what he means by that, he says: "Power to the people! Power to the roots, the congregation—not only is the March itself all about devolved power, each city doing its own thing, with facilitation, rather than instruction, from the center, but these grass-rooters from the U.K. . . . use their front rooms for prayer, rent a school hall for meetings, do the pastoring themselves." This was unlike America, reckoned Dan, where a church-planter's first instinct was to hire a pastor, get a mortgage, but it could be the difference between launch costs of a couple of thousand bucks and five hundred thousand dollars. The English groups, too, had created "grassroots, intermediate structures." In the U.S., one Charismatic leader would head vast, pyramid-shaped organizations based on mass meetings, with everything top-down, whereas the English started with house groups numbering maybe five, widening to local groups of maybe twenty, out to celebration groups of maybe a hundred—with all the energy coming from below rather than above. "Sort of bottom up," said Dan.

Sort of "small within big is beautiful," as the Greens would put it?

"That's the feel."

And you think of that line of John Naisbitt's: "Trends are bottom up, fads top down."

I kept in touch with Tom Pelton's organization, as it evolved, and watched it become more postmodern, even, than Ichthus. For what with Tom being a "right-brained" person, as he puts it, rather than a heroic, "top-down" administrator, his natural strategy, in synergy with the pressures, had been to give away as much organizational responsibility as he could, so that the naturally flat MFJ structure had become more pancake-like all the time.

It is true that the basic *raison d'être* of March For Jesus—a one-day praise march around the world—sounds simple enough, but the old-time way to arrange something like that, in any church, would have been a barrage of pastoral encyclicals from above: none of which suited Tom's outfit one little bit, either from the point of view of philosophy, flavor or funds.

"I'll give you an example," said Tom. "The way I've organized this thing is that if you come to me and say, look, Tom, I really think we ought to be getting U.S. MFJ's contacts on computer; and if it turns out, say, that you understand computers because it's your business, then I'll say to you: 'Okay, Ian! Absolutely! You're Computer Systems Organizer! That's your title! Take it away!'"

Indeed, said Tom, he must have said something like that more times than he can remember in Austin alone—so that now there were all these people wandering around town with these MFJ titles—Banner Task Group Leader, Choreography Task Group Leader, Sound and Equipment Task Group Leader, you name it—all of which was enough to give any old-time, left-brained, traditionally minded organizer heart failure.

"Yet actually," said Tom, "it's been the making of us: because the way I figured it, not only does this mean each title holder actually owns the project, feels responsible for the bit he's involved in, but our system sets up this huge, instamatic network.

"Did you know that sociologists tell us each of us has, on average, real influence over around seven other people in our lives? Well, we must have two thousand volunteers now, all fully involved, all running round town telling the seven people they influence how great this March For Jesus thing is, why, we've got ourselves this instant, self-activating relational network of at least seven times two thousand, fourteen thousand no less, all focused on that march date, June twelfth, all poised to actually join in. And all this," adds Tom, "With *no advertising*!"

This idea is itself impeccably postindustrial (Body Shop, for example, eschews adverts, preferring word of mouth) and is only one of many postindustrial, or postmodern, or Aquarian things about the way Tom's Austin MFJ office is run.

But its most Aquarian quality is its gentle Jesus, feminine flavor, so characteristic of the New Churches, for all the continued male dominance among the leadership. Such ethics are encapsulated in what Tom's March For Jesus "Organizer Manual" (page 6) calls "core values." The manual describes, for instance:

RESPECT

A consultative style of leadership expresses our heart of respect and inclusiveness of every part of the body of Christ.

SERVANT LEADERSHIP

It is intimidating to lead leaders, even presumptuous to take on that role. But it puts everything in proper perspective when we commit to serve leaders.

RELATIONSHIP

We are an expression of existing relationships and a growing network of people who recognize the value and significance of relationship.

Need one add that Tom's politics are anything but right wing? "Clinton's great," he said. It was that interest in reconciliation again, apparently; Tom liked Clinton's instinct for bringing people together, rather than springing them apart. "And he cares for the poor, the blacks, the minorities."

Interconnection, reconciliation, neo-socialism, do-it-yourself. . . . One of the more attractive things about Tom is that he seems genuinely puzzled by his own success. Yet it could be that he has just stumbled right into a genuine big idea whose time has come. It was H. G. Wells who pointed out that Lord Northcliffe, pioneer of popular journalism, didn't so much launch the Daily Mail as was launched by it, soaring geometrically, unexpectedly upwards on a mass popular readership unleashed by the Education Acts of the late nineteenth century.

Has something similar happened to Tom? To Roger Forster and Gerald Coates? To Ichthus, MFJ and all those New Christians worldwide? Little wonder that the delegates' mood for that February 1994 MFJ convention was riding so high.

In the States, U.S. MFJ did notice one problem: the Christian Coalition. That burgeoning, America-wide alliance of Christian conservatives did seem a touch aloof. Could this be jealousy? Or was it ideology? For MFJ does have a distinctly countercultural feel, more Clintonite than Reaganite, you might say. Whereas Christian Coalition, even in the Nineties, is perpetuating—

even exaggerating—every one of those Eighties, right-wing fundamentalist clichés. They have already achieved notoriety with their high profile at the 1992 Republican Convention, an event which Dan Quayle, for one, felt helped precipitate Bush's defeat. But in the mid-Nineties they are slugging it out with moderate Republicanism all over the U.S. In Texas, they inserted a strong anti-abortion plank into the Republican pitch for state governor, as moderates warned of Republican "marginalization." In Virginia, they came out in favor of good ol' patriotism in the shape of good ol' Colonel Oliver North, of Irangate fame. In Minnesota, the Liberal Republican candidate for governor, Arne Carlson, decided to run in defiance of his own local party machine, which was fundamentalist-dominated. While in Florida, the Christian Coalition-dominated school board of Lake County introduced a new curriculum which stressed America is "the best of the best," pointing out that if young people "felt our land was inferior or equal to others, they would have no motive to go to war and defend our country."

Yet simultaneously, there has been the clear emergence of this more liberal Christianity: centrist, all-embracing, even left wing. It has been showing up in the figures: where George Bush won 83 percent of the white Evangelical vote in 1988, in 1992 he managed only 55 percent. Almost one in three white Evangelicals had voted, specifically, Democrat.

"There's a definite bifurcation," said Harvey Cox, professor of Divinity at Harvard. "On the one hand, the radical conservatism of Christian Coalition, on the other, the new-look liberalism of March For Jesus. Yet in important ways—their common feel for decentralization, for instance—they have more in common than meets the eye. I think we'll see the two forces evolving side by side."

In the last few weeks before that "Day to Change the World," enthusiasm and support was surging. United Prayer Track (co-ordinator Peter Wagner, he of the demons, charts and grids at Dawn 2000) was also targeting 25 June 1994, as in "ten thousand neighborhoods of the world" a total of 160 million Christians would be focussing on a twenty-four-hour pray-in, billed as "the most massive prayer meeting in the history of Christianity." As for MFJ itself, having attracted 1.6 million marchers in 1993, this year its following would swell sixfold to 10 million. In Australia they got 250,000; in Ghana, the country's first marches drew 500,000 nationwide; in the Philippines, 700,000; in South Africa, 60,000; in Costa Rica, 200,000; in Brazil, already boasting one of the fastest Christian growth rates in South America, 1993's 500,000 figure countrywide hit a cool 2,500,000 in 1994. And as for Seoul, South Korea, that country which best fulfilled, in the whole world, the classical millennialist conditions—cultural transformation, boom-bust insecurity, the North Korean enemy just over the border and threatening to arm itself with nuclear weapons—no less than 1 million turned out in the city's parks.

As Erica Youngman of the U.K. office, world coordinator of MFJ, put it: "We're staggered. If ever there was an idea whose time has come, this seems to be it."

There were other reasons for this upsurge of exuberance. Week after week, from all over the world, news was coming in of the onward march of the Christian revival. There was the continuing progress in Eastern Europe, especially Albania. There were the figures from South Korea, where over 40 percent of the population were now Christian. There were news-from-nowhere statistics, like the 100,000 Pentecostals it turned out were active in Sicily, largely women. And then, to add to everything already happening in Africa and South America, by early 1994 news began to filter through of huge numbers of conversions in the most vast and hitherto virgin territory of all, mainland China: in Henan province, which has a population of around 50 million, official statistics admitted over a million converts, all house church members. As one startled China-watcher put it: "These scenes of worship are infused with an enthusiasm verging on hysteria. It is as if a Charismatic church had been transported from North London to North China."

So it was no surprise that there were a mass of new nations represented at Dallas. Since October 1993 Tom Pelton had been march coordinator for Latin America as well as North, and was now welcoming representatives from Brazil, Peru, Mexico, and Argentina. São Paulo, Brazil, which had already hosted the largest single march in the world in 1993 (300,000), was destined this year to top 700,000. In 1993, also, the first march had been held in Canada—124,000 Christians had marched in forty-seven marches country-wide—so now the Canadians were here in force at the conference. And what they lacked in numbers they sure made up for in enthusiasm, for if ever there were archetypal postindustrial Christians, then the Canadians were they.

As forty-three-year-old Rudy Pohl, Ottawa coordinator of March For Jesus, put it:

> We love this MFJ idea that you get out into the community, combine spirituality with action. We love the music—a lot of us are coming out of Sixties rock and roll—and for us, Graham Kendrick's like a latter-day John Wesley. But above all we love Ichthus, Graham's church: we love the way Ichthus members connect with the world around them, help the needy, work for the poor. And you know what we hate? We hate that "prosperity" stuff from the Eighties.

Forty-nine-year-old Don Kantel, president of Canadian MFJ, agreed: "The key is the counterculture. It started with the idealism around Sixties music and the Beatles, then as hippy culture groped its way out of the fog, people junked secularism and found Jesus."

It is no surprise that for the Canadians, too, that countercultural icon connection is a key phrase. (An Australian MFJ spin-off, stressing rebuilding family and school relationships, actually calls itself "Operation Re-connect.") Canadian "connection," naturally enough, is above all about reconciliation between English and French Canada—which translates on the ground into Protestant and Catholic. In 1993, thirty-five Catholic churches joined the Ottawa march, but Pohl and Kantel see those new-forged relationships, while crucial, as just the start. "Because a couple of years down the line," Rudy said, "you'll begin to see works programs coming out of all this. Housing, schools, welfare— just like Ichthus. A practical expression of spiritual advance."

This, it was increasingly emerging, looked like being the next stage for world MFJ: local marches as catalysts for a whole range of other interdenominational ventures, cooperatively planned. In the States, for instance, there was the interchurch work at Des Moines, Iowa, to aid the 1993 flood victims: 350 homes out of 900 were helped by Christian groups. There was Byron Mote, Texas, which brought together fifteen denominations to start a clothes, food and housing program, this in a town now almost entirely Christian-run—city government, police chief, mayor. Most typical of all, in the boundary-crossing way of MFJ, was interracial reconciliation. This has taken both macro and micro forms—from the 1993 line-up of marchers across the three-quarters-of-a-mile-wide bridge in Harrisburg, Pennsylvania, symbolic link-up of a city divided geographically and racially by the river; down to a whole series of small, intimate reconciliation services held to remember specific events, such as one held in Columbia, Missouri, for the 1925 lynching of a local black: there was a forgiveness service at the site, followed by an inter-racial service back at the local black church.

These two current emphases of MFJ "spin-offs," racial reconciliation and community works, were increasingly paralleled in Christian developments in the world at large. The most dramatic example of inter-racial reconciliation was, of course, South Africa, where by the early Nineties, largely unknown to the West, huge new racially integrated Charismatic churches were servicing up to 35 percent of the population. The result was that South Africa's Christians performed a crucial role as conciliators in the run-up to the historic elections of 1994: the word was, indeed, that Christian brokerage was crucial to Chief Buthelezi's last-minute agreement to join in.

Equally low profile, yet widely prevalent, was the community involvement of churches in mainland Europe: the classic example was Lille in northern France, where interdenominational co-operation had resulted in an elaborate medical and social services program which, since 1992, had garnered hefty local authority support. One of the Lille Evangelicals' favored ploys, it turned out, somewhat in the mode of the ghetto-busting Ichthus, was to take a central floor in a tower block and turn it into a Christian community center. They'd decorate the flat, offer worship, club facilities for children—then finally they'd Evangelize their fellow tenants on the floors above and below.

Not that, by the mid-Nineties, there was anything so very unique about the Lille project. Just as MFJ's boundary-crossing thinking was first cousin to the cross-departmentalization of modern business, so the community-orientation of groups like Lille (as, of course, Ichthus and Pioneer in the U.K.) formed part of the wider evolution of urban community throughout the West. Projects which might start as a school, a church, or even a small business, would quickly evolve, in the best spirit of postindustrial nonspecialization, into much broader, community-wide concerns. It's interesting to compare the Christian groups, for instance, with the St. Paul's project in Balsall Heath, Birmingham. Prominent at Balsall Heath was the work of Dick Atkinson, a sociologist who left academe to work in St. Paul's; his particular expertise was education, but as well as St. Paul's School, local, "bottom-up" initiatives created a nursery center, a community center, a language project, a newspaper, a printing facility, even a carnival. In St. Paul's case, an educational project was the catalyst; in Lille's case it was a church: what the projects share is this gestalt sense of the inter-relatedness of community life, and a belief that such schemes should grow from below, not be imposed from above.

The next stage is the prospect of alliances with governments which are thinking the same way. Cash-strapped administrations around the world are now thinking in terms of "steerers and rowers": at local and national level, you seek out those organizations which have already self-started and are, more or less effectively, doing their own thing; they then get behind their act-locally strategies with think-globally cash and vision. The grassroots provide the tactics, the government offers the strategy.

This form of thought is best articulated in David Osborne and Ted Gaebler's seminal *Reinventing Government* (1992), a book which not only crystallizes a process already spontaneously igniting throughout the world, but which has already had major influence on the Clinton administration. Clinton himself said: "I want a government . . . which is a catalyst for action by others . . . one that favors empowerment over just handing out benefits; one that believes in opportunity and responsibility more than entitlement."

Fans of Osborne and Gaebler may have noticed that in *Reinventing Government*'s acknowledgements they highlight the veteran economist Peter Drucker as their "single most influential thinker." Unsurprising—Drucker's 1968 "Age of Discontinuity" was THE predictor of the "discontinuities" of the last thirty years, in particular privatization.

Less known, however, is that the almost spookily prophetic Drucker—arch-rationalist though he is in many ways—was also one of the pioneer predictors of religious revival. In his 1959 *Landmarks of Tomorrow*, a book littered with early usage of the word "postmodern," he says: "The historian a century hence—should there be one to record our survival—may well judge the return to religion to have been the most significant event of our century and the turning point in the transition from the modern age."

Throughout the West, you can almost feel the pieces dropping into place. For what is the big problem, in the cities, if not sectionalism and racial confrontation? And what is the big social achievement of the Evangelical/Charismatic movement if not integration? The year 1995, in fact, was to see racial reconciliation as the bull priority for MFJ Christianity; such a target would seem perfect for government "steerers and rowers" support, however discreet.

You can see how Americans, in particular, might find such notions surprising. For as 1994 wore on, the media finally grasped that fundamentalism was not, in fact, the busted flush it had appeared. Nevertheless, it was the right wing, seemingly, of the fundamentalist movement that took on new life—most especially after the mid-term elections, which were so disastrous for Bill Clinton. The Christian Coalition, to media alarm, seemed to loom large in Republican successes throughout the land. The coalition sent out 30 million "voter guides" which effectively urged voters to vote Republican; clearly their supporters hated Clintonism with a passion. And yet, as so often with mid-term elections, only 40 percent of the electorate bothered to vote. Of that 40 percent, 25 percent defined themselves as "Evangelical Christians," and of that 25 percent, 60 percent voted Republican—recording a steep decline, seemingly, from that overwhelming Evangelical Republican vote in the 1988 presidential elections. Furthermore, when you totalled up that 1994 mid-term Republican Evangelical vote as a proportion of the total electorate, it came to just 6 percent. Not quite right wing Armageddon. . . .

Nevertheless, there was no denying that the Christian Coalition had reminded us, as with all comparable movements throughout history, that there was no knowing where Christian populism might end. Which reminder was underscored by the other most vivid Christian event of 1994, the worldwide outbreak of the so-called Toronto Blessing.

It started in a little church just off the runway at Toronto, Canada, called the "Toronto Airport Vineyard." It is home to extreme, expressive worship reminiscent of the wildest moments of that breakneck conversion of Jill and Edward's. Within weeks, its particular style had radiated out worldwide—in the U.K. alone, by the autumn, an estimated 3,500 churches were experiencing "manifestations." And while the message fanned outward down the network, the believers flowed inward by jet (it helped, of course, that the church was near the airport). By 1995, a conservative estimate was that 100,000 believers had flown in to taste the Toronto Blessing at source, and of these at least 20,000 were from the U.K., 40,000 from the U.S.

Everywhere the symptoms of a "Blessing" were the same: outbreaks of "holy" laughter, sweeping uncontrollably around the church; moaning, shrieking, barking as of dogs; believers thrashing around on the floor as if giving birth, or crashing down as if poleaxed, "slain in the spirit." In October, a breathless Gerald Coates was on the phone declaring this was "the most extraordinary thing" he'd seen in thirty years. He put it more succinctly to Christian friends: "This is it."

I went to some of the services and "extraordinary" was right. Perhaps most startling was the way this behavior was impacting on the mainstream—for as with the earlier, more clap-happy Charismatic forms, its effect on conventional denominations was out of all proportion to the size of the New Churches themselves. The highspot at one grave, creeper-bedecked C of E church I went to in Oxfordshire came when one of the shrieking congregation collapsed, symbolically, across the altar table; this was, to put it mildly, not the Church of England I had known.

But the moment I best remember took place at one of Gerald's own services, now being held, four years after we had first met, in a cinema in Esher: a congregation two hundred strong; sedate praise and hymn-singing for about twenty minutes; then, for an hour, the wildest, most rollercoaster worship scene you ever did see, with at least half the congregation ending up screaming in the aisles.

An unexpected influence was, apparently, the Disney film *The*

Lion King, then on release—a print of the Lion King was displayed on the screen, and the meeting, which had been titled "The Main Attraction," majored on highly expressive growls and roars. A believer would start by trembling, move on to shaking, and then bounce like a high diver about to leap off the board, finally exploding, with furious, outraged jungle roars, to the palpable danger of anybody within ten feet.

In short, that hyperexpressive Janovian end of the Charismatic continuum had finally moved center stage. Amidst all this, Gerald Coates still sailed blithely on, still upmarket, still aspirational, still Spirit of Retail, 1970.

We were all primal screamers now, for all Gerald's aplomb, and it was quite something to reflect on just how far Gerald's congregation have come since those innocent days just four short years ago. If they've come this far that quickly, what on earth will they be doing four years from now, as world hunger escalates, as ecosystems collapse, as the Western job market offers ever-dwindling security to an ever-dwindling proportion of its citizenry?

For we are heading into uncertainty as never before, and in the background, looming ever closer, is that most magical of numbers: the two-thousand-year, Third Millennium of Jesus Christ.

Index

abreaction theory, 114–15, 133–36; drug abreaction, 124–29
Anabaptists, 10–12
Anderson, Patrick, 79, 80–83, 86–88
Anderson, Robert, 160–61
Apocalypse, 97, 203–15
Atkinson, Dick, 236

Babin, Pierre, 171–72
Bebbington, David, 34–35, 211
Bell, Daniel, 37–38
Beyerstein, Barry, 192
Blizzard, Robert, 138
Body Shop, 92–95, 103–5, 106–8, 217, 218
Bond, Carol, 73–75, 109
Bouchier, David, 37, 42
Brown, Norman O., 45–46, 69, 110–11
Bucke, Richard Maurice, 38–39

Calver, Clive, 18, 61
Carey, George, Archbishop of Canterbury, 223–24
Carol (Ichthus member), 59–60, 64–65, 66, 70
Cerullo, Morris, 151–54
Chalmers, Thomas, 210–11
Charismatic Christianity. See Evangelical/Charismatic Christianity
child abuse, 28, 96–97, 112, 158–59, 187–88, 207–9. See also dissociation
Church Coalition (U.S.), 231–32, 238
Church of England, 16–17, 30–31, 223–24, 239
church-planting, 8, 53–54; Dawn 2000, 18, 268, 222
Churchill, Winston, 153, 158
Clark, E. T., 99, 110
Coates, Gerald, 6–8, 14–18, 26, 225, 239–40; on Cerullo, 152; childhood and youth, 153, 155–57; and March For Jesus 225, 226; meets Archbishop of Canterbury, 223–24; and Pauline Rawle, 91–92, 99, 102; and "Toronto Blessing," 239. See also Cobham Christian Fellowship; Pioneer organization
Cobham Christian Fellowship, 6–8, 14, 92, 95–96, 100, 101, 216
Cohn, Norman, 11–12, 34, 35, 214

Colson, Charles, 98–99, 112, 113
conversion: childhood trauma and, 109, 111–12, 153–59; depression and, 110, 153, 188–89; dissociation and, 159–62; drugs and, 124–32; individual stories of, 91–108; stress and, 98–99, 109–23, 153–54
Cox, Harvey, 232
Cruttwell, Patrick, 172–73, 175
CSICOP, 32, 33, 139, 142, 144

D'Antonio, Michael, 323
Davis, Dan, 228–29
Dawn 2000, 18, 268, 222
Devil as adversary, 23, 55, 81, 101–2, 129–30, 212–13; exorcism, 89, 130–31
dissociation, 159–62, 179, 187–88
drugs, 69, 119–20, 124–29

Edward (Ichthus member), 124–32
Ellen, John, ix–xiii
Ellen, Mary, ix–xiii, 109
Ellenson, G. E., 160
Evangelical/Charismatic Christianity: background, 1–13; defined, 5–6, 24–25

Fenwick, Dr. Peter, 155, 167–70, 171, 176, 178, 182
Forster, Chris, 222–23
Forster, Roger, 18, 21–22, 26, 52–53, 225
Fox, Matthew, 47, 172
Frady, Marshall, 154–55
Freeman, James, xii, xiii
Freud, Sigmund, 136–37, 158–59

"Ganzfeld procedure," 146
George, Susan, 205–6
Gott, P. S., 177
Graham, Billy, 4–5, 153, 154–55, 159
Grant, W. V., 143–44
Greven, Philip, 153, 154, 159, 160–61, 208

Hay, D., 111
healing, 87–89, 112–13, 128, 133–44, 146–50; by Cerullo, 151–53; investigated, 139–48; of Julie, 100–101, 219; psychology and, 133–39

241